CHASING
SOMEDAY

CHASING
SOMEDAY

#1 BEST-SELLING AUTHOR

LINDZEE
ARMSTRONG

Snowflake
Press

Copyright © 2017 by Lindzee Armstrong
Published by Snowflake Press

Cover Design by Novak Illustrations
Interior Design by Snowflake Press
Edited by Tristi Pinkston and Suzi Retzlaff

Tooele, UT
ISBN 978-0-9981667-1-1
Library of Congress Control Number 2017900739

To my husband, Neil,
who never let me stop believing that
one day our babies would come.
And to my sons, who proved that
miracles exist.

CHAPTER ONE
MEGAN

When Megan imagined life as a married woman, it didn't start at six a.m. each day with Beethoven's Fifth and a thermometer. The alarm interrupted her dream, and she wanted to roll over and burrow deeper into sleep. But any movement would raise her basal body temperature and skew the reading.

Trent leaned over to turn off the alarm, jostling the bed. Megan's eyes burned from lack of sleep, but she forced them open against the sandpaper begging her to keep them closed. Maybe packing until two a.m. hadn't been such a good idea.

"Open wide and say 'ah,'" Trent teased, slipping the thermometer under her tongue.

He thought he was so clever.

Trent rolled out of bed and changed into his running clothes. Really, today? Surely moving gave her a free pass from their daily run. He'd moved on to stretching by the time the thermometer beeped. Ninety-six point seven degrees. She didn't have to look at the chart in her phone to know she still wasn't ovulating. Her temperature hadn't peaked once in eight months.

"I'm ready to brave the cold when you are," Trent said cheerfully from where he stretched out his calf muscles against the door-frame.

She wasn't going to obsess about infertility. Not today. After five and a half years, she could afford to take a few hours off, especially with so many other things taking up brain space right now.

"Don't you think we should skip the run?" Megan asked. "We still have half the house to pack." They'd signed the papers two days ago, but the new owners agreed they had until five o'clock today to be out.

"You told me last night that under no circumstances should I let us skip our run today. You said if we did, it'd be easier to skip tomorrow." He leaned down and kissed her on the lips. "Let's go."

She had said that. Curses.

They were out the door within minutes. The brisk March air, so cold it took her breath away, made Megan long to be in her warm bed. Even packing sounded better than this. She hated running, but it helped keep her weight down—a necessity for favorable results when undergoing fertility treatments—and she loved spending time with Trent. Even though they were officially "on a break" from treatments, she couldn't let her daily rituals slide, or they'd lose ground when they started again.

They ran in silence for nearly ten minutes, mostly uphill toward campus. Megan mentally cataloged all the things she'd rather do: pack up the rest of their things, load everything up, clean the house for the new owners. "You're leaving to pick up the moving truck as soon as we get home, right?" Her words came in tiny puffs, clouds of condensation appearing with each breath.

"Megan, relax. Take this all in for a moment." Trent's breathing wasn't even labored. How annoying. There was no justice in the world. They'd been running almost every day for more than two years, but Megan still sucked at it. "This is the last time we'll run this path," Trent continued. "Enjoy it."

He was right. For the rest of the run she tried to soak in the view, but it only brought up painful reminders of how much she would miss the small town of Logan. There was the music hall, where Trent had picked her up after so many classes. The student center, where they'd first met. The statue of the A, where they'd stood so she could become a "true Aggie" by kissing Trent at midnight under a full moon. Logan was the only city they'd ever known each other in. Here they'd met, dated, married, bought their first house, graduated college . . . experienced their first disappointments as a couple. Megan's breaths came in ragged gasps, sending sharp pains through her chest.

"Are you going to miss it?" she asked as they rounded the road to their home.

"I'm ready to move on. I have a good feeling about this, Meg."

She glanced over at Trent and had to smile. His tall, lean body made running look effortless, and a scruffy beard and kind eyes complimented the country twang she adored. Most would call him average, but he had always been handsome to her.

The heat of the town house burned after growing used to the frigid air, and her hands tingled as they started to thaw. They weaved through the boxes littering their living room and headed toward the kitchen.

"I'm leaving to pick up the moving truck." Trent grabbed his wallet and keys off the kitchen table.

"Want me to drive you?"

"Nah. It's only a mile away—I'll run."

"Sure. It's not like we just ran five miles."

Trent grinned, giving her a quick kiss. "Be back soon."

Megan prepared her breakfast with a scowl. Too bad she didn't love running and eating healthy like Trent did. Instead she spent her mornings gagging down half a supposedly fertility-inducing grapefruit and three pills—a prenatal vitamin, folic acid, and Metformin. The Metformin helped with her insulin resistance, a common issue in women with Polycystic Ovarian Syndrome, but tasted awful. She tossed a handful of crackers into her mouth after swallowing to kill the taste and keep the nausea caused by the pills at bay, then started packing. She'd just opened the bottom kitchen cabinets when the front door creaked open.

"Knock knock," came a familiar voice.

Cami. Fan-freakin'-tastic. Of course she'd be the first one to arrive. Megan swallowed, trying to curb the jealousy that roared within her. Nothing had changed—not really. She was happy for Cami.

"Hey," Megan said. "Thanks for coming."

"What are neighbors for? I'm at your disposal." Cami removed her winter coat and laid it on a chair. Megan tried not to stare at the way her belly protruded. With each pregnancy she seemed to show sooner.

Megan forced herself to sound upbeat. "Do you want to wrap the dishes, and I'll pack them?"

"Sounds good to me."

Megan handed Cami the bubble wrap and packing tape. "Thanks. I really appreciate the help."

"I wouldn't miss it. I can't believe this is your last day here." Cami blinked rapidly, and tears stung Megan's own eyes.

Leaving would be harder than she'd expected.

"I can't believe it either," Megan said. It had only been four weeks since Trent accepted the manager job at the car mechanic shop in Riverton. "Trent's so excited about this promotion. I'm trying to be excited too."

Cami's shirt stretched over her rounded belly as she reached for a baking dish, and Megan looked away. Cami had moved in next door only two months after Megan and Trent bought their town house. At the time, they'd all been newlyweds eager to start a family. When Cami had announced her first pregnancy, Megan was thrilled. Surely she'd follow in Cami's footsteps soon. When Cami announced her second, it stung. Megan and Trent had been trying almost three years by that point. When Cami announced her third pregnancy a few months ago, it was an anvil to the chest.

It wasn't fair. Helpless rage welled in Megan's chest, and she fought to keep her face impassive. After five and a half years of trying, all she and Trent had to show for their efforts was a stack of doctor's bills and enough negative pregnancy tests to fill a bassinet.

"A new beginning will be good for you," Cami said. "I think you need a change of pace. Maybe in Riverton you can finally slow down and relax."

Megan rolled her eyes. Stress was Cami's favorite explanation for why Megan didn't have a baby. "Yeah, and if we relax, all our problems will disappear." As if PCOS—the disease causing Megan's infertility—would evaporate with a day at the spa.

"You know I didn't mean . . ."

And there Megan went, being a jerk again. Why couldn't she keep her comments to herself? "I know. Sorry." Time to change the subject. "'Relaxing' isn't the word I would use to describe this move."

"Uh-oh. Don't tell me you sold the house to obnoxious people. Were they a pain in the butt to work with? Am I going to have to move to get away from them?"

Megan laughed. "I got you good neighbors. Promise." As a real estate agent, Megan had sold dozens of homes over the past few years. Selling her own had been different. Harder. She hadn't realized how closely her dreams were tied to this house until they'd signed the papers.

Megan's phone rang, and she fished it out of her pocket. Trent. "Hey. I thought you'd be home with the moving truck by now."

"I'm on my way home. Without the truck." Weariness saturated the line.

"What?" She'd called last night and confirmed their reservation. "What's going on?"

"I got there, filled out the paperwork, took the keys out to the truck, and it wouldn't start. They're sending one up from Bountiful, but it won't be here for a couple of hours."

Megan ran a shaky hand through her hair, her heart racing with panic. "Isn't there one closer?"

"No. I made him check. Twice. For the inconvenience, they're delivering it to the house."

"How generous of them. What are we going to do?"

"There's nothing we can do. We'll work quickly when it gets there."

As soon as Megan hung up the phone, Cami asked, "What's wrong?"

Megan quickly explained the situation. "This will set us back hours, and we're already on such a tight schedule."

"We'll pick up the pace then."

Gratitude flowed through Megan, and for a moment she could almost forget Cami carried a child.

The moving truck didn't arrive until after eleven—four hours late. Helpful neighbors filtered in and out of the town house all day, but there were still a handful of boxes in the living room and the old piano to move when Laura and Dale Anderson's car pulled into the driveway.

Megan's stomach dropped. It couldn't be five already. She grabbed her cell phone. 3:58 p.m. The new owners were an hour early.

Frustration welled up inside, but Megan stamped it back. They were excited. She'd shown them enough homes before they picked hers to know that. Time to handle this professionally. She was the real estate agent, not the home owner.

Except she totally was the home owner. And she really wanted the chance to say goodbye to the house in private.

Megan walked toward Laura and Dale like a condemned prisoner facing her executioners. "I'm so sorry," Megan told them. "The moving truck arrived four hours late, and we're running behind. We'll finish up as quickly as we can." They still had an hour, after all.

Dale wrapped an arm around Laura's waist. "I know we're a little early. Laura couldn't wait."

"Do you mind if we start moving a few things in?" Laura asked.

Megan's smile froze.

"Laura, hon, leave them alone," Dale said. "We don't want to get our boxes mixed up with theirs."

"We could put them in a room that's already been emptied," Laura said.

Mine, mine, mine! Megan felt like a petulant child refusing to share. She didn't want them in her house. Not yet. How would she handle this as a real estate agent? "We still have things scattered everywhere," she hedged. A blatant lie, but Megan didn't care.

"Patience, dear," Dale said to Laura. "We can wait an hour."

"I appreciate it," Megan said, relaxing. "We'll hurry."

Cami came up behind Megan as Laura and Dale pulled away. "Are those the new owners? A little anxious, aren't they?"

"It's their first home." Megan stuck her hands into her back pockets and hollered to the moving truck. "Let's pick it up, Trent." She was desperate to have a chance to say goodbye.

Soon the ancient piano, a hand-me-down from Trent's mother, was the only thing left. Five years ago Megan had insisted it be the first thing into the house, and now it was the last thing out. The wood held countless chips and dings from fifty years of moving trips, and a few stray pen marks decorated the side from when Trent was a toddler with artistic aspirations. It wasn't the grand piano Megan dreamed of, but it played beautifully. She'd make sure it was the first thing unloaded in Riverton, where she already had new piano students lined up.

Megan kept glancing at her phone as they rushed to load the last of their belongings. Fifty-eight minutes. Forty-five minutes. Thirty-nine minutes. One by one their friends and neighbors left. As Megan thanked them for their help, her phone burned against her thigh. When everyone but Cami had gone, Megan pulled out her phone. Twenty-two minutes until the house was no longer hers.

"I guess this is it," Cami said, tears glistening in her eyes.

And that's when it hit Megan. They were really leaving. No more spending lunch breaks at the park with Cami and her daughters. No more complaining about the homeowners association. No more whispering in church.

Megan pulled Cami into a hug, the growing stomach pressed between them. Megan froze. She loved Cami, but it was good Megan was leaving. Watching Cami's stomach blossom with new life a third time, while Megan's remained empty, was unbearable. She'd be a better friend from far away. But she would miss Cami all the same.

"Thanks so much for your help today," Megan said.

"I'm going to miss you. We'll keep in touch, right?"

"Absolutely."

Cami left, and at last Trent and Megan were alone. The house was theirs for eighteen more minutes. As they wandered through the rooms, a thousand memories assaulted Megan—the carpet in one corner of the living room, slightly discolored from spilled hot chocolate. The pantry door that wouldn't stay shut because of the broken latch. The living room carpet with permanent creases from where the piano had sat.

Goodbye. Why was it so hard?

They ended up in the master bedroom. "Are you okay?" Trent asked, taking Megan's hand into his.

"Moving feels like giving up." She stood in the middle of their empty room, overcome by the urge to sit down and cry. The house felt strange and alien with all the pictures taken down and the furniture absent. So empty. So lifeless. She ran her fingers along the sage green paint until it met with the bathroom door-frame. How many pregnancy tests had come back negative in here? Fifteen? Twenty?

"We're not giving up, Megan."

"I never imagined we would leave here as a family of two."

Trent wrapped his arms around her shoulders. She clutched at his hands, leaning into him.

"We'll start over in Riverton," he said. "Let's forget all the bad memories and make new ones. Good ones."

"I bet we could've bought a grand piano with all the money we spent on pregnancy tests."

"Let's not talk about that today."

She sighed. "I know, I know. If we can laugh at our infertility, we can live with it."

He tapped the tip of her nose with his finger. "And don't you ever forget it."

A knock at the front door interrupted them. Megan checked her cell phone and closed her eyes, wanting to scream in frustration. She still had nine minutes.

"I'm not ready to leave," she told Trent. "I need to say goodbye."

He gave her a quick kiss. "I'll distract them for a few more minutes."

She wandered alone across the hall. In her mind, this guest bedroom had always been dusted in pink, with a white crib in the corner and a baby mobile crooning a lullaby. In the beginning, when a baby had seemed like a certainty, she'd even purchased a few items on clearance. So many dreams.

None of them had come true.

A burst of laughter floated up from the front entryway, stealing the moment from her. Megan looked down at her phone. Five o'clock exactly. This room would now forever belong to what should have been. She gave the nursery one last longing look, then shut the door.

In the front entryway Laura glowed, her eyes bright with excitement. "Sorry, we didn't mean to rush you."

"I know you're excited," Megan said.

Dale put an arm around Laura's waist. "For more reasons than one. We found out last week that Laura's pregnant. I want to hurry and get the furniture brought in so she has somewhere to lie down if she gets tired."

Megan inhaled sharply, the revelation a slap in the face. A baby. In this house.

Not hers.

"Congratulations," Megan stammered, her voice shaking. "The room upstairs is perfect for a nursery."

It would happen for her. Just not here. She couldn't give up hope.

They said their goodbyes, and the door shut behind them with a finality that stung.

Trent squeezed Megan's hand. "You okay?" he asked, helping her into his truck.

She nodded and shut the door. Tears pricked her eyes as she drove away from the home that was no longer theirs. But she refused to look back.

They weren't giving up.

They threw back shakes and bottomless fries at Angie's Restaurant before heading down the road. Though it was only six o'clock, darkness encompassed the landscape. Snow began to fall as they entered Sardine Canyon. At least she was driving Trent's four-wheel drive pickup truck instead of the moving truck towing her car. She squinted through the snow, struggling to see Trent's taillights up ahead. She hoped the moving truck would handle the snow well.

They were halfway to Brigham City when the pickup truck slowed, pulling to the right. Megan called Trent, irritation making her voice clipped. "I'm pulling over. Something's wrong with the truck."

Outside the snow fell heavily all around, coating her in seconds. The hazard lights clicked from the dashboard, grating on her nerves.

Trent appeared, flashlight in hand. "You've got a flat."

Megan groaned. "Seriously?"

Trent pulled out the jack, positioning it under the truck. Megan knelt down beside him, trying to balance on the balls of her feet so her jeans wouldn't get wet. She clutched the lug nuts in one frozen hand and a flashlight in the other, blinking snowflakes out of her eyelashes. Things would look better in the morning. If only they could leave behind their infertility as easily as they'd leave behind the difficulties of today. It wasn't like this day could get any worse.

And that's when the flashlight burned out.

CHAPTER TWO
CHRISTINA

Christina pulled her silver Lexus into the parking lot of Riverside Elementary and killed the engine. 7:30 a.m. on the dot. Weak sunlight illuminated the falling snow, and a thin layer of white blanketed the ground. Thank heaven she'd worn a coat with a hood. If her hair got wet, it would frizz, and that was the last thing she wanted with the principal conducting her yearly evaluation today.

Inside, she unlocked her classroom door and flipped on the lights, the smell of dry erase markers and disinfectant calming her nerves. Twenty-eight miniature chairs sat on top of twenty-eight miniature desks. Students' artwork papered the walls and the carpet showed lines from the janitor's vacuum. A brightly colored bulletin board featured commonly used phrases in both English and Spanish. Christina had spent hours making sure everything was perfect before school started in August, certain this would be her final year teaching. Now she wasn't so sure.

Christina was placing reminders about the book drive in student cubbies when the click of heels made her pause. Stacey

Applegate, a fellow first grade teacher, walked into the room, her long auburn ponytail bouncing with each step. A full smile, teeth and all, lit up her entire face.

"Good morning," Christina said. Stacey had married over Christmas break and was still in the giggly newlywed stage that drove Christina nuts. Stacey would get over the newness of marriage soon enough.

Stacey bounced on the balls of her feet as her hair continued to swish. If she wasn't careful, her cheeks would split from all that smiling.

Christina dropped a slip of paper into the last cubby and gave Stacey her full attention. "What's up?"

"I'm pregnant!" Stacey let out a squeal, wrapping her arms around Christina. "Ohmigosh, can you believe it? Me!"

Christina's feet were cemented to the berber carpet as rocks tumbled in her stomach. Mechanically, she returned Stacey's embrace. "Congratulations." Christina winced, hearing the jealousy in her voice. Hopefully Stacey didn't. "When did you find out?"

Stacey's smile grew impossibly wider. "Yesterday after school. I was like a day late and fah-reaking out because that never happens, and T.J. said to take a test, and I did, and it was positive. It was a total surprise too. I'm on the pill and everything, but sometimes I forget to take it. I'm not very far along, and we haven't been married a long time like you and Gary, and it wasn't exactly planned, but we're excited."

Christina gave Stacey her best fake smile. Stacey was so . . . young. Barely twenty-two, although her maturity level was more concerning than her actual age. The first year of marriage was hard enough, and now Stacey was pregnant on top of everything else? Just like that?

"I'm happy for you," Christina said. "How are you feeling?"

"So far so good. I haven't puked yet or anything if that's what you mean. I made an appointment with the doctor, and they don't need to see me until eight weeks, and since I'm not even five, it's going to be a while."

Well, wasn't she lucky. She'd probably bypass morning sickness entirely. Why did Stacey's body function perfectly, when Christina's screwed up more often than not? She continued to smile, nodding and feigning pleasure at the news.

Maybe she had no reason to be jealous. She was three days late. At least, she was pretty sure she was late—her periods weren't regular, so it was hard to be sure. Christina hadn't taken a test, but maybe she was finally pregnant. She and Gary were definitely ready for a baby, unlike Stacey and T.J.

Christina's hope lasted until lunch, and then a quick trip to the restroom squashed it completely. She wasn't pregnant this month. Again.

She walked down the hallway, her face hot and legs trembling. So much for using lunch to mentally prepare for her evaluation. All she wanted was to sit at her desk and cry. *Hold it together, Christina.* She forced a smile as she passed a co-worker in the hallway. Just a few more minutes, and she'd be alone.

Her classroom door came into focus, the bright yellow butcher paper covered in multicolored hand prints visible even from the end of the hallway. Christina let the tears pool in her eyes. Solitude. That's all she wanted.

She crossed the threshold, letting her shoulders slump.

Not alone. Stacey sat at her desk in the exact position Christina wanted to be—arms on desk, head on arms, shoulders shaking with sobs.

Christina's stomach dropped. Why her? Why today?

Her own tears would have to wait.

Christina stiffened her spine and walked over to Stacey, placing a hand on her back. "Stacey, what on earth is wrong?"

Stacey didn't look up. "What am I doing, Christina?" she asked, the words muffled. "We must be insane to have a baby now. I'm excited, but I'm so scared."

This was her big problem? Christina sighed, pulling over a chair. "Stacey, look at me."

Stacey straightened, smudged mascara highlighting her swollen eyes.

"What's going on? I thought you were happy."

Stacey grabbed a tissue and wiped under her eyes, smearing the makeup even more. New tears appeared. "Of course I'm happy but the timing is so bad. T.J.'s still in school, and we live in a crappy one-bedroom apartment, and I barely make enough money to pay the interest on all my student loans. We're practically at poverty level and can't afford a baby."

Christina closed her eyes, fighting down the jealousy. She and Gary could afford a baby. They could afford three or four easily. So why did Stacey get pregnant accidentally, and Christina couldn't even get pregnant on purpose?

"Stop crying," Christina said sternly. "You're going to be a great mother. This baby will be loved and cared for. You can do this."

The tears had slowed down at least. Stacey's eyes begged for reassurance. "Do you really think so?"

The crazy thing was Christina did. She smiled, pushing the box of tissues closer to Stacey. "You take care of twenty-five six-year-olds every day. After teaching, a baby will be a cake walk. Now dry your eyes. Lunch will be over in a few minutes."

Stacey laughed. It was shaky, but happy too. "You always know the right thing to say." She walked over to the mirror hanging off a cabinet door and dabbed under her eyes, then grabbed another tissue and blew her nose. "How do I look?"

Christina smiled, hoping it didn't seem sad. Stacey was beautiful and happy and luckier than she could imagine. Irresponsible, perhaps. But lucky all the same. "I think you've got the pregnancy glow."

The bell rang, signaling the end of lunchtime.

"I'm sorry," Stacey said as they walked outside to pick up their classes. "I know you have your evaluation this afternoon, but I was scared, and I knew I could talk to you, and you'd calm me down. T.J. and I probably should've been smarter about things like you and Gary, but we can't do anything about that now."

Smart. It seemed that word defined Christina and Gary's entire five-year plan. But now she had to wonder—were they being punished for waiting? Christina had always looked down on girls who got pregnant right after the wedding. She and Gary had decided early on they weren't going to be that couple. Responsible adults finished school and established their careers before having children.

"Smart" had translated into waiting nearly four years before trying. First Gary was in law school, and Christina was in the middle of her bachelor's degree. After Gary's graduation Christina had wanted to start trying, but he'd said it was better to start their careers and buy a house. When laid out in his courtroom voice, it seemed logical enough. Now they had everything in place to welcome a baby except a positive pregnancy test.

Was something wrong with her? With Gary? They'd been trying for thirteen months, and all the books said it should happen within a year.

"Don't worry about it. I'm ready for my evaluation," Christina said. She could cry in solitude later.

"Of course you are," Stacey said. "You're such an awesome teacher. Half my lesson plans are copied from yours. You would be a great mom, too. Maybe you should have a baby soon. We could be first-time moms together. We could quit our jobs and go to the park with our strollers and have play dates with the babies and everything. What do you think?"

Christina was not about to explain her personal struggles to Stacey. The girl was so fertile she got pregnant on birth control. "I think I really love my job." It wasn't a lie, but it wasn't the truth either.

The rest of the day dragged. Christina did her best to stay upbeat and positive during her evaluation. It must have worked because Principal Gardner gave her glowing compliments.

After the evaluation, the familiar heavy cramps began, and it was all Christina could do to stay at school until contract time instead of leaving as soon as the kids did. Promptly at four o'clock she drove home. After changing into pajamas, she curled up on the couch and turned on the TV. It didn't take long for the tears to come.

Two hours later, Christina heard Gary place his briefcase on the counter. A tentative hand rested on her shoulder. "What's wrong? Did your evaluation go poorly?"

Christina glanced at his concerned face, then shook her head. "It's just cramps." Her mouth felt thick, her voice scratchy from too long crying.

"Oh, is that all?" He sat down beside her, gray slacks still crisp and starched even after a ten-hour day at the office. "I'm sorry, babe. Do you need some Midol?"

She stared at the floor, telling herself not to get upset. He didn't realize what this period meant—at least, not fully. "No. Sorry I didn't make dinner."

Gary brushed away a lock of her hair. "Don't worry about it. I'll heat up some leftovers. Want anything?"

She'd already eaten half a jar of chocolate frosting and a package of graham crackers, but Gary didn't need to know that. "No thanks. I'll watch TV. Maybe grade some papers."

"All right. I have some work things to finish, so I'll eat in my office. Let me know if you need anything."

She should've told him when she had the chance.

At nine o'clock Christina turned off the TV. Looked like she'd be going to bed alone again. When Gary started working at his father's law firm shortly after graduation, they'd been thrilled. Over a year later, Christina wasn't quite so excited. Maybe a baby would bring them closer together. Help them find that spark again.

Christina wandered into the office to grab her laptop, making as little noise as possible so she wouldn't bother Gary. He didn't even look up from his computer screen. A tennis racket leaned against the closet door, marring the otherwise spotless room. Gary must've played with a client today. And once again, he hadn't bothered to put away his equipment. Stifling a sigh, Christina quietly opened the closet, wincing when the hinge squeaked. She glanced over at Gary, then opened the door the rest of the way.

Stuffed animals tumbled down from the top shelves. A pink elephant bounced off her head and a giraffe hit her shoulder. She put up a hand, grabbing a panda bear and two penguins before they hit the ground. Fifteen or so animals littered the floor around her feet. Soon there wouldn't even be room for sports equipment in the closet. The stuffed animals were taking over.

Gary spun around in his chair, eyebrow raised. "Everything okay?"

So much for not disturbing him. "Just fine." Christina set the tennis racket inside the closet. She crammed the stuffed animals onto the shelves with their fuzzy friends, then leaned her weight against the door until it clicked shut. They should donate the darn things to a children's hospital. But Gary would never allow it.

Two minutes later she climbed into bed with her laptop and a hot water bottle. She tried to enter grades but couldn't concentrate. Thirteen months. She had promised herself she wouldn't borrow trouble until now. After all, the books said not to worry unless it had been more than a year.

She pulled up the internet browser and stared at the screen for nearly a minute. *Just do it, Christina.* She typed "signs of infertility" into the box and clicked search. Within seconds over nine million hits were populated. Christina clicked on the first one and read. Her eyes scanned through article after article as her heart climbed into her throat.

Was it really possible? She'd never seriously considered that once they wanted a baby, they might not immediately get one.

"What's this?"

Christina jumped, slamming the laptop lid shut. "Nothing."

Gary raised an eyebrow. He sat on the edge of the bed and took the laptop from her. She wanted to grab it back, tell him it was a surprise and he couldn't see, but didn't. She had promised herself she wouldn't worry Gary.

Until this month.

"Infertility?" Gary clicked on a few of the open web pages before setting the laptop aside. "Christina, what's going on?"

"I . . . I'm not sure."

His eyes narrowed, the planes of his face hardening into his lawyer look. There was no keeping it from him now. After months of agonizing alone, it was time to let Gary know. Even if it meant she'd have to tell him *that*.

"You think we're having problems?" Gary asked.

It sounded awful when said out loud. Christina picked up the edge of the quilt and fidgeted with a loose string. "Maybe."

"Because your period started again?"

She nodded, avoiding eye contact.

He scooted closer and wrapped an arm around her. "Why didn't you tell me that's why you were upset? I thought it was the cramps."

She turned her face into his shoulder. "It seemed stupid."

"It's not stupid if it worries you. It says on the website you should see a doctor after twelve months of trying. It's been like, what, nine months? Ten? It could still happen."

And there it was. She would have to tell him now.

Christina remembered so well the day he told her they should start trying—last June, the morning of their fourth wedding anniversary. Gary had surprised her with breakfast in bed. He'd brought her a tray of pancakes, pretty much the only thing he could cook, with a single red rose and a tiny box.

"I thought we agreed not to get each other presents," she said with a smile. They were going on a Caribbean cruise in a few weeks as their anniversary present to each other. "I didn't get you anything."

He twisted a dish towel in his hands. "Open it."

Christina picked up the box, the crisply precise lines a dead giveaway it had been wrapped by the department store. She carefully unwrapped the box and pulled off the lid. Inside lay a pair of beautiful white baby booties.

"I think we should start trying," he said. "We did agree on this summer. My job is going really well, and we have the house now—"

Christina leaned over and kissed him before he could finish the sentence, her heart soaring. She'd gone off birth control a few months earlier. Now he'd never have to know.

She snapped back to the present and blurted, "We've been trying for thirteen months." She clapped a hand over her mouth, wishing she could take back the words. She could have eased into it, explained the circumstances first.

Gary blinked. "Excuse me?"

"I've been off birth control for thirteen months, not nine." She whispered the words as though a lower volume would lessen the consequences.

Gary stood, running a hand through his hair. "I . . ." He shifted from foot to foot. Blew out a breath. Scrubbed a hand over his face. Christina could see him struggling to keep his cool, to not explode. To find out all the facts before passing judgment. "Why didn't you tell me?"

She thought of all the reasons, but finally said, "It didn't come up."

"You didn't think it was important to mention you were off birth control?"

"It wasn't like that."

"By all means, tell me what it was like."

"It was when we were buying the house, okay? We were fighting with the bank over the short sale price, and then we were closing and moving in and getting settled. I completely spaced getting the shot, and by the time I remembered, it was nearly summer."

Gary's jaw muscles neared spasm status. "I thought you set a reminder in your phone for that."

Christina knelt on the bed, desperation making her hands shake. "I did. I was going to get it on the way home from school, but a parent showed up, and by the time I was done, the doctor's office was closed." All true. "That night we found out our offer was approved. With closing and moving, I forgot."

Gary continued to shift from foot to foot. "Why didn't you tell me when you remembered? Or go get the shot?"

Because they'd already waited four years to start trying.

Christina hung her head, tears gathering in her eyes. She blinked furiously. Now was not the time for a waterfall. "Since we agreed to start trying soon, I didn't think it was a big deal. The nurse told me it would take a few months for the effects of the shot to wear off. I wasn't trying to go behind your back. I was planning for summer." She reached for his arm, but he backed away. "After our anniversary, I didn't see the point in telling you."

"And what if I changed my mind? How long would you have kept it a secret—until you brought the baby home from the hospital? I thought we made major decisions together."

Christina shrank away. "We did make the decision together. We decided on summer."

"I can't talk about this right now. I need to think." He pinched the bridge of his nose, eyes raised to the ceiling.

"We need to—"

"I'm going for a drive. I can't be around you right now." He grabbed his keys off the dresser and headed out the door.

She lurched off the bed. Her foot caught in the sheet, and she stumbled, then raced after him. "Let's talk about this. Garrison!"

"We'll talk when I get home." A door slammed shut.

Christina held a hand to her chest, squeezing her eyes closed. Stupid, stupid, stupid. Why hadn't she told him?

She hadn't tried to deceive him. Withhold information, maybe. But not trick him.

Christina cried and prayed and paced. It was nearly two a.m. before Gary came home. He dropped his keys and wallet on the dresser, not meeting her gaze.

"You left," she accused.

"I was upset. Still am."

"And you have every right to be. But that doesn't mean you can run away."

"You kept a secret from me. I left in the middle of an argument. Let's call it even."

Christina raised an eyebrow. "Do you mean—"

"I did a lot of thinking while I was out."

"Me too."

"And I know you weren't trying to trick me. I was angry and stupid and surprised."

Her heart leapt. "You believe me?"

He gently grasped her hand and led her to the bed. "Yes. You caught me off guard. The idea that we could have gotten pregnant when we weren't planning on it terrifies me."

"But we were planning on it. We always planned for summer."

"I only told you we could start trying because I ran out of excuses."

Her stomach dropped as though she'd plunged over a fifty-foot waterfall. "I don't understand. You seemed so excited."

The muscles in his forearm bunched and relaxed as he ran a hand through his hair. "I pretended to be excited. But I'm scared of being a father. I kept making up reasons we should wait, and every time you agreed, I felt relieved. But then we had the degrees and the careers and the house, and I ran out of reasons to put it off. So I gave in."

Their five-year plan was a product of fear. Unbelievable. "Having a baby is giving in?"

"You know my father was never really there for me. I'm scared of being like that with our baby. I'm scared one day our kid will tell his wife how much he resents me."

Christina knew Gary was desperate for Alexander's approval, that it was a big reason behind his sixty-hour work weeks. But this went much deeper than that.

She leaned into Gary, holding his hand tight and resting her head on his shoulder. "You will be a great father. I know it." Her voice caught, and she swallowed. "I want a baby so badly. Every month when my period comes, my heart breaks. I love my career, and I love you. But something's missing. Don't you feel it?"

"All I feel every month is relief."

She flinched. "Why didn't you tell me that, instead of agreeing? I feel horrible. Horrible I didn't tell you about the birth control, and horrible I never knew how you really felt about this." Horrible that he didn't want a baby and she did.

"I thought you'd think less of me if you knew."

How had their marriage arrived here? "If you'd told me, we could've worked on it together."

"I'm telling you now." They were both quiet for a moment, and then he spoke again. "I'm sorry you didn't feel like you could tell me about the birth control. I don't care what I'm doing or how busy and stressed I am, you can always come to me."

Christina nodded, holding him tight. "No more running away. For either of us."

"Agreed. How long did you say it's been?"

"Thirteen months. I was supposed to get another shot last February."

"Thirteen months." He fiddled with her wedding ring, looking at their clasped hands. "You think there might be a problem?"

"I think we should see a doctor to rule out the possibility."

"I hate doctors."

"I know."

"I don't know if I can deal with all this right now—if I'm ready to have a baby."

"Are you saying you want me to go back on birth control?" The thought made her sick.

He smoothed hair away from her face. "Let's sleep on it. We can talk about this more tomorrow."

As they crawled into bed, Christina felt the gulf between them widen. It filled with water, and the water crashed over her in waves, making it hard to breathe.

CHAPTER THREE
KYRA

One thousand dollars for a twenty percent chance at pregnancy. Those were the odds Dr. Mendoza had given Kyra and David. That one thousand dollars might as well have been ten thousand, as hard as it had been to come up with the cash. But they wanted a baby badly enough to take the gamble.

And it had paid off. Kyra was six weeks pregnant, and today they would see their baby for the first time. She couldn't tell if the butterflies in her stomach were from nervous excitement or a sign of morning sickness. That one thousand dollars was worth every penny.

The waiting room at the Center for Infertility and Reproductive Medicine was all warm browns and soothing oceanscape paintings. David and Kyra sat on the earth-toned couch, their three-year-old daughter, Sophie, between them. David's glasses had slid to the end of his nose as he focused on the flat-screened TV playing the latest Disney movie. Kyra shook her head at the choice. Disney, when most of the patients were childless.

Sophie tugged on Kyra's hand. "When do we get to see my baby, Mommy?"

Kyra smiled, brushing a lock of Sophie's honey-brown hair behind her ear. "Soon, baby girl. Try and watch the movie."

David nestled Sophie against his side. "Your favorite part is coming up, Soph."

Kyra pulled out her cell phone and snapped a picture, her heart nearly exploding with happiness. She'd spent more time in this office over the last few months than she cared to remember. But at least now they were here for a happy reason.

Unexplained secondary infertility. After months of tests, that had been Dr. Mendoza's official diagnosis. There had been no medical reason why David and Kyra couldn't get pregnant. And yet somehow, after a year and a half of trying, they hadn't.

"I think your best bet is intrauterine insemination, or IUI," Dr. Mendoza had said.

"Is that the same thing as artificial insemination?" David asked.

Dr. Mendoza nodded and pointed to a chart on her desk. "We directly inject the sperm into Kyra's uterus, bypassing the cervix, to give you the best chance at pregnancy."

Kyra could still remember the way she'd wound her purse strap around and around her finger. "What happens if we decide to move forward?"

"You take Clomid on days three through seven of your cycle," Dr. Mendoza said. "It's a pill that should make you ovulate two or three eggs instead of one, further increasing your chances of getting pregnant. We do an ultrasound right before ovulation to ensure conditions are optimal for fertilization and implantation, and then you give yourself an HCG trigger shot. On the day of ovulation, we collect David's sperm sample and wash and concentrate it so only the healthiest sperm are used. You come in that same day, Kyra, and I insert a catheter into your uterus and inject the sperm. You wouldn't even have to both be here."

Kyra remembered thinking how strange it was that she could conceive a baby without her husband present.

They took a few weeks to pray about the decision, and decided to give IUI a try. Kyra had taken the Clomid, a drug that made her totally unbalanced, as evidenced by her three-hour sob session when David forgot to bring home a pint of Ben and Jerry's. David gave her the HCG injection to trigger ovulation. They'd done the IUI.

And it had worked. Kyra still couldn't believe they were in the twenty percent.

A nurse walked into the waiting room, pulling Kyra back to the present. "We're ready for you now," she said. Sophie jumped up from the couch and impatiently waited for David and Kyra to do the same.

"Hurry," she said. "I want to see my baby brother."

The nurse laughed. "How do you know it'll be a brother? Maybe you'll get a sister."

Sophie shook her head vehemently. "No. A brother."

The nurse laughed again, directing them to an exam room. "Undress from the waist down, Kyra. Dr. Mendoza will be with you shortly."

Minutes later Kyra sat on the crinkly paper of the exam table, a thin paper sheet covering her lower half.

"Can I name my baby brother?" Sophie asked.

David chuckled. "Don't you think your mother and I should do that?"

"No," Sophie said.

Sophie wasn't the only one who'd been dreaming about baby names. "I was thinking Hunter if it's a boy," Kyra said.

Sophie wrinkled her nose. "Hunter like Grandma and Grandpa Hunter?"

Kyra nodded. "And I think Theresa is pretty for a girl."

The door swung open, and Dr. Mendoza walked into the room. "Already picking out names I see." She shook David's hand, then Sophie's. "Hello, Sophie. It's nice to see you again."

"I get to see my baby brother." Sophie wiggled in her chair, her face bright with excitement.

"Maybe. We won't know if it's a boy or a girl for a while yet." Dr. Mendoza squeezed clear goo onto the ultrasound wand. "Let's see how baby is doing."

Kyra's eyes eagerly scanned the ultrasound screen, trying to pick out a person from all the wavy lines and shadows. "Where's the baby?"

Dr. Mendoza pointed to a tiny white speck in the middle of all the squiggly lines. "Right there. Congratulations, you three."

Awe enveloped Kyra. Their baby. She stared at the white speck, her heart overflowing with love. Their miracle. Her eyes found and held David's. He smiled and mouthed *I love you.*

"That doesn't look like a baby," said a pouty voice.

Kyra tore her eyes from David's and focused on Sophie. Her lips were turned down in a frown, arms folded across her chest.

"It won't look like a baby for a long time." Dr. Mendoza pointed. "Right there is how your baby gets food, Sophie. It's called a placenta."

"Can we hear the heartbeat?" Kyra asked.

Dr. Mendoza tore a photo from the printer and handed it to Kyra. "It's still too early for that. At this point, all we can tell for sure is that there's a baby, sack, and forming placenta. We'll know a lot more at your nine-week appointment."

Kyra stared at the tiny jelly-bean in the photo. It was hard to believe this was real.

Dr. Mendoza flipped open a chart. "Your HCG levels are continuing to double, which is good. Continue your progesterone suppositories each night, and we'll see you in three weeks. Congratulations again."

As soon as the door shut, Kyra hopped up from the table, the paper sheet clutched around her waist. "We're having a baby!" She threw her free arm around David. He leaned down, kissing her softly as he held her close.

"When can I see my baby brother?" Sophie asked.

Kyra released David and picked up her pants. "We just saw him, Soph."

"That wasn't a baby."

"I promise, sweetie, it was. He still has to grow."

Sophie wrinkled her nose like she didn't quite believe her mother, but nodded anyway.

The green-and-rust color of their Honda Civic was easy to spot, even from across the parking lot. Sunlight reflected off the duct tape on the passenger side window. David struggled with the handle on the back door, but finally opened it with a screech and buckled Sophie into her carseat.

"This calls for a celebration," he said once they were all in the car.

"McDonald's!" Sophie exclaimed.

"We don't have money for that," Kyra said quietly.

"We'll get something off the dollar menu." David gave her a reassuring smile. "We'll keep it cheap."

Their budget didn't even allow for that small splurge. "Another baby is going to be expensive."

David leaned over and kissed her. "We can afford to spend five dollars on a celebration."

Five dollars in treats was enough for an entire home-cooked meal complete with leftovers, if they didn't have a meat.

"I want chicken nuggets," Sophie said from the back seat.

Definitely not on the dollar menu. But Kyra gave herself over to the celebration. "Okay."

At McDonald's, Sophie scarfed down her chicken nuggets and ran off to play. David and Kyra ate at a slower pace, watching from their table as Sophie bounded up the stairs and shot down the slide.

David reached across the table and placed his hand on Kyra's. "Thank you."

"For what?"

"For giving us another child." His eyes glistened. "I know how hard Clomid was on you. I know the IUI wasn't fun. But it was all worth it, right?"

"Absolutely."

David pulled his hand from hers and returned to his cheeseburger. Kyra watched him eat, her fingernail finding its way between her teeth.

"Are you still hungry?" David asked.

Kyra shook her head. "How are we going to afford this baby? We had to save for the IUI for three months, and still ended up pulling a couple hundred from our emergency fund. A baby is going to cost a lot more than one thousand dollars."

"We prayed about this, Kyr." He pointed to her stomach. "That child is meant to join our family. Everything else will work itself out."

Kyra rested her hand on her stomach. She wasn't experiencing any pregnancy symptoms yet—if this pregnancy mirrored her first, she wouldn't for another few weeks—and she definitely wasn't showing. But she still felt the baby's presence, small but reassuring. "You're right. I just worry."

"I know, but enjoy the moment. We worked hard for this."

Sophie chattered the whole way home from McDonald's. At their rented home in Riverton, Kyra got out of the car as the neighbors pulled into their driveway. The minivan door slid open, and four children piled out. Cassandra Everhart emerged from the driver's side, her dark chocolate skin and corkscrew hair a faint outline against the night sky.

"Malachi!" Sophie ran across their lawn toward Cassandra's house while he raced to meet her.

"Hi, Sophie."

"I've got it," Kyra told David. "Meet you inside in a minute."

He nodded and headed inside, and Kyra went to meet Cassandra. The other three children had disappeared inside the house.

"Hey," Kyra said. "How are you?"

"Great," Cassandra said. "I've been meaning to come over for a few days now. I've got some books for the school drive. Aren't you collecting them?"

"Yes," Kyra said. "Christina asked if I'd be willing since I'm home during the day."

"I think it's great you're helping out," Cassandra said. "I have almost an entire box full of books we don't read anymore. Let me go get them."

"We went to McDonald's," Sophie told Malachi.

"Ah man." He frowned. "We didn't."

"We went cuz there's a baby in my mommy's tummy."

Cassandra froze, then took a few steps toward Kyra, eyebrows raised in surprise. "Are you pregnant?"

Kyra couldn't stop the silly grin from spreading across her face. "Six weeks today. We just got back from our first ultrasound."

"Congratulations!" Cassandra wrapped her in a tight hug. "Wait, six weeks? Why are they doing such an early ultrasound? Is something wrong?"

"No, just standard procedure at my doctor's office I guess." Time to change the subject. For months, Kyra had been making up excuses to explain away the babysitting favors she'd asked of Cassandra. There was no reason anyone needed to know about their short and humiliating stint into the world of infertility treatments. "We're not supposed to tell people about the baby yet, Sophie. Remember?"

"My mom doesn't have a baby in her tummy." Malachi squinted up at Cassandra. "Do you?"

"I certainly hope not. Four kids is plenty for me."

"Time for bed," Kyra told Sophie. "Maybe you can play with Malachi tomorrow."

"Let me grab those books for you really quick," Cassandra said. "Congratulations again, Kyra. Your secret is safe with me."

"Thanks." And somehow, that made it real. Not the IUI, or the positive pregnancy test, or even the ultrasound. But the moment Kyra shared her news with a friend who was happy for her.

CHAPTER FOUR
MEGAN

Trent jumped onto the lift of the moving truck and released the latch for the roll-up door. Megan put a hand over her eyes and squinted, trying to block out the blinding morning sun. They'd finally made it to Riverton well past their projected arrival time last night and had decided to hold off on unloading things until this morning.

The door slid into the ceiling, and they both stared at the piano. It sat in front of the other boxes and furniture, blocking everything else. They'd have to move the piano into the house first, just like Megan had wanted. But it was bulky. And heavy. She should've thought that part through better.

"How are we going to move that by ourselves?" Megan asked.

Trent grunted in response, unwinding straps from the flat dolly. "We'll get it on here, and you can help me guide it out of the truck."

"We'll break our backs," Megan said.

"Hello?" A man in jeans and a University of Utah Law hoodie peered into the truck. He was tall and slim, with dark hair and a clean-shaven face. A woman, also tall and slender, stood next to him, her wild red-orange hair pulled up in a ponytail with curly tendrils escaping every which way.

"I'm Gary Vincent from next door," he said. "This is my wife, Christina. You must be our new neighbors."

Trent hopped out of the truck and brushed a hand on his jeans before extending it toward Gary. "Sure are. I'm Trent Burke, and this is my wife, Megan. Happy to meet you."

Christina held up a loaf of bread, so fresh it still steamed inside the bag. "We made banana bread for breakfast and had extra. Do you need any help unpacking?"

Megan closed her eyes and sent a quick *thank you* heavenward. "We would really appreciate any help you can give us. That bread looks amazing. Thank you."

Gary pointed to the piano and pulled out his cell phone. "I'll see if I can scrounge up a few neighbors to help with that."

By the time they each ate a slice of banana bread, there were four men in their driveway, ready to help. Megan couldn't stop smiling. She liked this neighborhood already.

With a lot of grunts and a few curses, the men managed to haul the piano into the house. It fit along the wall of the front room perfectly. The bay window opposite illuminated the space with a soft light that would make reading sheet music a dream.

"It's perfect." Megan gave Trent a quick kiss. "Already this place feels more like home."

Once most of the boxes were unloaded, Christina and Megan left the heavy furniture to the men and went inside to start unpacking. "Where do you want to start?" Christina asked.

Megan looked around the front room, overwhelmed by all the boxes. "Um, maybe the kitchen. I'll feel a lot better once we have dishes in cupboards."

"I know what you mean. The kitchen is my sanctuary. I love to bake."

Megan stared at Christina's slender figure with a raised eyebrow. "How on earth do you stay thin?"

The tips of Christina's ears pinked. "I do Pilates, and we eat mostly organic, but I think a lot of it's good genes. I've never struggled with weight."

Megan slapped her own ample hip. "Yeah, me either."

Christina smiled uncomfortably. Time to change the subject.

Megan picked a box and set it on the kitchen counter, pulling off the packing tape. "So, how long have you lived in Riverton?"

"Almost a year." Christina opened a box filled with plates and silverware. "How about I unpack boxes so you can put things where you want them?"

"Sounds like a plan. Do you like the area?"

Christina nodded. "There are a lot of good people here, mostly young families or couples just starting out. Have you and Trent been married long?"

"Five and a half years. What about you guys?"

"We're coming up on five years this summer." Christina finished unloading the box and placed it, now empty, on the kitchen floor. "Do you have children? I haven't seen any around."

Megan had known the question would come up, but it still stabbed like a knife. She wanted so badly to be able to say "yes."

To pull out her cell phone and bore Christina to tears with a dozen pictures. "No kids yet. We've been trying for years, but it hasn't happened."

Christina's hands stilled, then slowly removed glasses from the box once more. "I'm so sorry. I didn't mean to be nosy. I should know as well as anyone how annoying that question is. Gary and I don't have children yet either. We've been focusing on our careers, and the timing hasn't been right."

Megan shrugged. "You didn't know."

"Do you mind if I ask what the problem is?"

"Of course not. Trent and I are pretty much an open book." Megan smiled, hoping Christina could see she was being genuine. "I have PCOS—polycystic ovarian syndrome. Basically my hormones are completely unbalanced, and I don't ovulate without fertility medication. It has lots of fun symptoms like inability to lose weight, insane sugar cravings, and struggling to get pregnant." And it had a lot of embarrassing ones she avoided mentioning, like excessive facial hair growth and acne. "Trent has a low sperm count too."

"I'm sorry." Christina looked like she wanted to cry.

"We're dealing with it."

Christina shifted, tugging at the packing tape on a box. "Gary and I want kids one day, but he just got out of law school and is trying to get established. And I really love teaching elementary school."

"That's great. What grade do you teach?"

"First."

"I saw a poster on a telephone pole for a book drive. Is that your school?"

"Yeah. I'm in charge, actually. A woman from church is helping me out by collecting the books during the day."

"I'd love to help, if you still need people."

Christina raised an eyebrow. "Are you serious?"

"Yes. We were very involved with our church and community in Logan, and I'd love to do the same here."

"That would be great. I'll need help sorting the books once Kyra's collected them all. Um, I don't think this is kitchen stuff." Christina pulled a DVD case out of the box, examining it. "You guys are *Criminology* fans?"

"Oh yeah. We own all the seasons."

"Gary mentioned he's interested in watching this show." Christina set the DVD in the box. "Where should I put this?"

"I'll put it in the living room." Megan grabbed season one of *Criminology* out of the box. "Here, you guys borrow it. We'll swap for season two when you're done."

Christina took the DVD case hesitantly. "You won't miss it?"

"Not at all." And now they'd get to talk again when Christina brought the DVDs back.

By one o'clock, the truck was unloaded, and Megan and Trent shooed everyone away to enjoy their Saturday. Christina and Gary suggested getting together soon, and Megan hoped it wasn't just one of those polite things people said but didn't really mean.

Trent and Megan worked feverishly the rest of the day. By two a.m., they had managed to unpack all the essentials and called it quits.

"It's starting to feel like home," Megan told Trent as they lay in bed in the dark.

Trent leaned over and kissed her softly on the lips. "Home is wherever you are. I love you."

She smiled, snuggling in closer. "I love you too. Marrying you was the best decision I ever made."

CHAPTER FIVE
CHRISTINA

"Babe, are you ready to go?"

Christina looked up from her magazine and glanced at the kitchen clock. Right on time. Gary had gone into the office for a few hours after church, but had assured her he'd be home by three. "Give me five minutes," Christina said, setting aside the magazine.

Gary placed his iPad on the counter. "I don't want to listen to my mother complain if we're late for dinner."

Neither did Christina. But Elauna would insist they were late even if they showed up fifteen minutes early. "I just need to box this up." Christina motioned to the apple pie cooling on the counter. It was made from all organic ingredients, with no refined sugars or processed foods. She had spent most of the afternoon on it, and it looked beautiful. Perfect, in her book.

Elauna would find something wrong with it, Christina was sure. The latticing lay crooked. The outer edge of the crust was crisper than she liked. Elauna was in the mood for cherry pie, and Christina had made apple.

"Okay, well hurry. I'm going to use the restroom, and then I'm ready to go." Gary looked down at Christina's jeans. "You're putting your dress on, right?"

Christina sighed and gave a "really?" eyebrow raise. They'd spent nearly every Sunday dinner with his parents since their dating days. She knew how this worked.

Ten minutes later they were in the Lexus and were pulling out of the driveway. "How was work?" Christina asked as they drove toward the mountain bench in Draper, where Gary's parents lived.

"Good." He didn't elaborate. Christina knew he wouldn't, but it seemed rude not to ask, so they played out the same conversation every day.

"So . . ." Christina wasn't sure how to bring up what she really wanted to talk about. They had successfully avoided bringing up anything important all weekend, namely their fight. They'd discussed the Burkes last night (they were nice) and today's church services over lunch (the sermon had been pleasant, and they were happy to see the Burkes attend). They had run out of small talk, and the elephant in the room was driving Christina nuts. She decided there was nothing to do but dive in. "Have you thought any more about what we discussed on Friday?"

Gary sighed, his hands tightening on the steering wheel at exactly ten and two o'clock. "Now isn't the best time to discuss this. We'll be at my parents' in twenty minutes."

She wouldn't let him put her off any longer. "You said we'd talk about it yesterday, and we never did. I think I should make an appointment with my gynecologist so we can go in for some tests. Maybe this has something to do with my painful periods."

Gary's jaw clenched. Christina was getting nowhere fast. "You said yourself it can take a few months after you go off the shot for things to go back to normal. So really, if you take that into account, it hasn't been a year since we started trying to get pregnant."

"I think there's something wrong with me." Christina said it quietly, hoping if she didn't act angry, he wouldn't get more upset. "I want to know what we're dealing with. If there is a problem, we can take it from there. Don't you want to know?"

His knuckles were white now. "Not really. I'm still trying to get used to the idea of being a father. I don't think I can handle the thought of not being one."

That did it. She slammed her hand on the dashboard with a *crack*, causing Gary to swerve.

"What the crap, Christina? We almost wrecked."

"'What the crap' to you too. First you make this huge romantic gesture, telling me you're ready to be a father. Then you tell me you've felt nothing but relief I'm not pregnant yet. And now you tell me you actually want kids and don't want to find out if something's wrong?" She shook her head. "I don't know what to make of you these days. You are the biggest contradiction I've ever seen in my entire life. And I teach six-year-olds!"

"I want to wait a few more months," Gary said, his lips tight. "We've waited almost five years. What's a little longer?"

They had waited five years. That was part of the problem. Christina folded her arms. "It's a big deal to me."

"Let's not talk about this anymore. We don't want to upset Sunday dinner with things like infertility."

"I have a better idea. How about we don't talk at all?"

"Christina . . ."

She focused on the scenery outside her window.

Gary sighed. "Please don't be like this."

She pursed her lips and refused to answer.

The rest of the drive passed in uncomfortable silence. The car wound up the peaceful neighborhood streets of the bench, a sharp contradiction to the mood inside the vehicle. Guilt gnawed at Christina for being petty—the silent treatment wasn't exactly mature—but she refused to apologize. Gary was wrong. They needed to see a doctor. Why didn't he understand?

An intimidatingly large wrought-iron gate had the name "Vincent" scrolled in intricate, swirling letters across the top. Gary rolled down his window and entered the security code, then drove down the long driveway to the sprawling Vincent mansion. They walked up to the massive solid wood doors and rang the bell.

"Please don't make things awkward," Gary said. "I don't want to get into this with my parents."

Christina gave him a scathing look but didn't reply. As if she would ever discuss anything substantial with the Vincents. It was best to be fake and skim the surface of life with them.

"Christina, Gary, why don't you have children yet?"

"Well, Elauna, Gary and I might be infertile. We're not sure since he refuses to go to the doctor."

"Oh my! Don't let the ladies at the country club know. I couldn't handle the humiliation. I always knew there was something wrong with you, Christina."

Yeah. She wasn't about to have that conversation.

The door swung open, revealing Elauna dressed in an expensive designer suit. "I was beginning to think you weren't coming," she said. Her smirk, too wide and filled with unnaturally white teeth, screamed Botox.

Christina plastered on her fakest smile and followed Gary inside.

"We're ten minutes early, Mom," he said.

Elauna hung up their coats and waved her hands dismissively. "It's no matter. Dinner's warming in the oven." Since the staff had Sundays off, the cook always made something Elauna could easily heat up.

"I'll put the pie in the kitchen," Christina said.

"Nonsense, I can do it." Elauna grabbed the pie and lifted the lid of the box to look inside. "Oh no. Apple pie."

Christina gritted her teeth. "I'm sorry, is that not okay?"

"Oh, it's fine, dear. I meant to call and ask you to bring a chocolate cake. Looks like you burned the crust, but I'm sure it'll still taste fine."

Christina wanted to rip that smile right off Elauna's spray-tanned face.

"I asked her to make an apple pie, Mom." Gary placed a hand at the small of Christina's back. "I've been craving one all week."

"Hmmm. Your father's in the living room. Go in, and I'll take this to the kitchen. I have something for you."

Not another one. It took monumental effort for Christina to keep her shoulders from sagging. She should've guessed. They just returned from their cruise to Alaska, after all.

In the living room, Alexander reclined in an easy chair, the Sunday paper held out in front of him.

"Hello, Dad," Gary said.

"You're late." Alexander rose and shook both of their hands. "Your mother was starting to worry."

Elauna rounded the corner and held out a box, wrapped in shiny white paper with crisp lines and an unnaturally perfect bow. "Here it is."

Crap.

Christina forced herself to smile as she took the box. "That's so nice of you, Elauna. You didn't have to get us anything." She slid a finger under the tape and the tiniest rip appeared in the wrapping paper. Christina froze. Had Elauna noticed? No. She was too busy frowning at Gary.

"It's not for you," Elauna said. "It's for the grandchildren."

Christina gritted her teeth and purposefully aggravated the tear in the paper. Gary glanced at her, his eyes warning.

Alexander snorted from behind his paper. "If you're this bad before the grandkids are even born, Elauna, you'll bankrupt us when the children are actually here."

Christina turned the box around to work on the other corner. She put her nail underneath the tape and yanked. Another rip.

"Careful, Christina," Elauna said. "If you attack my gift like that, I'll think you don't like it."

"Sorry."

Gary sat close to Christina, his arm around her back, just as expected. "She's overly eager to see what you've given us."

"Of course I am." Christina pulled the rest of the wrapping paper free and lifted the lid off the box. Nestled in satin lay the most beautiful stuffed polar bear she had ever seen. She pulled it from the box with trembling hands. It was pure white, and softer than a feather. In its hands it held a cut-out of Alaska with the state name across it. How many more stuffed animals could they cram into the office closet before the doors would no longer close?

"Thank you," Christina said, proud her voice remained steady. "It's beautiful."

"We love it," Gary added.

"And so will the baby," Elauna said. "How long are you going to make me wait before I'm a grandmother? Some of my friends already have grandchildren starting kindergarten."

"And how was Alaska?" Gary asked, his voice strained.

Alexander snapped the paper shut, giving Gary his full attention. "Highly successful. I was able to get everything cleared up with the Jorgensen account."

"Must we talk shop on Sunday?" Elauna sat down across from Christina and Gary, hands clasped in her lap. "I want to have a frank discussion with my son and his wife. I've been giving this a lot of thought lately, and I really think you two are shirking your duties as a couple."

Here we go. Time to buckle up for a bumpy ride.

"Mother," Gary began, but Elauna held up a hand and cut him off.

"I have been buying you stuffed animals for nearly three years now in the hopes you would get the hint."

"Last I checked, stuffed animals aren't what makes a baby," Alexander said. Christina choked back surprised laughter.

Elauna ignored her husband. "Every place we go, I seek out the perfect stuffed animal for my grandchild. But eighty-seven stuffed animals—"

Eighty-nine, Christina thought. There were now eighty-nine stuffed animals.

"—later, you two aren't getting the hint. You are my only chance at grandchildren, and I would like to see them before I die."

Gary rolled his eyes. "You have at least thirty good years left."

Elauna frowned. "That is beside the point. God wants you to have children."

If God really wanted them to have children, why couldn't they get pregnant? Was it punishment for their refusal to have them earlier?

"It breaks my heart you aren't giving me grandkids," Elauna continued.

"Mother," Gary said.

It broke Christina's heart, too. Why couldn't Gary see that?

"Don't you want to see your mother happy?" Elauna asked. "All I want is a few grandchildren to spoil. I think two or three would be a nice number. What do you think, Alexander?"

Alexander disappeared behind his newspaper again. "I think you should leave the kids alone."

Elauna shook her head. "It's a mother's duty to warn her children when they stray from what's truly important." She leaned forward and grasped both their hands. "I know your careers are important to you. But is that a good enough reason to put off having children?"

The humor of the situation was gone, and tears stung Christina's eyes. She hoped Elauna wouldn't notice her hands trembling.

"Mom, that's enough." Gary put an arm around Christina's shoulder, and she leaned into him, hoping the Vincents wouldn't interpret it as a sign of weakness. "Christina and I have always done what we think is best. It would have been difficult to have children while still in school."

"But you're not in school anymore," Elauna said. "So what's the problem? Money? It's the only reason I can think why Christina is still working. Vincent women don't work." Elauna nudged Alexander's foot with her toe. "Alexander, aren't you paying this boy enough?"

"He's paying me plenty," Gary said. "Christina works because she enjoys it."

"Then is it fertility problems?" Elauna said the words as though they were dirty. "One of the ladies at the country club has a daughter-in-law who is barren."

It was too much. Christina was going to crack, and in front of the Vincents, no less. The panic on Gary's face would have been funny if she wasn't struggling not to cry.

"Now you're being ridiculous," he said. "We don't want to talk about this anymore." *Please, keep quiet,* his eyes begged Christina.

"Elauna, stop harassing the children." Alexander put down his paper and stood. "They've done what they think is best, and we should respect that. I'm sure they don't plan on living childless forever."

"Of course not," Gary said. "Is dinner ready? We can't stay too long tonight. I still have some things I need to get done before work tomorrow."

"I'm trying to help you," Elauna said.

A tear splashed onto Christina's wrist. She turned her hand over so it would disappear into the fabric of her skirt before anyone saw. She couldn't believe she'd let her composure crack.

"I'm just saying—" Elauna continued.

"If it's okay with you, Elauna, I'll pull the food out of the oven and put it on the table." Christina rose quickly and went into the kitchen.

"Mother, please, not today," Christina heard Gary say as she walked away.

As soon as she was alone, the tears escaped. Christina blinked, trying to clear her vision. She was pulling the roasted duck out of the oven when Gary appeared.

"I'm sorry," he said quietly. "I tried to stop her, but once she gets going . . ." He grabbed some hot pads and pulled out the garlic potatoes.

"Let's get through dinner and go."

Within minutes they all sat around the dining room table, loading up their plates with food.

"I didn't intend to make you uncomfortable, Christina," Elauna said.

Christina's back stiffened. "It's fine," she said, forcing her voice to sound cheerful. "I really do love the polar bear. It'll go great with the eighty-eight other stuffed animals."

"Gary is such a joy to me. My life would be meaningless and empty without him. When you're young, children seem like such an inconvenience, but when you're old like me, you realize what a blessing they are."

"We want to establish our careers," Gary said. "It would have been unfair of me to ask Christina to put her education on hold so we could have children."

"I'm sure teaching those underprivileged children is very rewarding, dear," Elauna said.

Christina swallowed. "Most of them are from middle-class families." It drove her crazy that as soon as people found out she taught Spanish immersion, they assumed she taught homeless illegal immigrants.

"I'm sure they are."

"For the love of heaven, woman, leave the kids alone." Alexander cut off a piece of duck and shoved it into his mouth. "They don't want to talk about this anymore."

The only good thing to say about dinner was it ended quickly. After eating dessert—too crispy a crust for Elauna's taste, and the apples were definitely soggy, though she was sure Christina had tried—Gary made their excuses, and they left. It was all Christina could do to keep her smile in place until she was safely in the car, where their tinted windows and the darkness of night hid her expression.

"I'm so sorry," Gary said as they pulled onto the main road. "I had no idea they were going to attack us like that. Mother was way out of line."

Christina pursed her lips. "I want to go to the doctor."

"Why can't we wait a few more months? That's no time at all in the big scheme of things."

"Because, Gary. We've been married almost five years, and everyone is looking at us like, 'Why don't they have children?' Everyone already thinks we're destitute or infertile or worse. I want to know."

Gary's jaw clenched. "No one thinks we're infertile. And okay, the financial comment was annoying. I don't want people thinking that either. Maybe you should quit and stay home. We don't need your income."

"And what am I supposed to do at home all day, with no kids to take care of?"

"You could do charity work, like Mother. Get involved in some of the organizations she supports."

Christina laughed. "I'd rather die."

"Something different, then. An organization she isn't involved with."

"I'm not quitting my job."

"It was just a suggestion."

"Five years, Gar." Christina turned away from him, looking out the window at the glittering lights of Draper. "We're coming up on five years. It might as well be five hundred. All our neighbors, the young couples at church—they all have kids within a couple of years of getting married."

"I didn't realize we had to conform to some stereotype."

"Remember my old college roommate, Deena?"

Gary glanced over at her, eyebrow raised. "Yes."

"They got married a few months after us."

"I'm not sure where you're going with this."

"She announced on Facebook she's expecting baby number three. They have three kids, and we can't even have one."

"Stop saying that." Gary pounded the palm of his hand on the steering wheel. "Why are you so convinced something's wrong?"

"Because it's been thirteen months. Doesn't that bother you? Do you even care?"

Gary scrubbed a hand over his face and signaled into the far left lane. "I do care. I'm just scared."

"I'm scared, too. But we can be brave together and see a doctor."

"I'm not ready. In a few months we can discuss it again, but for now . . ."

She turned away.

"Christina, don't be like that."

She clamped her lips shut, not saying a word.

CHAPTER SIX
KYRA

Kyra was dreaming of playing house with Sophie when a sharp pain tore through her middle. Her eyes jerked open as another cramp hit. She gasped, rolling onto her side and pulling her legs up to her chest. A fiery hot sensation consumed her.

No, no, no.

This wasn't happening.

The pain subsided, and she lay curled in a ball, her whole body trembling. The thudding of her heart echoed in her ears. A clock in the bathroom ticked. David let out a snore.

Another gasp forced itself from her throat. The cramp started in her midsection and worked toward her back. Kyra squeezed her eyes shut and tried to breathe.

When the cramp subsided, she stumbled out of bed, shivering from the thin sheen of sweat covering her body. She stubbed her toe on the door-frame. Banged her shin against the bathtub. Barely noticed the pain. She was too busy counting her heartbeats, trying to ignore her worst fears.

The wetness she felt was unmistakable. A sob tore from her throat.

Please, please, please . . .

Kyra flipped on the bathroom light, squinting at the sudden brightness. She blinked, willing her eyes to quickly adjust. Red stained the white of her underwear.

Blood.

She sat on the toilet, heart hammering until she wondered if it would explode. Kyra fumbled to open a pad, her hands shaking almost uncontrollably. She barely remembered to flush the toilet. At the sink, Kyra focused on the water washing away the damp sweat coating her palms, on the warmth slowly infusing her fingers.

Another cramp hit, and she gasped, a single tear trickling down her cheek. Kyra turned off the water, stumbled to the bed, and roughly shook David. He snored loudly in response.

Another tear. "David." Kyra shook him harder. "David, please. Wake up. David!"

His eyes slowly opened, still clouded with sleep. "Kyra?" He sat up in bed, reaching for his glasses. "What's wrong?"

"I'm bleeding."

"Oh my gosh." He flicked on the bedside lamp. "How bad? Are you cramping?"

"Yes. Not a lot of blood, but . . ." A sob caught in her throat. "We can't lose this baby."

"Shhh." He brushed her hair away from her face. "Don't panic. Didn't you bleed with Sophie?"

"Y-yes. But I don't remember ever having cramps."

"You're shivering." He pulled her into bed, tucking the covers tightly around her. "It's almost six o'clock. We'll call the clinic when they open and see what they want us to do, okay?"

Two hours later they dropped Sophie off at Cassandra's and headed to the clinic. After having her blood drawn, Kyra undressed and sat on the exam table, a thick pad beneath her.

"It's going to be okay," David told her, his face white. "Everything will be okay."

When Dr. Mendoza opened the door, her eyes were soft and solemn. She squirted hand sanitizer into her palm and sat on a swivel stool. "I understand you're having some problems."

Kyra nodded. "I woke up at about five-thirty this morning with cramps. I was bleeding."

"Lie back," Dr. Mendoza said. "I'm going to do a quick exam, and then we'll do an ultrasound."

Kyra obeyed, scooting to the edge of the table and putting her feet in the stirrups. She tried to relax, but her shivers made it nearly impossible. "I bled with Sophie," Kyra said. She had to fill the silence. "Not this bad, though. Just spotting for about a week. Bleeding isn't always a bad sign, right?"

"Right. But the cramping is concerning." Dr. Mendoza withdrew the speculum. "I'm going to do the ultrasound now."

"Did you find anything wrong in the exam?" David asked.

"Nothing obvious."

Dr. Mendoza inserted the ultrasound wand, and Kyra's eyes glued to the screen. "Where's the baby?" she asked. Had it really been less than two weeks since they'd sat in this same room, seeing their baby for the first time?

Dr. Mendoza pointed. "Right there."

"Is it okay?" Kyra curled her fingers into her palms, nails biting her tender flesh.

Dr. Mendoza motioned to something that looked indistinguishable from all the other wavy lines. "I can see the blood flow here, but I can't tell where it's coming from. Let me take some measurements."

The next fifteen minutes were agony. As Dr. Mendoza took measurement after measurement, Kyra watched her face grow more and more grim.

"Please tell me what's happening," Kyra whispered.

Dr. Mendoza sighed. "I'm so sorry. I think you're miscarrying."

Rushing waves filled Kyra's ears, and black spots darted across her vision.

"The fetus hasn't grown since our appointment ten days ago, and there's still no movement or heartbeat. By seven and a half weeks, we can usually hear one." Dr. Mendoza withdrew the probe, and Kyra sat up, her eyes fixed on the screen. It was blank now, the baby gone. Just like Kyra's hopes and dreams. "Have you noticed the cramping or bleeding getting worse?"

Kyra wrapped her arms tightly around her waist. "Maybe. It's hard to tell."

"At the last appointment you hadn't experienced any pregnancy symptoms. Have you had any since then? Nausea, sensitivity to smell, headaches?"

Kyra shook her head. "Most symptoms didn't hit with Sophie until about eight weeks, so I haven't questioned it."

A knock sounded at the door, stealing Kyra's focus.

"Come in," Dr. Mendoza said.

A nurse entered and extended a folder. "The lab finished Mrs. Peterson's blood work."

The nurse left, and Dr. Mendoza flipped open the file, her eyes scanning the chart inside.

"What does it say?" Kyra asked.

"Your HCG levels are dropping. I'm sorry. The baby's gone."

Gone. Kyra struggled to process the reality. How could it be 'gone'? The baby was right there. Kyra had seen it.

"What happened?" David croaked, eyes red and watery behind the lenses of his glasses.

"I'm not sure," Dr. Mendoza said. "It's almost impossible to tell with miscarriages this early. At the last appointment, you measured on the small end of normal for six weeks. But it's hard to get accurate measurements that early, and I wasn't concerned. The fetus probably stopped growing shortly after implantation." She smiled sadly at Kyra. "Unfortunately, miscarriage happens in about ten percent of all pregnancies. It was probably a spontaneous abortion, and not an indication that something is wrong with your body."

As though that was supposed to comfort Kyra. "The baby's really dead?"

"I'm sorry," Dr. Mendoza repeated. "We won't know for certain until you pass it, but I think so."

Kyra hunched over, her hands clutching her stomach as a sob tore through her.

Dr. Mendoza spoke quietly with David, then left the room. Kyra numbly got dressed, her movements clumsy. David put an arm around her, and she let him lead her to the car.

Gone.

David called Cassandra and quietly explained the situation, asking if Sophie could stay at her house until bedtime.

Gone.

Soon they were home. David led Kyra up the steps and into the house.

Gone.

David lay next to her on the bed while they cried. The cramping grew steadily worse, as though the mere mention of a miscarriage had given the baby permission to leave. Kyra's shivers grew more pronounced as her temperature rose to a fever. When she went to the restroom, the bleeding was much heavier.

The doctor had been right. They were losing this baby.

Kyra lay in her bed, curled into a ball of pain nearly as intense as labor. It took all night to pass the baby. After it was over, she cried and cried and cried while David held her.

Empty.

Alone.

Devastated.

Cheated.

Why did You let me down, Lord? Kyra prayed angrily. *I'm a good person. I'm a good mother. Why did You take my baby? Why did You have to be so cruel?* Being unable to have children was bad enough. But having a child, and then losing it . . .

There were not words to describe that type of agony.

Eventually Kyra fell asleep. When she woke next, it was to David stroking her hair. Sunlight streamed in through the closed window blinds.

"Sophie's awake and wants to see you," David said. "Is that okay?"

Kyra closed her eyes and nodded. She wanted Sophie's arms around her neck and warm body cuddled close more than almost anything.

It could've been five minutes or five hours before Sophie entered the room. Her soft little body climbed onto the bed next to Kyra. "Mommy?" Her voice was tiny and scared.

Kyra wiped away her tears and rolled over. She smiled and tried to make her voice cheerful. "Hey, baby girl."

Sophie frowned, looking uncertain. "Daddy said our baby isn't coming home. Is that why you're crying?"

Kyra's tears spilled over, and she nodded. "Yes, sweetie."

"But why not?"

"Remember how I told you the baby would have to grow in my stomach for a really long time?"

Sophie nodded.

"The baby got sick and couldn't grow any more. It went to live in heaven with God instead."

Sophie leaned forward and wrapped her small arms around Kyra's neck. Kyra closed her eyes and breathed deeply, clutching her daughter close. Whatever else happened in life, she was lucky to be Sophie's mother.

"Don't cry," Sophie said, patting Kyra's cheek. Kyra captured Sophie's hand and kissed it. "My brother is coming soon. God told me."

Kyra's brows furrowed. "How did He tell you?"

"He just did. My brother has yellow hair and is fat and cute."

"There's not a baby in my tummy anymore, Soph. The baby's in heaven now."

"I know. But he's coming soon. I can't wait to play with him."

Kyra buried her face in Sophie's neck. "I can't wait to play with him either."

"Don't be sad, Mommy."

"Sometimes mommies have to be sad for a little while." Kyra kissed Sophie's cheek and stroked loose strands of hair behind her ear. "But that doesn't mean I don't love you. It just means I'm sad our baby can't come live with us right now."

Sophie cuddled in closer to Kyra. "I'm sad, too. I love you, Mommy."

"I love you, too."

CHAPTER SEVEN
MEGAN

Megan's first day with her first piano student in Riverton. A Juilliard hopeful. She nervously rearranged sheet music on the magazine rack, then turned to the piano. Light from the bay window bathed it in warmth, making the thin coating of dust visible. So much for cleaning yesterday.

She wiped down the piano, then gave the picture of Christ hanging over it another dusting for good measure. Moved the kitchen chair she'd placed beside the piano bench a fraction of an inch to the left.

I'm Sexy and I Know It blared from the speakers of her cell, making her jump.

"Hey, Trent. You changed your ringtone."

"Just a reminder of why you love me. I wanted to call and wish you luck on your first piano lesson. Isn't she coming soon?"

"About thirty minutes," Megan confirmed, looking around the living room. There was nothing else to fix.

"Don't worry. You'll do great."

"I don't know why she wants me to teach her. She should be studying with a PhD."

"She's studying with you because you're the best."

Megan rolled her eyes. "Yeah, that's gotta be it."

"I'm going to pretend you aren't being sarcastic. Hey, have you made an appointment with the new RE yet? I meant to ask you last night."

Megan winced, running her fingers over the piano keys. She'd avoided thinking about the new reproductive endocrinologist as much as possible. "I kinda hoped you wouldn't ask."

Trent's voice turned soft and soothing. "Is there something you aren't telling me? I thought you'd be jumping to make this appointment, but we've already been in Riverton more than a week. You said you'd make the appointment last Monday."

"Do we really have to talk about this right now?"

"I'd like to."

Megan sighed. "Fine. I don't want to be infertile again. Happy?"

"Babe, we never stopped being infertile."

"I know." Why did he have to be so logical? She perched on the edge of the piano bench. "But I didn't feel infertile when we were on our break. I knew I wasn't ovulating, so I never expected to get pregnant and wasn't disappointed when my period started."

"We're here. We're settling in. We have a house. Aren't you ready for the next step?" His voice pleaded with her. "You know we'll never get pregnant without help."

She hated it when he was right. Megan angrily swiped her hand over the piano keys, causing them to play discordantly. Sometimes life sucked. "I'll call and make the appointment today."

"Do we need to talk about this? I don't want you to feel like I'm forcing anything."

She wanted a baby so badly—was more than ready to be a mother. But she wasn't ready for fertility treatments. Again. "You aren't forcing me. I'll call the new office right now." She'd never be able to focus on Sienna's lesson unless she did, now that she'd promised Trent.

"Are you sure?"

"Yes. I'll text you the appointment information."

"Okay. Thanks for doing this for us, babe. I love you. And good luck with the lesson."

"Love you too, Trent."

Megan hung up and glared at her phone. It glared back.

"Fine," she said. "You win. I'll call the stupid doctor." She scrolled through her contacts and found the number, pushing *call* before she could talk herself out of it.

A voice answered after one ring. "Center for Infertility and Reproductive Medicine. This is Natalie speaking. How may I help you?"

"Uh, hi." The prompt answer threw her off. "My name is Megan Burke. I need to schedule a new patient consultation."

"Burke . . . Burke . . ." Megan heard the click of a keyboard. "That's right. Dr. Faulkner's office in Logan forwarded all your files a few weeks ago. He spoke personally with Dr. Mendoza about your case." A rustle of papers. "Dr. Mendoza said to get you in as soon as possible."

"Great." Megan didn't know whether to be impressed with the personal treatment or depressed she needed special attention.

More clicking. "Your timing is excellent—I just had a cancellation. Dr. Mendoza has an opening on the twenty-third at ten o'clock. Does that work?"

"Of March?" That was a week and a half away. Megan had anticipated a wait of at least a month, maybe two.

"Yes. If that doesn't fit your schedule, the next available appointment is April twenty-eighth at noon."

For a split second, Megan considered taking the later appointment. Another month's reprieve from the endless round of ultrasounds and medications sounded heavenly.

But then she pictured Trent holding a baby wrapped in a pink-and-blue striped hospital blanket. A tiny face smiled up at him in sleep. A baby was worth it. It would all be worth it. "No, March twenty-third works. Ten a.m., you said?"

And just like that, they were trying to have a baby again.

The roar of an engine stole her attention, and she stood, straightening the piano bench. A red Suburban pulled up to the curb outside her house. Megan's breath hitched, and she wiped wet palms on her jeans. Time to switch gears. Right now was about piano, not infertility.

The doors to the Suburban flew open, and two little boys tumbled out, practically on top of each other. A woman emerged from the driver's side. Her short, honey-colored hair looked like it hadn't seen a brush since morning. She grabbed an arm of each child, her face scrunched together as she spoke to them. They bowed their heads in apparent contrition and walked ahead of their mother toward the front door. A girl who could only be Sienna rounded the front of the SUV and followed behind the woman. She was of average height and slender, with long blonde hair that flowed around her shoulders.

Megan's stomach lurched as the doorbell rang. "Stay calm," she reminded herself. Loud pounding started and abruptly cut off. Megan opened the door as the woman caught a little boy's hand mid-air, apparently poised to knock again. Her other hand held tightly to the other child's.

"Hi," Megan said, making her voice purposefully light. "You must be the McBrides. I'm Megan Burke."

The woman glanced at the little boy who had tried to knock, then dropped his hand and held hers out to Megan, giving it a quick shake. "I'm Annabelle McBride. Sorry I had to bring the twins today. I was hoping to come alone, but my husband got caught late at work." She nodded toward the girl standing next to her. "This is Sienna."

"It's nice to meet everyone. Please, come in." Megan stood back, and they entered.

Sienna gave Megan a nervous smile, looking every bit as young as Megan knew her to be—only seventeen. "Hi, Mrs. Burke. Thank you so much for taking me on as a student."

"It's my pleasure."

One of the twins bent down near the baseboard and flicked the door stopper. *Boing!*

Annabelle rushed forward. "Connor, don't play with that."

The lights flicked off, and the living room grew dim as the overcast March sky became their only light.

"Cameron, turn the lights on right now," Annabelle said.

"No!"

"Cameron—"

The lights flicked on, and Cameron ran across the living room to the magazine rack holding the sheet music Megan had so laboriously straightened. He grabbed a piece and flung it to the floor. Megan flinched.

"Cameron!" Annabelle left Connor to play with the door stopper and rushed to Cameron, putting the sheet music back on the rack. Cameron started crying. Annabelle reached down and picked him up, then turned to Megan as though nothing was wrong. "You come highly recommended," she said.

"Remind me again how you found me?" Megan asked. And why did Anabelle think Megan was qualified to prepare Sienna for Juilliard?

"Sienna heard you play at a wedding reception a few months ago," Annabelle said. "Landon and Alizabeth Burke. Sienna's friends with Alizabeth's younger sister."

"Of course," Megan said. "Landon's my nephew."

Cameron let out a scream, wiggling free from Annabelle. He darted over to his brother. *Boing!* They were both playing with the door stopper now.

"I've never heard someone play with so much emotion." Sienna blushed as though she was embarrassed to admit it. "My piano professor is great at technique, but I want to learn how to play with feeling like you."

"Wow," Megan said. *Boing!* It took a lot of effort to avoid looking at the twins. "I'm flattered."

"Sienna just got back from her live audition for Juilliard," Annabelle said.

"That's great, Sienna," Megan said.

"Connor, don't you dare touch that!" Annabelle yelled. Connor stood on top of the piano bench, leaning toward the framed picture of Christ. Megan held her breath, waiting for the painting to come crashing down. Annabelle pulled Connor to the floor. "You know you aren't supposed to do that. Cameron, if I tell your brother no, that means no for you, too." A twin in each hand, Annabelle dragged them toward the front door. "Sorry about this. I'll pick Sienna up in an hour, *without* the twins. We can talk more then."

"I look forward to it." Megan tried not to show her relief as she shut the door behind them. Her house wasn't made for twins.

Sienna clutched the strap of her music bag, her face red. "I'm so sorry, Mrs. Burke. The twins are crazy. I told Mom I could drive myself, but she was worried I wouldn't find your house on my own."

"Please, call me Megan. Mrs. Burke makes me feel like an old woman." Megan motioned to the piano. "I thought we could start with some scales."

Sienna sat obediently, dropping her bag on the floor next to her. She adjusted the piano bench, then took up position, hands poised over the keys. "What would you like me to start with?"

"C major, both hands, and go from there."

Sienna worked her way up to F minor, her scales flawless and quick. Megan smiled, pleased as Sienna finished the last scale.

"Excellent," Megan said. "Now play me the piece you've been working on with your piano professor."

Sienna didn't pull out any sheet music, and Megan's smile grew as she played Beethoven's Concerto Number Five from memory. About halfway through she stumbled, and the rest of the piece was choppy, but Megan's smile didn't sag.

Sienna played the last note. She turned to Megan, her expression unsure. "I know it's not great. I just finished memorizing the piece, and am working on perfecting it."

"It was beautiful. I think your odds of being accepted to Juilliard are fantastic if you played like that at the audition."

Sienna's eyes lit up. "Really?"

"Really. Now pull out the sheet music for the concerto. We've got work to do."

CHAPTER EIGHT
CHRISTINA

When Christina walked into her classroom Monday morning, it felt like coming home. She was happy here, and so were her students. This is where she felt most at ease. Christina flipped on the lights, breathing fully for the first time since leaving on Friday afternoon.

It had been two weeks since the fateful dinner with Elauna and Alexander. Two weeks, and all Gary and Christina had done was pretend their fight had never happened.

When had everything changed? While dating, Gary had been the perfect boyfriend. He'd brought Christina flowers at least once a week. He let her pick the movie. He told her to order whatever she wanted at restaurants. They had stayed up long past when they should have, talking for hours about everything and nothing. Communication had flowed. Now everything felt impossibly hard.

Christina was writing some simple equations on the whiteboard for the morning lesson when her desk phone rang. "Mrs. Vincent's room," she answered.

"Hi, Christina." It was Linda, the front desk secretary. "I figured you'd be in already. Principal Gardner wants to see you in his office."

A shiver of nerves shot down Christina's spine. She ran over her last few weeks of teaching. Nothing unusual had happened—no problems with students or upset parents. She had received her evaluation back from Principal Gardner with high praise. There was nothing bad to warrant a trip to his office. Hopefully that meant it was something good. "Is everything okay?"

Linda laughed as though Christina had made a joke. "Why wouldn't it be?"

Christina blushed. Now Linda would think she'd done something to be ashamed of. "Of course. Tell him I'll be right down."

Three minutes later Christina paused outside the office door. The silver plaque beside it read PRINCIPAL DAYTON GARDNER in all caps. She took a deep breath and knocked. "Come in," the principal said.

Principal Gardner was middle-aged, with thick salt-and-pepper hair. He was of average height and average weight. Average in pretty much every way. The only thing intimidating about him was his job title and PhD. Principal Gardner didn't stand when Christina entered, but the smile on his face calmed her nerves. "Christina, sit down please." He motioned to a chair. "Don't worry. You're not in trouble."

Christina pretended to laugh, but it came out shaky. "That's a relief. What can I do for you?"

He leaned forward, elbows on the edge of his desk and fingers steepled. "I have a proposition. The district wants us to introduce an after-school program for at-risk students. The curriculum will include education on bullying, suicide prevention, that sort of thing. We'll do it on a trial basis through the end of the year, and if it's successful, the district will introduce the program in all elementary schools next year."

Christina's eyebrows rose.

"With your minor in child psychology, I thought you'd be perfect for the job. I already spoke to Trista." Trista Goodryn taught fourth grade. "She's agreed to be one of the co-chairs. I'd like to offer you the other position. You'd meet with the kids for an hour after school on Monday, Tuesday, and Wednesday. Of course you'd get a pay increase too. Not substantial, but it's something."

More opportunity. More respect. More time teaching. Christina didn't have to think twice. "I'll do it."

Principal Gardner blinked. "You can talk it over with your husband first."

Gary. Christina hadn't even considered his reaction to this. He wouldn't like it, but why should he get to make this decision for her? Her students needed her. And Christina needed teaching. She loved how her students looked at her with near hero-worship. She loved Michael's victory shout last week, when he finished his first chapter book without any help. She loved watching Sarah's shy smile give way to excited chatter as the year progressed and Christina gained her trust. Helping at-risk students would be even more rewarding because they needed the help so badly.

Principal Gardner stared at Christina, his eyebrows raised in question. Christina blushed. She had taken too long to answer. "My husband will be fine with it, I'm sure." The program wouldn't take too many extra hours. She'd still be home before him. If Christina explained it right, Gary would get on board. If he wasn't home in the late afternoons, why did she need to be?

"Great." Principal Gardner pulled out a folder. "I had Linda get all the information together on the off chance you'd agree. You and Trista have free rein, as long as you follow the district guidelines."

Christina took the folder, leafing through it. Her eye caught on the pay raise. Principal Gardner was right—it wasn't a lot. But she hadn't taken the job for the money. "Thank you. I'll email Trista so we can get started."

"We want the program up and running by the first week of April. You have two months to make it a smashing success."

"No pressure," Christina murmured.

Principal Gardner smiled and stood. Christina rose as well.

"I'm sure you two will do great," Principal Gardner said. "I have every confidence in your abilities."

"Thank you." Christina shook his hand and left, the file folder clutched against her chest. Back in her room, she sent a quick email to Trista, asking when they could meet. As Christina hit send, Stacey walked into the room.

"Hey, Stacey. How was your weekend?"

"I had my first experience with morning sickness." Stacey flopped into a chair near Christina's desk. "It sucked. T.J. made fried chicken for dinner on Sunday because I *love* fried chicken. He started cooking it, and the smell made my stomach churn. And I thought 'that's weird' and sprawled on the couch until dinner was done. I took one bite of chicken and bam, I was puking."

Christina's fingers curled around the computer mouse. "I'm sorry to hear that." She would give anything to experience morning sickness.

"I barely made it to work on time today. I can tell you've been here for a while already, as usual. You're like the most dedicated teacher I know. Were you coming back from the front office?"

"Yes. Principal Gardner asked me to co-chair an after-school program with Trista."

Stacey's eyes widened. "I hope you said no. Gosh, don't we spend enough time in this place? I love teaching, but they don't pay us nearly enough for all the time we put in."

Christina frowned. Teaching wasn't about the money. It was about the kids. "I think the program will really help at-risk students. I said I'd do it."

"You're joking. I mean, what will Gary say? I can't wait to go home and see T.J. at the end of every day."

Had Gary and Christina ever been like that? The early days of their marriage, when leaving for school each morning had been painful, seemed like another lifetime. "Gary's gone most evenings, so the program won't interfere with our time together. He's putting in a lot of hours at work right now. And besides, we've been married almost five years. After you and T.J. have been married a while, you'll start to have lives apart from each other again."

"I hope not." Stacey made a face. "Wouldn't that suck? The whole reason we got married in the first place was to be together. If we ever get to the point where we want to do things without the other, that means our marriage is in trouble."

Was Stacey right? Christina shook her head to clear it. Of course not. It was normal for a married couple to have separate interests and hobbies. Healthy. "Just wait a few years. Things will be different."

"You're really going to do the program?"

"Yes, and I'm even excited about it."

Stacey narrowed her eyes. "Are you and Gary having marriage problems?"

How on earth did Stacey come to that conclusion? "Of course not. Don't be silly."

"I'm serious! You don't even care that you're going to have, like, a bazillion less hours a week with him."

Why did she get stuck with Stacey as a co-worker? Only Christina's sense of professionalism kept her from rolling her eyes. "The program's not going to take up that much time."

Stacey snorted. "That's what they tell you now. But soon you won't have a second to spend with Gary. What did he say when you told him?"

"I haven't told him yet."

"Wait. You didn't even ask him if it was okay?"

"He's not home much, so he's not going to care." The lie burned on the way out.

Stacey stood, clasping her hands dramatically. "I'll pray for you guys. You make such a great couple. I don't want you to break up."

"Good, because we're not." Could she be any more dramatic? Gary wouldn't be thrilled. But he wouldn't leave Christina over it, either. Whatever their problems, they were committed.

Stacey ignored Christina, heading toward the door. "I've got to pick up some worksheets from the copy center. I'll see you at lunch." The door clicked shut behind her.

Christina sighed loudly. Stacey was so obnoxious.

Christina decided to eat lunch in her classroom to avoid Stacey. Besides, she needed to call Kyra. The book drive had ended over the weekend, and Christina needed to collect the books so she and Megan could sort them tomorrow after school. Christina had wondered initially if Megan's interest was merely polite, but Megan had caught her at church on Sunday and insisted on helping.

Christina quickly ate her turkey and avocado sandwich on pita bread, then pulled out her phone and found Kyra's number in the contacts. It rang and rang. Christina clicked her nails on the desk, debating whether she should leave a message or call back later.

"Hello?" The voice sounded small and childish.

Christina stopped drumming her fingers. "Hi. Is your mom there?"

"Yeah." A long pause.

"Is this Sophie?"

"Uh-huh."

"Hi, Sophie. My name is Mrs. Vincent. We go to church together. Do you know who I am?"

"Nope."

Six-year-olds Christina could handle without a problem. But Sophie was only half that age, and Christina wasn't sure what to do now. "Oh. Well, can I talk to your mommy?"

"She's crying again."

"Crying?" Christina frowned, trying to figure out what to say next.

"The baby in her tummy went to live with God."

"Oh." Shock was quickly replaced by an ache in Christina's heart. She'd had no idea.

There was a rustling, and Christina heard an adult voice—obviously Kyra's—mutter something. "Hello?" Definitely Kyra.

"Hi, Kyra. Sorry to bother you. This is Christina Vincent, from church."

"Oh. Hi."

Christina swallowed. Clearly Kyra hadn't wanted to answer the phone, and didn't want to talk to anyone. Should Christina bring up the miscarriage or not? She vacillated back and forth before deciding it would be more awkward to avoid the topic now and then bring it up the next time they spoke. "Sophie said you had a miscarriage. I am so sorry."

Christina heard a quiet sniff. "Thank you."

"I was calling about the book drive, but obviously that can wait. Sorry to bother you. I had no idea."

"Oh yeah," Kyra said distantly. "I've got quite a few boxes downstairs."

"Megan Burke—she just moved into the neighborhood, maybe you've seen her at church?—was going to help me sort them tomorrow. But I can pick them up another time."

"No," Kyra said quickly. "No. Come by tomorrow and get the books."

"Are you sure?"

"Yes. Does four o'clock work for you?"

Christina agreed that it did, and they ended the call. If a phone conversation was that uncomfortable, Christina dreaded tomorrow's visit, even if it was just a quick pickup. She dialed Megan's number next. It only rang once before being picked up.

"Hi, Megan," Christina said.

"Hey. I'm glad you called."

Christina couldn't help but smile. Megan genuinely sounded pleased. "I spoke with Kyra. We can pick up the books tomorrow at four o'clock. Does that fit your schedule? If not, I can pick them up alone."

"No, that's fine. I'm showing houses in the morning, but my afternoon's free." Christina heard what sounded like a chair squeaking. "Man, I've been looking at listings all morning and my back's killing me. There are so many more options here than in Logan. How's your day going?"

Christina blinked. She had expected to relay the information about their appointment, then hang up. Megan seemed relaxed, however, and willing to continue the conversation. "It's going well," Christina said. Usually she would've left it at that, but Megan seemed interested, and Christina wanted to be friends. "I found out I'll be co-chairing an after-school program for the rest of the year. It's for at-risk children."

"Wow, that's awesome."

"Yeah."

"You don't seem excited about it."

Christina paused. She wasn't used to people being so straightforward. "I'm excited."

"But?"

Christina surprised herself by opening up. "I haven't told Gary yet, and I don't think he'll be thrilled."

Megan laughed. "Cook him something amazing, then tell him while his mouth's full. He'll be so busy eating he won't even care. Oh, there's my other line. Sorry, I've got to go. Let's meet outside our houses at five minutes to four tomorrow, and we can drive over to Kyra's together."

They said their goodbyes, and Christina hung up the phone. Maybe Megan had the right idea. Christina pulled out a piece of paper and made a shopping list. It was time to make nice.

CHAPTER NINE
CHRISTINA

If Christina wanted to convince Gary the program was a good idea, she had to apologize for their fight. They should've apologized days ago. The problem was that neither of them were very good at saying "I'm sorry" or admitting when they were wrong.

Megan's suggestion had given Christina an idea. Even if she wasn't great at apologizing, she was a great cook. She called Gary to verify he'd be home by seven, then stopped by the grocery store on the way home from work, and raced to start dinner—grilled halibut on a bed of rice pilaf, Gary's favorite.

"What's this?" Gary asked when he walked in the door at 7:05. Christina had the table set with their wedding china. Two candles in crystal candlesticks glowed in the middle of the table.

"An 'I'm sorry' dinner." Christina took his coat and hung it up in the closet. Gary sat at the table, and she joined him. "I know I've been difficult the last two weeks."

Gary reached across the table and took her hand. Once one of them took the initiative, the rest was easy. "We're both to blame. I'm sorry too." They said a prayer and loaded up their plates. "This is delicious," Gary said around a bite of halibut.

"Thanks." Christina had spent hours in the kitchen perfecting this meal during the early days of their marriage. "How was your day?"

"Productive. What about yours?"

If she didn't mention the program now, it would seem like she was hiding something. "Interesting. Principal Gardner asked me to co-chair an after-school program for at-risk students. It'd only be an extra three hours a week, and I'd get a couple hundred more a month until the end of the school year." The money wasn't likely to sway Gary's opinion, especially when they didn't need it, but it was worth a shot.

Gary frowned, wiping at his mouth with a napkin. "Is that a good idea? We barely see each other as it is. I don't like the idea of your job taking time away from us."

Christina's mouth dropped open. She had known he wouldn't like the idea, but how hypocritical could he be? She was taking the job because he was always at his. "I already told Principal Gardner I'd do it."

Gary paused, his fork halfway to his mouth. "Without consulting me?"

She shrugged. "He needed an answer quickly." A half lie.

Gary set his fork down, clenching his jaw. "Are you doing this because you're mad about the infertility thing?"

"What? No." It was Christina's turn to set down her fork. "I thought you'd be happy I'd have something to fill my free time. It's not like you're home in the afternoons. It won't interfere with our time together, I promise."

"Ever since you brought up infertility, you've been shutting me out. You're still mad because I don't want to see a doctor."

Christina gritted her teeth. "This has nothing to do with that. If anything, it might distract me." Another lie, but she'd dangle the bait just the same.

"It wouldn't."

"It's a good opportunity to help students. We can visit my parents in France this summer with the extra money." Maybe he would come with her this year, if only for a few days.

"If you want to go to France, we'll work something out. Money isn't stopping us."

Christina took a deep breath, trying to stay calm. "This isn't only about France. I get lonely sitting at home while you're off saving the world one court case at a time."

"You know I have to work harder than anyone else in the firm to prove myself."

"You choose to work harder than anyone else."

His voice was controlled, but angry. "I refuse to let people think I'm only there because I'm a partner's son. I have to prove myself. And now, when I'm working sixty-hour weeks, you go and do this. Are you trying to sabotage our relationship?"

"I can't believe you asked that." Christina picked up her fork and stabbed at her halibut. "I didn't do this to hurt you. It sounded like an interesting career opportunity." An opportunity to feel needed. To feel important.

"I'm sorry I'm not ready to do the infertility stuff. I'm trying to be okay with it. But right now I'm not."

He was relentless. Christina regretted bringing this up. He never would have found out about the program if she'd kept her mouth shut.

"This has nothing to do with wanting a baby," Christina said.

"I'd rather you don't do the program. Tell Principal Gardner you changed your mind. It'll end up taking time away from our relationship."

Christina pushed back her chair, standing. "What relationship? You're never home, and even when you are, your head is still at the office. I'm lonely. I thought this would fill some of the empty hours. Stop making this about you." Christina stomped out of the room, slamming the bedroom door behind her.

A few seconds later the door flew open. Gary stood in the doorway, his chest heaving. Christina stared in shock. Usually he left her alone when she stormed off.

"We are not going to be this couple," Gary said. "I am sick and tired of getting in fights and never solving our problems."

"You want to solve a problem? Fine. Let's talk about why you really don't want me to do the program. You're worried what your parents will think. What the people at the country club will think. This is all about you."

Gary's jaw clenched. "*I* support my family, Christina."

"Support is more than bringing home a paycheck. I don't need your money."

His Adam's apple bobbed. "I'm trying to build a career. To prove myself. And you're angry about that? I feel like I don't even know you anymore."

Christina stared at him, then hung her head and cried. Gary lurched forward, probably in surprise. "Who are we?" she asked. "What happened to us?"

Strong arms wrapped around her, tight and comforting. She stood stiff, surprised, then sank against him. For a moment the man she fell in love with was there, holding her. "I don't know," Gary said.

"I really didn't think you'd be this upset. If you're that concerned, I won't do the program. But you have to come home more. I need you, Gar." Christina knew she was losing the fight, and when it came right down to it, the program wasn't worth their marriage. If he was willing to be home more, to work on them, she wouldn't even care.

"I don't want people to think we're having financial troubles. If you take on extra hours at work, it'll look like I can't provide for you."

"But I know that's not true, and you know that's not true."

"I know. But it still bothers me. You know how my parents are. Please, let's go back to dinner. You worked really hard, and it doesn't seem fair to let it go to waste."

Christina nodded, letting him take her hand and lead her to the dining room. All was silent for a few minutes as they ate.

"I think you should do the program," Gary said. "You love your students, and you'll be great at it."

Christina looked down at her plate. He had heard her offer, and had chosen to risk his image over spending time with her. He'd rather be at work.

"And you're right," Gary continued. Her head jerked up. "I do spend too much time at the office. I'll try to cut back, be home at six like I'm supposed to be."

Christina's heart lifted. Did she dare hope? "And not bring work home with you?"

He flinched. "You know I can't promise that. But I'll try and minimize it." His eyes caught hers across the candlelight. "I want to work on us. I don't want our marriage to fall apart, and lately I feel like it is."

"I don't want that, either. I'll tell Principal Gardner I can't do the program if it bothers you that much. Or you can tell people I'm doing it as charity work."

Almost immediately, Gary shook his head. "No, you should do it. You're right. You'll still be home before me, and it's something you'll enjoy. It doesn't matter what other people think."

And there he was—the man she'd married. Tears pricked her eyes. They would be okay. "I love you, Gar. I don't want us to float by on 'okay' anymore."

"Me either."

The rest of dinner was quiet and a little uncomfortable, but she knew they were both trying. All their problems weren't solved, but it was a start. They were finally heading in the right direction.

CHAPTER TEN
KYRA

In the three years Kyra and David had lived in Riverton, she could count on one hand the number of times she'd had visitors, especially from church. So why did they have to come pick up the books now, after Sophie spilled the beans? Kyra wasn't in the mood for chitchat and sympathetic smiles. She sighed. She should've accepted Christina's offer to wait and had David drop the books off sometime this weekend. Too late now.

"Why are they coming over?" Sophie asked, scrunching up her face as she helped Kyra straighten the living room.

"To pick up the books people have been bringing over. Mrs. Vincent is a teacher, and she's going to take them to her school."

"That sounds boring."

The doorbell rang. Kyra tossed a throw pillow on the couch. "You can play upstairs. It won't take long."

Sophie followed Kyra to the front door. "I want you to play with me."

"I can't right now. We'll play when they leave." Kyra opened the door, forcing a smile. "Hi." She recognized Christina Vincent, with her knee-length pencil skirt and curly red-orange hair pulled back in a French twist. The other woman could only be Megan Burke. She had a round face and full figure without seeming overweight. Blonde curls hung loosely halfway down her back. She wore a bohemian style skirt in a brilliant turquoise that flowed to the ground, and bracelets jangled on her wrist.

She held out a hand. "Hi, Kyra. I'm Megan. It's nice to meet you."

Kyra shook her hand, then motioned the two women inside. "It's nice to meet you too."

"We're so sorry about the miscarriage," Megan said.

Kyra wished they hadn't brought it up. As if either of these women had any idea what Kyra was going through.

"Thank you. Please, come in." Kyra motioned to the living room. "The books are right in there. We managed to collect eight boxes worth."

"That's fantastic," Christina said. "Thank you so much. It would've been hard for me to collect everything without being home during the day. I don't think we would've had as many donations if people had to drop it at the school."

Sophie scampered over to Megan. "Are those cookies?" She pointed to the plate Megan held, wrapped in plastic.

"They're the best kind of cookies in the whole world—double chocolate chip." Megan glanced at Kyra. "I know it doesn't fix things, but chocolate always helps."

"Can I have one?" Sophie asked.

"Well, I brought them for your mom, so only if she says so."

Sophie looked at Kyra with big, pleading eyes, and Kyra nodded. Megan smiled, pulled one from the plate, and handed it to Sophie.

"Thank you," Sophie said. She took a bite. "Mmmm."

"Can you take the plate into the kitchen for me, Soph? Then go play in your playroom," Kyra said.

"Okay." Sophie shoved the whole cookie in her mouth, then took the plate from Megan and scampered off.

"Thank you, Megan. You didn't need to do that," Kyra said.

"It's the least I could do." Megan's eyes were soft and full of compassion. "How are you doing?"

A stab to the chest. Kyra chose to answer the question in regards to her physical health. "It was an early miscarriage. The recovery hasn't been too bad, and I'm feeling better."

"I'm glad," Christina said.

But Megan shook her head. "That's not what I meant. How are you doing emotionally? I don't think it hurts any less because it was early."

"No." Kyra blinked back tears and looked at these two women with newfound respect. They seemed genuinely sorry for her loss. "We were all really excited about the baby. It's been hard."

"I can't even imagine," Christina murmured.

Kyra was suddenly desperate to know if they understood— *really* understood. "Have either of you had a miscarriage?"

They both shook their heads. "Gary and I are focusing on our careers right now," Christina said.

Kyra nodded, deflated. Of course they were. Christina was always so poised and put-together. She had a perfect husband and a perfect house, and they had perfect careers and lots of money. She would never understand Kyra's problems.

"I've never been pregnant, but I understand how badly it hurts to want a baby," Megan said. "My husband and I have struggled with infertility our entire marriage. I'm so sorry, Kyra."

Infertility. Kyra wanted to pepper Megan with questions. What was her diagnosis? How long had they been struggling? What treatments had they undergone? But Kyra clamped her mouth shut.

It was too hard. She could barely handle the miscarriage right now. She didn't want to deal with the questions and advice and condolences they'd give if she admitted to infertility. Kyra bowed her head and tears fell. "I'm sorry." Kyra wiped under her eyes. "The doctor said it would take a couple of weeks for my hormones to stabilize."

"Hey, it's okay." Megan moved to Kyra's side and wrapped an arm around her shoulder. "You have every right to cry."

"We're here for you, whatever you need," Christina said.

"I'm so angry," Kyra whispered. Snot trickled out of her nose, and she wiped it with the corner of her shirt, embarrassed.

"Anyone would be," Megan said. "I've never had a miscarriage, but I have failed a lot of fertility treatments. I'm always angry, too. But you can do hard things, Kyra Peterson. You're strong enough to get through this. I promise."

The book pickup-turned-visit with Christina and Megan was healing, but exhausting. They mostly listened while Kyra talked, and that felt good. She didn't have many girlfriends, and none she'd wanted to confide in. After they left with the books, Kyra put in a movie for Sophie and took a nap on the couch. When she woke up, it was nearly dinnertime. Kyra decided to make spaghetti.

Sophie had just finished helping Kyra set the table when David arrived home. Sophie ran to him with a squeal, and he picked her up and spun her around. He planted a kiss on the cheek, then set Sophie on the floor and walked over to Kyra.

"How are you doing?" He leaned down to kiss her. "I could've made dinner."

This was the first time since the miscarriage—had it really been a week?—that Kyra had cooked. It was time to return to a semblance of normality. "I'm feeling a little better. Some ladies from church came over today."

He took the cups from Kyra's hand and went to the freezer to fill them with ice. "Why?"

"To pick up the books, but we—Christina Vincent and Megan Burke—ended up visiting for a while. The Burkes just moved in and started attending our congregation. Megan mentioned they've struggled with infertility."

"Did you tell them?"

"No. But visiting with them helped."

"I'm hungry," Sophie said.

"We're ready," Kyra said. David grabbed the spaghetti, Kyra got the sauce, and then they said the prayer and started eating.

"How was your day?" Kyra asked David as she picked at her food, not really hungry. It felt weird to ask such normal questions, as though they hadn't lost a child.

"It was weird," David said.

Kyra paused, her fork halfway to her mouth. "What do you mean, weird?"

"My boss got fired today."

For the first time in days, Kyra felt something other than grief—interest. "Are you serious?"

David nodded. "It's been all over the office. A woman accused him of" —his eyes flicked to Sophie— "a certain kind of harassment. The company did an investigation and found out the problem was widespread. And then there were all the allegations of unfair treatment and verbal harassment."

"What's harassment?" Sophie asked.

"It means he was being really mean," Kyra said. "So what happened?"

David took a bite of garlic bread. "All day, higher-ups kept coming and going. About an hour before the end of my shift, security showed up and escorted him from the building. We're all glad he's gone."

"Why, Daddy?"

"He isn't a very nice man, Soph. He made me not like going to work."

"Mean people are bad." Sophie shoved a big spoonful of spaghetti into her mouth as if for emphasis.

"What's going to happen now?" Kyra asked.

"I assume we'll get a new boss quickly, but until then I'm not sure."

"Who will they hire?"

"I bet it's someone internal. I have no idea who, though. There are quite a few people who would fit the bill."

"Well, I'm glad he's gone for your sake." David's boss had been a thorn in his side since the day he was hired.

David nodded. "Me too."

On Friday, Christina called to check up on Kyra. It brightened Kyra's day in a way she hadn't expected. It was nice to feel like someone cared.

The hole in Kyra's heart throbbed, but she was sick of wallowing. She took Sophie to the park, and they had a picnic despite the chilly March air. When Sophie went down for her afternoon nap, Kyra pulled out her laptop. She needed to indulge, and digital scrapbooking was just the thing.

An hour later she was interrupted by the sound of the garage opening. "Kyra?" David's voice. She set her laptop aside, rising.

"What's wrong?" Kyra asked as he walked into the room. It was nearly two o'clock, well past his usual lunchtime. *Please don't let something else be wrong.* She couldn't take any more bad news.

His smile nearly split his face. "Right before lunch, the vice-president of my department pulled me into his office."

Kyra's heart skipped a beat. "Okay, I'm guessing that's a good thing."

"He asked me to apply for my old boss's job." David laughed, pulling her into a hug. "He said they've been impressed with my work and think I'd be a great fit for the position. Applying is on a by-request basis. And they asked me."

Kyra stood there, stunned, then hugged him back. "That's great! How many people are applying?"

"I'm not sure. I probably won't get the position, but being considered is awesome."

"Don't be so hard on yourself. You're going to get it."

"It'd be a decent pay increase, Kyr. We could do another IUI."

Kyra flinched at the reminder of their lost baby. The miscarriage was still fresh, and most painful of all was the knowledge they didn't have the money to try again. "I want to try again too. I'm not ready to give up."

He hugged her. "Are you okay? I have to get back to the office. We're scrambling to catch up on work with Mark gone. I should've called, but I wanted to tell you in person."

"I'm fine." Kyra kissed him. "Go. You don't want to be late."

David pulled her in, giving her a longer, much more satisfying kiss. "I love you."

A potential raise. The possibility of another IUI. Another baby.

Kyra didn't understand why the Lord had taken their baby away. But it seemed like that while He'd closed a door, maybe— just maybe—He was opening a window.

CHAPTER ELEVEN
MEGAN

Tomorrow Megan would once again be infertile. The reality of her forthcoming appointment gnawed at her nerves all day.

Sienna's afternoon piano lesson proved a welcome distraction. Megan blissfully lost herself in Beethoven's Concerto Number Five, amazed at the improvements Sienna had made in only a week.

"You did great today," Megan told Sienna as she packed up her piano bag. "Do you play in the school orchestra or anything?"

"I play for the choir mostly, but I also play for the orchestra when they need me. That's where I met my boyfriend."

"I didn't know you had a boyfriend. How long have you been dating?"

Sienna grinned, the excitement of new love making her glow. "We started dating this summer. His name is Dane, and he's a senior, like me. He plays the cello but only because his mom won't let him play football otherwise. He's pretty bad, actually—at the cello, not football. He's got colleges scouting him from all over the country." A horn honked, and Sienna stood. "There's my mom. See you next week, Megan."

So Sienna had a boyfriend. Megan wasn't surprised. Sienna was beautiful, with a bubbly personality and thoughtful nature. The boyfriend didn't seem to interfere with her dedication to the piano in the least.

How would it be to be seventeen again, with nothing more than piano lessons and a boyfriend to worry about? If Megan was seventeen, she wouldn't have an appointment with a fertility specialist tomorrow. But she'd also have a curfew and no car. Maybe the appointment wasn't so bad.

Would the doctor make them rerun old tests? What course of action would she recommend? Megan's stomach churned as she obsessed about the possibilities.

When the squeak of the garage door reached her ears, Megan raced to the mud room, throwing the door open.

"Hello to you too," Trent said, stepping inside. "And how was your day?"

"We're infertile," Megan said.

"So that's where all our money's gone."

"Trent, be serious. Starting tomorrow, we're infertile again."

He shrugged. "We've been dealing with infertility every day. Tomorrow we'll just get back to fixing the problem. I thought you'd be happy."

Megan turned in frustration, heading into the living room. "You really don't get it."

He grabbed her hand, pulling her onto the couch. "Explain it to me. I feel like we're finally heading in the right direction, so why are you mad?"

"I'm not mad. I'm scared. I don't get how you can be calm about this. Tomorrow we have to go back there." Megan pointed, as though the Land of IF—the term those "in the know" used for infertility—was a physical place you could visit. Not that anyone ever would. "The last eight months have been nice."

Trent raised an eyebrow. "How so?"

"We haven't had to obsess about treatments or worry if they're going to work. I haven't had to take those crazy hormone drugs."

"Okay, I'll admit that has been nice."

During the last round of Clomid—their sixth straight cycle—Megan had seriously worried Trent would temporarily move in with his mother. Especially after Megan decided she hated the wall between their kitchen and living room and took a sledgehammer to it, determined to rip it out.

"Well, tomorrow, that's all over," Megan said. "We go back to being infertile. We go back to the hormone treatments and counting our cycle days and the endless doctor appointments. I'm not sure I'm ready."

"There's always adoption," Trent said, his voice gentle. "We could put all the treatments behind us."

Megan pressed her lips together. "I'm not ready for that either."

"I think we should consider it."

"No. Not yet."

Trent nodded. It wasn't the first time they'd discussed the subject, and unless they got pregnant, Megan knew it wouldn't be the last. But she continued to resist the idea. It wasn't just a baby she craved. It was the ultimate experience you could have as a woman—pregnancy.

"Get your coat," Trent said, standing.

"Why?"

"We're going out. If tomorrow we have to be infertile, then tonight we're going to enjoy ourselves. What do you want to do?"

Megan stared at Trent, falling in love with him all over again. He always knew exactly how to make her feel better. "I get to pick?"

Trent pulled his shoes on. "Yup."

"I want to go to Roberto's."

"Done."

"And I want to go see *A Love that Lasts*. And eat popcorn. With extra butter."

"No problem."

"And I want to finish the whole night off with the biggest bowl of moose tracks ice cream I can find. I want to eat so many unhealthy calories that it takes me a week to run them off."

Trent shrugged into his coat. "Your wish is my command."

Megan hugged him. "I love you. You're the best."

"I know. Now let's go."

Megan laughed and followed Trent to his truck, allowing him to open her door and help her inside.

"We need to set some ground rules," Trent said as they drove toward the restaurant.

"What is this, a first date? I think we're past that."

Trent gave her a stern glare. "Not those kind of rules. The making-this-date-a-good-date rules."

Megan folded her arms and pretended to pout. "If you insist. What are these rules?"

"There's only one—no talking about babies or infertility."

"You don't think I can do it."

"Nope."

Did he think she spent every waking minute obsessing about infertility? Megan could go a few hours without discussing it, easy. "Well, Mr. Pessimistic, I'm going to prove you wrong. I won't say another word about infertility or babies for the rest of the evening."

Since it was a Thursday, Roberto's was dead. They were seated quickly, and Megan started perusing the menu.

"Why are you even looking at that?" Trent asked. "You order the same thing every time."

"I'm feeling adventurous tonight. Maybe I'll order something new."

"Maybe pigs will fly."

"Maybe we'll have a—" *Baby.* The word was on the tip of her tongue, but she stopped.

Trent pointed a finger at her. "You lose."

"I was going to say maybe we'll have a bird attack our car on the way to the movie. Maybe we'll be dive-bombed."

"You were going to say—"

Megan waggled her finger. "Ah ah ah, if you say it, you lose."

The waitress appeared, pad and paper in hand. "Are you ready to order?" she asked.

"Yes," Megan said. "I'll have the cheese ravioli with the Alfredo sauce, and a frozen raspberry lemonade."

Trent raised an eyebrow, but placed his order too. After the waitress left, he said, "I thought you were going to order something different."

"I was, but then I thought, 'why mess with a good thing?' So I stuck with the ravioli."

Trent shook his head and laughed.

They had a fabulous time at dinner. They laughed and joked and flirted. But it was harder than Megan had expected to not talk about babies or infertility. Halfway through the meal, they were stretching for topics of conversation.

"This is ridiculous," Megan said as they waited for the waitress to bring them their check. "We've been here for an hour, and already we're struggling to find things other than you-know-what to talk about."

Trent reached across the table and stole a sip of Megan's lemonade. "That's why this night is so important. We can't lose ourselves this time. You can't lose yourself. I need you. And I need to not re-drywall the kitchen."

"I make no promises. You give me Clomid, and I lose all rational thought."

"You can do it. Now what was the rule? Come on, we have a movie to catch."

The movie was everything a romantic comedy should be, the popcorn was drenched in butter, and the ice cream afterward was divine, even if Megan would pay for it by running extra miles every day next week. She couldn't have asked for a better evening.

"Thanks, Trent," she said as they walked into the house. "I really needed this."

He leaned down and kissed her. "Thanks for going on a date with me, pretty lady. I had a good time."

"Even though the movie was mushy?"

"I'll deny this if you ever tell anyone, but the movie wasn't as bad as I thought it would be."

Megan put a hand to her chest and did her best Scarlett O'Hara impression. "Trenton Burke, I do declare. You liked that movie!"

"Now don't put words in my mouth. Frankly, my dear, I didn't give a—"

Megan cut his words off with a kiss.

When she pulled away, Trent smiled. "Feel better about things now?"

"No. I'm terrified tomorrow will catch up with me."

"We can still cancel if you need more time."

"But you really want to move forward."

"I really want a baby. But not at your expense. Not if it means I'm going to lose you."

Megan looked away. "I have to be ready. Eight months was a long enough break. It won't be like last time."

Trent nodded, but she caught the worry in his eyes. He grabbed the TV remote off the coffee table and held it up like a champagne glass. "To tomorrow."

Megan laughed. She grabbed a DVD case, clinking it against his remote. "To tomorrow. And to finally being parents."

CHAPTER TWELVE
MEGAN

Dr. Mendoza's office looked eerily similar to Dr. Faulkner's office in Logan. The muted earth tones of the furniture. The oversized desk. The nondescript paintings on the wall. It brought back a flood of memories Megan would rather forget. She fidgeted with her purse strap, her toe tapping impatiently against the carpeted floor. Trent lounged against the love seat while flipping through a magazine, looking totally at home.

"Aren't you nervous?" Megan asked.

He glanced up from the magazine. "Why? We already know what the problem is and what to expect."

That was exactly what made this so hard. Even after last night, he still didn't get it. Not really. It wasn't only the physical toll the treatments took. It was the emotional one. "I hope the word 'Clomid' doesn't leave her mouth. I hate that drug."

"Our kitchen wall wasn't too fond of it either," Trent said, his mouth curled up in a smirk.

The door opened, and Trent and Megan both rose.

"Hello," the woman said with a smile, extending a hand. The barest of wrinkles framed kind eyes, and her chin-length brown hair was streaked with gray. "I'm Dr. Mendoza. You must be Trenton and Megan."

"I go by Trent." He smiled to soften the words.

"Trent it is." Dr. Mendoza sank into the swivel chair behind the desk. She perched reading glasses on her nose and opened their charts. "Let's get right to it. Dr. Faulkner's office faxed your medical records, but I want to verify everything's accurate. It looks like we're dealing with PCOS and low sperm count."

"That's us," Megan said with fake cheerfulness.

"You worked with Dr. Faulkner for almost three years?"

Megan shifted in her chair. "Yes. And we tried the holistic route for a year before that. Trent's also worked with a urologist."

"It says here you've attempted IUIs."

"We were scheduled for eight," Megan said, her throat tight. "But we've only done five. The others three had to be canceled either because I didn't ovulate or the sperm count was too low to proceed."

"How did you respond to Clomid?" Dr. Mendoza asked.

Emotionally? Not well. Megan shrugged. "It depended on the cycle. In the beginning I did well on Metformin. For about six months we did timed intercourse, but then I stopped ovulating again. That's when we switched to Clomid. We started out at fifty milligrams and gradually worked up to one hundred fifty milligrams."

Dr. Mendoza pursed her lips, appearing to be deep in thought. "I spoke to Dr. Faulkner about your case. He approaches fertility treatments a little differently than I do. I usually recommend three IUIs on Clomid and three on injectables before moving on to IVF. I rarely see couples get pregnant from IUI after more than six attempts. If it's going to work, it should by then."

Megan's heart sank.

"Where does that leave us?" Trent asked.

Megan wasn't sure she was ready to hear the answer.

"We have a few options," Dr. Mendoza said. "We can do a cycle of IUI on two hundred milligrams of Clomid and see if Megan ovulates. If not, we can move to injectables and try two or three IUIs on those and hope we're successful. Or we can skip the IUIs, since you've already tried that route, and go straight to IVF."

Megan looked at Trent. "What would you recommend?" he asked.

"I think we should try IUI with Clomid. I'm sure Dr. Faulkner is proficient at his job, but we have a great success rate here, and I think it would be worth our time to explore that option again. It's so much more affordable than in vitro. Since we don't know what's changed in the last eight months, I'd also like to do blood work and another semen analysis."

It was more or less what they'd expected, but Megan's stomach still tied itself in knots. Clomid. Again.

"What do you think?" Megan asked Trent.

"I think we should go with Dr. Mendoza's recommendation." His eyes apologized, but his voice was resolute. "It's worth it if it works, right?"

Megan closed her eyes, breathing deeply to ease the tightening in her chest. She imagined a tiny pink face with her lips and Trent's nose. It was time to push forward. "Okay, let's try IUI with Clomid. I really don't want to do in vitro unless it's our only hope."

"I think that's a good choice," Dr. Mendoza said. "Let's talk about your cycles. How long has it been since your last period?"

"Seventy days," Megan said.

"I'll write you a prescription to see if we can get it to start. We want to get this ball rolling."

They talked for a while longer. Trent and Megan had their blood drawn, and he gave a sperm sample. They left with plans to call when—make that if—Megan's period ever decided to start.

"How do you feel about things?" Trent asked on the drive home.

"Cautious," Megan admitted.

"I'm sorry if I pushed you into the IUI. I know you don't want to do Clomid. But I'm ready to be a dad."

"No, you were right to push. I'm not ready to jump into IVF." If Clomid was bad, Megan was sure to be a mental case on all the hormone drugs required for IVF.

Trent frowned. "Are you saying you won't consider in vitro?"

Megan didn't have to think about it for long. "If it comes to that, I'll do it. But we should give IUI one last shot. Even if it's already failed five times."

"Yes, but never on two hundred milligrams of Clomid. Maybe the higher dosage will make a difference."

Or maybe it would make her crazier. Megan fingered the prescription in her hand. Prayed it would help her period start.

"I hope it does make a difference. I'm ready to jump off this infertility ride and be done."

"So after we have one, you don't want to go through it all again for a second child?"

Megan sighed. "Ask me again when the time comes. I always wanted a houseful of kids. But lately, all I want is one or two to call my own and the relief of never having to take another hormone pill." The fertility drugs increased their chance of having multiples, but Megan wasn't holding her breath that they'd get that lucky.

Trent and Megan went out to dinner and a movie again that evening. Surprisingly enough, the next morning her period started. Usually it took the pills longer than a day to take effect. She pulled out her cell phone and opened the fertility app. A wheel spun on the home page, indicating Megan was on day seventy-one of her cycle. She marked that her period had started, and the wheel circled back to one.

Here we go. She prayed they'd be able to hang on tight for the next few months.

CHAPTER THIRTEEN
KYRA

Saturday night after Sophie went to bed, David cornered Kyra. "We need to talk."

Kyra didn't look away from the bookcase she was alphabetizing. "About what?"

He took the book from her hand and placed it on the shelf, then guided her toward the couch. "About doing another IUI."

The miscarriage had made Kyra more desperate for a baby than ever. But she couldn't see a way around their current financial situation. She chewed on a fingernail. "Why even discuss it? That IUI was our one shot. If you get the position, we can re-evaluate."

"Do you need more time, Kyra?"

She played with a loose thread on the couch. They'd bought it at a yard sale when they were first married, and it really looked the worse for wear. "For what?"

His hand fell over hers. She finally looked up. "Are you ready to have a baby?" David asked.

She didn't have to think twice. "Yes. But—"

"No buts. If you're ready, we'll figure out the money. Let's go over the finances again and make this work. I'll go get the laptop and meet you at the kitchen table."

Forty agonizing minutes later, a baby felt further away than ever.

"There's nowhere else to cut corners," Kyra said. "There's not enough money to make it happen."

"Not true. I think if we're really careful, we can make it work."

"We have your student loans now." Bitterness crept into her voice. The loans had been in deferment until this month, and now they had to start making payments.

"There's enough left from our tax return that we can squeeze in one more."

"And what happens when that doesn't work?" She pointed to the computer screen. "We're barely able to make ends meet as it is. Between the medical bills and student loans, we're treading water. That tax return is the only savings we have. What do we do when an unexpected expense comes up if we spend it?"

"I have my six-month review at work in a few weeks. I should get a decent raise. And maybe I'll get the promotion."

Kyra folded her arms and shook her head. "Who are we kidding? We can barely afford the one child we have. Maybe the miscarriage was God's way of telling us we shouldn't have another baby."

"No." David's hand clamped tight on her shoulder. "Don't think like that. We prayed about that first IUI. We knew it was the right thing to do. And I think emptying our savings for another one is the right thing to do now."

The hole in her heart begged her to take another chance. "It really would be the last IUI we can afford."

David nodded. "I know. Promise me we can at least think about it?"

"Okay."

On Sunday morning, Kyra, David, and Sophie fell into their seats mere moments before the pastor started the services. The choir sang a hymn while Sophie played with a rag doll, and then the pastor stood to begin his sermon.

"Mommy," Sophie said, a bit too loudly.

Kyra pulled Sophie onto her lap, holding her close. "Shhh, baby girl," Kyra whispered. "We use our quiet voices at church. What do you need?"

Sophie held the doll out to Kyra. "I want her to wear the pink dress."

"As of late, I have felt impressed to speak to our congregation about the dangers of debt," the pastor announced.

Kyra's hand froze on the doll. After last night's conversation, she wasn't sure if she wanted to hear this. Sometimes debt couldn't be avoided, and they had more than their fair share.

"What I say today may be hard for you to hear," the pastor continued. "Many of you will argue that there are many things worth going into debt for. But I think the Lord would disagree. I strongly encourage each and every one of you to pray for guidance before going into any more debt. Avoid it whenever possible."

Kyra's hands fumbled with the button on the doll clothes she was changing. David and Kyra had tried their best to avoid debt. They didn't use credit cards. They hadn't bought a second vehicle. But what about a baby? Surely the Lord wouldn't want them to put off having a family. They wouldn't exactly be going into debt for this IUI, if they decided to do it. But they would be emptying their savings account, which could translate to more debt if an unexpected expense arose.

"Mama," Sophie whined. "Change faster."

"Sorry." Kyra switched the doll into a ballerina leotard. But the pastor's words kept floating around in her head. Kyra listened carefully to the rest of his sermon, alert and attentive for the first time all morning, but he never said anything specifically about going into debt for a baby. Not that she had expected him to.

After the services, Kyra and David dropped Sophie off at the nursery and headed to their Bible study class. David saw a neighbor and wandered over to talk with him while Kyra took a seat.

"Hey." Megan slipped into the seat beside Kyra. "How are you doing?"

Kyra forced a smile. "I'm good. How are you?"

"I'm loving today's weather. It's so warm for March."

Kyra hadn't noticed. "Must be spring."

"Spring comes much later in Logan. It's nice to have some warmth and sunshine."

Kyra barely heard Megan. A baby or financial solvency? The two batted around in Kyra's head, like a ping-pong ball. Which took precedence?

Ask Megan. Kyra pushed the thought away. Megan might know about the world of infertility treatments. But with two incomes, Kyra doubted the Burkes struggled financially.

"Can I sit here?" Christina pointed to a seat on the other side of Kyra, leaving an empty space between them. "I'll leave a spot for your husband."

"Sure," Kyra said.

Christina smiled her thanks. They made small talk until the assistant pastor stood, signaling the beginning of Bible study, and David slipped into his seat.

"Today I wanted to focus on the Bible's teachings about raising a righteous posterity," the assistant pastor said.

Kyra's heart sank. Maybe she should go home and sleep the day away.

Megan reached out and squeezed Kyra's hand. Kyra looked up in surprise. Megan's eyes were full of empathy. "Sorry," Megan mouthed.

Kyra gave a tiny smile of thanks.

The assistant pastor went on and on about how man and woman had been created to multiply and replenish the earth. How it wasn't something they should put off for any reason.

Like financial difficulties.

Each word was a knife to the heart. *I'm trying!* Kyra cried to the Lord. *I'm willing. But You took our baby away.*

How did this lesson fit with the earlier sermon? What if the only way to have more children required going into debt? If the next IUI worked and they were careful for a few months, maybe everything would be fine. But if they had to do a third IUI, they would need a loan. Which commandment was more important to obey? Kyra felt like Eve in the Garden of Eden, being told to multiply and replenish while also being asked to not eat the fruit.

She wasn't ready to give up. They couldn't stop trying now. If the IUI hadn't worked last time, maybe Kyra would call it quits.

But it had worked. And their baby had died.

Tell me what to do, Lord. Should we be financially responsible? Or should we move forward with infertility treatments?

A slow warmth spread through Kyra, and tears sprang to her eyes. *Thank you.* Maybe it wasn't the right decision for everyone. But for their family, they needed to move forward with the IUI. The money was worth it.

It'll work, Kyra told herself as the assistant pastor finished the lesson. *The next IUI will work.* She bowed her head for the prayer. They wouldn't have to take out any loans. David would get the promotion. Things would go in their favor.

A collective "amen" sounded from the room, and Kyra's eyes popped open. "Are you okay?" Christina asked, peering around David.

"Lessons like this suck," Megan said. "Geez, I'm sorry, Kyra."

"I'm fine," Kyra assured both of them, ignoring David's raised eyebrow. She knew which direction they needed to head.

They said their goodbyes, and Kyra and David picked up Sophie from the nursery. "Look, Mommy!" Sophie shoved a picture toward her. "I colored it for you so you won't be sad anymore."

Kyra took the picture. It was mostly scribbles, with the words "Jesus Loves Me" typed across the top. "Thanks, baby girl." Kyra gave Sophie a kiss on the cheek, then took Sophie's hand in hers. "I love it."

In the car, David asked, "Is everything okay?"

Kyra nodded. "I think we should do the IUI."

"Really?"

"It feels right."

He grinned. "It does. Things will work out this time. I know it."

"Dr. Mendoza said with such an early miscarriage, as soon as I have a period, we can try again."

"Do you need more time?"

"No. I already feel like we've waited so long." *Don't let anything bad happen again,* Kyra prayed. *Please, please, please.*

CHAPTER FOURTEEN
CHRISTINA

Stacey was right. Christina never should've agreed to the after-school program.

She tried to keep her eyes from widening as Trista droned on and on about her ideas for the class. When Christina had agreed to the job, she'd envisioned empowering downtrodden students. It was something to fill the empty hours until Gary got home, and had the added bonus of that warm glow that comes from helping others.

What Trista had in mind was an intense, two-month program designed to encompass even the most obscure risky behaviors. Trista's curriculum involved way more work than Christina had anticipated. Her ten-hour a week side-job would become a thirty-hour a week second career if she didn't redirect Trista soon.

"I thought maybe you'd like to teach the lesson on verbal manipulation," Trista was saying.

Time to derail this train before it derailed Christina. "These are some great ideas, Trista. But we have one chance to get the district to fund this program. I really feel like we should focus on the most common and easily recognized risky behaviors. That's what the district will look for, and I think that's what Principal Gardner had in mind. Once the program is successful, maybe they'll want to include a more comprehensive list of concerns."

Trista's eyebrows knit together in displeasure. "Anybody can conduct that type of program. If that's what Principal Gardner wanted, he could've asked any first-year teacher or intern." She inclined her head as though to say, *Maybe that's why he asked you.*

Christina frowned. "I think Principal Gardner asked us to *co*-chair the program because we both have a lot to offer."

"I think we should be thorough and include all information."

What would Gary say if he knew what a disaster this was turning into? Not that Christina would tell him.

Christina left Trista's classroom feeling tired, frustrated, and overwhelmed. How was she supposed to work with such a difficult co-chair? And how on earth were the kids going to get the instruction they needed with Trista around?

Christina wanted to go home and unwind. Maybe she'd allow herself a couple spoonfuls of chocolate frosting and thirty minutes with the TV before starting dinner.

Linda stepped out of the front office as Christina walked past, blocking her exit. "Hey, Christina. Do you have a few minutes?"

Christina hitched her bag up higher on her shoulder and smiled. "Sure. What can I do for you?"

"Principal Gardner wants an update on the outreach program. I was going to schedule something for tomorrow, but he's free now."

"Sounds great," Christina said, less than enthusiastic.

Principal Gardner's door was open, and he looked up, obviously hearing her approach. "Oh good. I wanted to talk to you." He stood behind his desk, gathering papers to place in his briefcase. "How's the program coming along?"

If Christina mentioned Trista, would Principal Gardner think Christina incompetent? Would he regret asking her to co-chair? "It's coming along."

Principal Gardner frowned. "Is something wrong?"

"Not exactly." She'd better mention the situation before Trista skewed the story. "Trista and I had a disagreement today. She's under the impression you want a detailed program encompassing every possible at-risk behavior, whereas it was my understanding our job was to give an overview and teach coping skills."

Principal Gardner sighed, snapping his briefcase shut. "I know Trista can be difficult to work with, but she's a dedicated teacher."

Christina's shoulders relaxed.

"I'll talk to her tomorrow. While a comprehensive program would be great down the road, right now the district is interested in seeing student awareness and coping skills improve. I found out today they want us to offer a test at the beginning and end of the program to measure how much improvement took place."

Just as Christina had suspected. "Is the district providing the test?"

Principal Gardner grimaced, walking toward the door. Christina stepped aside, letting him pass, and followed. They waved to Linda and headed toward the parking lot.

"No. They want you to create it," Principal Gardner said. "And here's the real kicker. They want it next week. They need to 'approve' the test before we administer it, and we need to administer it on day one of the program." He sighed. "The red tape in education is enough to drive me crazy. I'm really sorry, Christina. I know they're asking a lot."

Creating that test would take at least ten hours by itself. Christina wanted to sigh too, but instead plastered on her teacher smile. "I'll talk to Trista first thing tomorrow, and we'll get right on it."

"I knew I could count on you. I'll let Trista know we can't afford to waste time on less prevalent behaviors this year." Principal Gardner waved, heading toward his car. "Come back and update me on Friday, okay?"

"Sure thing," Christina said.

Once inside her car, she flipped to a rock station—her guilty pleasure. She looked around to assure herself Principal Gardner had left and no cars were nearby before she turned up the volume.

"Happy Monday," she muttered to herself as she drove away. It was going to be a long, painful week.

◆◆

Gary was home by seven. It wasn't the six o'clock he'd promised, but it was better than eight or nine.

"Hey," Christina said from where she stood near the stove.

Gary leaned down to kiss her, making her heart flutter in a way it hadn't in a long time. "I missed you today. I would've been home earlier, but a last-minute issue delayed me. What's for dinner?"

"Fish tacos."

"Sounds great." He unbuttoned his shirt sleeves and rolled them up to his elbows. "What can I do to help?"

Christina froze. In the early years of their marriage, dinner had always been a team effort. But since starting at the firm, Gary usually disappeared into his office until dinner was on the table. "Um, you can grate the cheese. I'll sear the fish, and we should be ready."

Fifteen minutes later they sat down to dinner. "You haven't said anything about the outreach program," Gary said. "How's that going?" He took a big bite of his taco and looked at her expectantly.

Was he asking to be polite? Or hoping she'd tell him the program was a disaster so he could gloat? "It's going well."

Gary's eyes narrowed. "You always play with your hair when you're holding something back."

Christina's finger tangled in a curl. She quickly unwound it, dropping her hands into her lap.

"How's it really going?"

"I didn't think you'd want to know." She reached for a glass of water, avoiding his eyes.

"I thought we agreed not to do this. I always want to know. Tell me what's wrong."

If he was going to make an effort, so was she. "My co-chair, Trista? She's a complete control freak."

Gary's mouth twitched, and he burst out laughing.

Christina glared. She shouldn't have opened her mouth. "If you're going to be a jerk, I won't tell you anything else."

Gary pursed his lips together as though trying to keep a straight face, his shoulders hunched from the attempt. "I'm sorry. I know it must be hard to work with her. You're so particular about things."

Christina flinched, feeling the words as though they were a whip. "You say that like it's a bad thing. I just like things done right."

"I'm sorry. Really." He reached across the table and grabbed her hand. She pulled away, but he recaptured her fingers. "I'm done laughing. Tell me why she's being controlling."

"No."

"Please?"

She sighed. "Trista can't seem to focus on the specific aims of the program."

"How so?"

"She's trying to do too much with the time allotment we're given."

"Have you talked to Principal Gardner about it?"

As Gary showed concern and asked thoughtful questions, Christina opened up. She told him about her conversation with Principal Gardner and how she hoped things would go better next time she spoke with Trista.

"Enough about me. How was your day?" Christina asked.

"Good," Gary said.

Christina's heart sank. The typical one-word response. She went back to her plate of food.

"We played a prank on one of the new interns today."

Christina's head shot up. Not only had Gary helped with a prank, but he was going to tell her about it?

"The guys always razz new interns. We flipped the screens on their computers so everything was upside down. Totally harmless. But it felt good to be a part of, even if it was juvenile. They had to call the IT guys to flip them back. I felt like a co-worker for the first time, and not just the partner's son."

Christina beamed. "That's great, Gar. I'm glad they're accepting you."

She stood and started to clear the table. Gary stood as well, grabbing his dishes and following her into the kitchen.

"Don't you have work to do?" Christina asked.

He shook his head. "I promised I'd leave things at the office, and I will as much as possible. Do you have work tonight?"

"Some worksheets to grade, but I can put it off."

"Good. I thought we could watch TV for a while."

"Sounds great," Christina said. And it really did.

As they sat cuddling on the couch, watching episodes of *Criminology*, she felt closer to Gary than she had in a long time. It felt like she had back the man she'd married.

"Want some crackers and hummus?" Gary asked, pausing the DVD.

"Sure," Christina said, trying not to sound surprised at the thoughtful suggestion.

Christina went to the restroom while Gary got their snack from the kitchen. She stared in shock. She counted in her head. No, she hadn't lost track of time. It had only been twenty-one days since her last period.

Things were getting worse. Christina's periods had never been regular, but even this was unusual for her.

"I'm pushing play," Gary called from the living room.

Christina slowly made her way back to Gary. It wasn't just about a baby anymore. If something was wrong, her health could be in jeopardy. Maybe that would convince Gary to go to the doctor with her.

Gary munched on a whole-wheat cracker, the TV still paused.

"Gary," she said, standing behind him.

"Okay, I'm pushing play for real now."

"Gary."

He turned around, brows knit together. "What?"

Christina slowly took the remote from his hands, staring at him.

He set the plate of crackers and hummus down on the coffee table. "Is everything okay?"

"My period started."

"Oh." He glanced at the TV, then at the hummus, then back at her. She knew he was trying to decide how she wanted him to respond. "I'm sorry."

"It's a week early."

"Okay." More silence. "But that's not too weird for you, right?"

"This is unusual, even for me. I really think we should see a doctor." She could already see his face muscles tightening, but she held up a hand. "It's not only a baby we're talking about. It's not normal for a period to be so short. Or unpredictable."

"Yours have always been that way."

"But it's getting worse. Lately I never know when to expect my period or how long it will last. And the cramps are more awful every month. Sometimes it's so painful I can barely walk."

"Why haven't you said anything?"

Because he was never around to talk to. He wasn't around to see how physically painful it was for her each month. "I didn't want to worry you. But now I think we should be open to the possibility of finding out what the problem is. Because clearly there is a problem."

"Christina—"

"Just because we find out what's wrong doesn't mean we have to do anything about it right now."

"Is this an excuse to see about a baby?"

Christina had to consciously will herself not to play with her hair. "Now that's insulting. Of course I want a baby. But this is about my health too. I haven't gone to my yearly exam for a few years now."

Gary's jaw muscles relaxed. "I guess I never thought about your period pains in terms of your health. Has it really been that long since you went for a checkup?"

Christina tried to keep her face calm and impassive. "Yes. I think something's wrong." She held a hand to her abdomen where the cramps were starting to make it ache. "I can feel it in my gut. Literally. We should be pregnant by now, and we're not."

"These are two separate issues. I don't know if I'm ready to be . . ." He swallowed hard. "Infertile."

Christina reached for his hand. "I don't know if I'm ready, either. But what if it's a really simple fix? Medical science can do so much for people these days. Maybe we'll go to the doctor, and a baby will magically appear nine months later."

That made the corner of his mouth quirk, and Christina was pleased she'd put that half smile there. "Okay."

Christina tightened her hand on his arm. "Really?"

"Really. Make the appointment with your doctor. I'm not saying I'm ready to address any" —he grimaced— "fertility issues. But we definitely need to look after your health. If you need to get a checkup, I'm not going to discourage you."

Christina wanted to jump with joy. She wanted to be ecstatic. But she feared Gary would change his mind if she made a big deal about it. "I really think that's best," she said coolly. "I'll do it first thing in the morning." Now to change the subject before he changed his mind. She unpaused the DVD. "Let's finish this episode then go to bed?"

"Sounds like a plan."

At eight o'clock the next morning, Christina started calling the doctor's office. The first three times she got a pre-recorded message saying they were out of the office, but on the fourth call someone answered. She gave her name and date of birth, and the receptionist pulled up her charts.

"And how may I help you today, Mrs. Vincent?" the receptionist asked.

"I'd like to make an appointment with Dr. Blakely."

Christina heard tapping on the keyboard. "What is this concerning?"

Christina chewed on her lip. She knew what Gary expected her to say. But they needed to move forward. "My husband and I have been trying to get pregnant for over a year. I think something's wrong."

Ten minutes later, she had an appointment scheduled in two weeks. Christina called Gary to give him the news.

"So soon?" he said.

"Is that a problem?"

She heard his sigh through the phone. "I don't know about this. Maybe we should wait a little longer."

"I already made the appointment. If you won't go with me, I'll go alone."

"No, I don't want to do that either," Gary said quickly. He probably wanted to make sure she didn't make any baby-making decisions without him. "I'm willing to see about your health. But I'm not ready for the other stuff."

"The two are probably connected, Gar. To find out about one we'll have to find out about the other."

"Christina."

Time to end the call. "You're cutting out. I can't understand you. Gar . . . I . . . talk . . ."

"I know you're faking."

Christina sighed. It had been worth a shot. "I'm going to the appointment. Please don't make me go alone."

"Can we please—"

"Oops, there's the other line. It's my mother."

"Aren't they on a cruise in Greece right now?"

"I'd better get this. See you at home."

"Christina!"

CHAPTER FIFTEEN
MEGAN

Megan glared at the four small round white pills sitting on the counter as though they were the enemy. "I don't like you very much," she told the pills. "Last time you were hateful, and I really didn't appreciate it."

The pills sat there, staring innocently up at Megan. Probably calling her crazy for talking to them.

"I know it's not your fault. You were created to do this. And I guess if you make me a baby, I'll be happy. But right now, I really don't want to take you. Let's make a promise. I'll be nice to you if you be nice to me, okay?"

The pills didn't answer. Megan sighed, flopping onto one of the barstools. "This is stupid," she said to herself. She had just returned home from her baseline ultrasound. Everything looked good, and she was given the go-ahead to start Clomid. But she'd been staring at the pills for ten minutes now, trying to convince herself to take them. The thought of returning to that cold, dark place full of needles and crazy hormones and shattered possibilities and mountains of bills . . .

It was better than never being a mother.

"Fine." Megan grabbed the four pills and angrily tossed them into the back of her throat before she could reconsider, chasing them down with water in one large gulp. Megan slammed the cup on the table. Too late to turn back now.

As Megan made calls for a client, the symptoms started. She grabbed a magazine off her desk and fanned herself, trying to focus on the other end of the phone conversation. *It's already happening,* she thought, heart racing. The pills were taking effect. She put a hand to her mouth, swallowing back the bile rising in her throat. Her body blazed with heat, and a buzzing filled her ears.

It had only been forty-five minutes since she'd taken the Clomid. It was all in her head.

Then again, maybe not. As the evening progressed, her symptoms worsened. Megan tried ignoring them, but that didn't work.

"Time for a breather," Megan said aloud, pushing back from her computer desk. She headed toward the laundry room. She'd switch the loads and play the piano for a while. Maybe watch TV. She couldn't work anymore tonight.

Megan opened the door and zeroed in on Trent's dirty socks. They sat on the floor, two inches from the hamper.

She let out a scream. "It would take you two seconds more to put them in the hamper," she yelled to the empty house. "Two. Freaking. Seconds!"

Megan slammed the laundry room door shut without switching the load. If Trent couldn't be bothered to put his socks in the hamper, then she couldn't be bothered to put his pants in the dryer.

Ten minutes into furiously pounding out Tchaikovsky, the guilt hit. Megan put the clothes in the dryer, then lay morosely on the couch watching mindless reality TV.

By the time Trent got home, she was a wreck. Megan pounced on him as soon as he walked through the garage door. "How can I feel crazy already?"

Trent didn't seem surprised by her presence or the question. "What's got you feeling crazy?"

"You didn't put your socks in the laundry hamper. You left them right next to it, like you couldn't be bothered to make the extra effort to help me out."

"Sorry. I'll make sure to put them in the hamper next time."

"I am so mad at you right now."

He raised an eyebrow. "They're just socks. I'll go put them away."

"This isn't about the socks! It's about the Clomid. I feel irrationally mad right now."

"You took the pills like what, five hours ago?"

Megan's eyes narrowed. "This is all your fault. Do you remember what I was like last time on Clomid, Trenton? I didn't want to take it again, but you pushed until I said yes. Well, this is what you pushed for." She flounced out of the room.

"Megan, wait. I didn't mean it like that."

"Put your socks in the hamper!"

Trent tiptoed around the house for the rest of the evening, avoiding Megan as much as possible.

The next morning, she felt even worse. She went for her morning run alone, but not even that helped pound out her frustrations. While showering, Megan discovered Trent had used all the soap and not bothered to replace it. "Trent," she yelled.

He popped his head into the bathroom. "What?"

"You. Didn't. Replace. The soap." She bit out each word.

Trent handed her a new bar, and they finished getting ready for the day in silence. He left for work without kissing her. Fine. She was still mad at him over the socks anyway.

Megan reached for the box and popped four pills from the blister pack. Her hand shook as she filled a glass with water, but she swallowed all four pills anyway.

She worked in her office all morning, then took a break to prepare for her afternoon piano lesson with Sienna. Megan took a few deep breaths and mentally stepped into her teacher persona. *Don't be crazy,* Megan commanded herself when the doorbell rang.

"Hi, Sienna," Megan said.

Sienna nodded, walking inside and slipping off her shoes. "Hey."

Well, someone was super chatty today.

"Play me your assigned scales to warm up, and then I want to hear the first piece," Megan said.

Sienna nodded and started playing scales. A discordant note made Megan curl her fingers around the notebook.

"Sorry," Sienna muttered, playing the correct note and continuing. After she finished her scales, she started on her piece for the week, pulling out the sheet music since she hadn't yet memorized it. The chords were messy, and Sienna frequently played incorrect notes. Megan watched Sienna's fingers tremble.

Megan's own stress melted away, and her brows furrowed in concern. Something must be seriously upsetting Sienna. She never played this poorly.

Halfway through the song, Megan dropped her notebook to the floor. She splayed her fingers across the sheet music, covering the notes. Sienna froze, her fingers suspended over the keys.

"Let's take a breather," Megan said.

Sienna nodded, placing her hands in her lap and lowering her eyes to the keys.

"Talk to me, Sienna. You're usually flawless. What happened this week?"

Sienna raised her eyes, and Megan was shocked to see they sparkled with tears. "I'm really sorry, Megan. I swear I'll practice next week."

"Hey, that's not what I meant." Megan waved a hand toward the music. "This can wait a week. What I'm worried about is you. What's going on?"

"I got some bad news this week." Her voice was so quiet Megan had to strain to hear it.

That didn't sound good. Was someone sick? Had Sienna broken up with her boyfriend? Did she fail a history test? "You don't have to tell me anything you don't want to, but I'm here to listen."

Sienna blinked, and a single tear rolled down her cheek. "I made a really big mistake, and I can't fix it."

"I'll help if I can," Megan said softly.

"I'm pregnant." Sienna dropped her head into her hands with a sob.

Waves crashed against Megan, knocking the breath from her lungs. Buzzing filled her ears, and her vision blurred.

Pregnant. No, it couldn't be true. She'd misheard Sienna.

"What?" Megan said stupidly.

Sienna's shoulders shuddered. "I took a test yesterday at school. Then I took three more. My period was a week late, and Dane and I . . . I didn't mean for it to happen."

Sienna didn't mean for it to happen. After five years of begging for it to happen—of planning and praying and paying—it still hadn't happened for Megan. But one moment of passion was all it took for Sienna and Dane to accidentally create life.

"Have you told your parents?" Megan's voice cracked. Of course Sienna hadn't told her parents. There was no way she'd be here at piano lessons if she had.

Sienna shook her head. "I'm scared. They'll be so disappointed."

Disappointed. A beautiful baby, and yet everyone would be disappointed. Because Sienna was seventeen. She should be worrying about prom dresses, not maternity clothes.

Megan closed her eyes as the pain rolled over her. *Don't let me make a mess of this,* she prayed. *Don't let me fall apart.* Somehow, Megan had to put aside her own feelings—and the raging hormones from Clomid—and not make things worse.

She took a deep breath and opened her eyes. "Your parents love you. You need to tell them. You need to go to the doctor." Megan swallowed hard. "You need to make plans. For the baby."

Sienna's sobs came louder. "It'll break their hearts. I was so stupid. I'm never irresponsible. And now . . . They'll . . ." Her shoulders shook.

"Hey." Megan wrapped an arm around Sienna and pulled her close. All Megan could think about was Sienna, and how this was every bit as sad for her as it was for Megan.

Sienna had her whole life ahead of her. And now she also had a baby.

"You have to tell them, Sienna. You know you have to."

Sienna turned, and Megan's arm fell off her shoulders. "Help me, Megan. Please." Her voice caught on the word. "I know I have to tell them, but I don't know how."

They spent the rest of Sienna's lesson carefully planning how she would approach her parents. Sienna broke down a few times, but seemed determined to figure this out.

Megan gave Sienna a long hug before she left. "Your parents are good people," Megan reminded her. "They'll be disappointed, but they love you, and they're going to help you through this."

Sienna nodded, hugging Megan back. "Thanks."

"I want a text letting me know how things go tonight."

"Maybe I should do it tomorrow."

Megan shook her head, making her voice firm. "You need to get this over with. It's going to get harder the longer you wait."

Sienna sighed, then nodded. "I should've never let this happen."

The knife twisted in Megan's heart until she wanted to scream. "But it did. And now you have to deal with it."

Megan stood on the front porch and watched Sienna drive away. Then she went inside and stared at the piano. With a yell, she swiped all the sheet music onto the floor.

"Why?" she screamed. "Why do you give her a baby and not me? It isn't fair. Not to either of us." The hurt cut deep into her soul, a physical pain she feared she'd drown in. "I'm a good person. I read the Bible and say my prayers and go to church every Sunday. Why won't You give me a baby?"

Silence was her only answer.

She pushed the piano music aside with her foot and slid the bench out to accommodate her longer legs. She pounded on the keyboard with a ferocious intensity. *Am I not good enough?* Megan wondered as the tears streamed down her face. *Would I not be a good mother? Is that why You won't give me children?* She couldn't shake the feeling that she was the problem, and not just because of her physical difficulties in conceiving.

The music flowed through Megan, each note pulled from her soul and strung together to sing of her anger and despair. She hunched over the keys, pounding. The minor chords pulsed through her arms.

In the middle of a particularly furious section, the doorbell rang, echoing through the whole house.

Megan stopped playing. She should ignore it. But whoever stood outside would've heard her playing—and would've heard her stop. What's more, they'd probably seen her through the bay window as they walked up the front steps.

Sighing, Megan walked to the door. If it was a solicitor, she would send them running away in tears.

But it wasn't a solicitor. Christina stood on the front steps, looking embarrassed. She wore a cream-colored pea coat that nearly covered her dress, leaving a few inches of the skirt exposed at the bottom. Her gloved hands were clasped around a DVD case. "Hi," she said. "I wanted to return this before I forgot." She held out the *Criminology* DVD box.

Why couldn't Christina have stopped by any day but today?

"Thanks." Megan took the DVDs from Christina. "How'd you like it?"

"It was great. We really enjoyed it." Christina opened her mouth as though to say something, then pursed her lips. "Well, thanks again." She turned to leave, then spun back around. "I'm really sorry, but I have to ask—is everything okay?"

Megan laughed, and it sounded bitter even to her own ears. "Of course. I'm Megan Burke. I'm always okay in the end. Nothing can bring me down."

Christina shuffled her feet. "Do you want to talk about it? I'm a good listener."

Megan did want to talk. But Christina wouldn't understand. "I don't want to bother you with my problems."

Christina nodded. "Is it weird to ask if we can borrow season two? I promised Gary I'd ask."

"Oh." Megan opened the door wider, motioning Christina inside. "Of course it's still okay. Sorry, I'm not thinking clearly today."

Christina followed Megan inside. "I feel bad asking. I can see you're upset."

Tears pricked Megan's eyes, and she blinked. She didn't want to cry in front of Christina. She wanted them to be friends, and crying might convince Christina she was a crazy person to be avoided.

Megan led Christina into the family room and went over to the DVD cabinet, putting *Criminology* back and grabbing season two. "I've had a really rough day."

"Can I ask what happened? If you don't want to tell me, I understand. But I really would like to help if I can." Christina sat on the edge of the couch, her hands clasped tightly in her lap, gloves still on.

Megan handed Christina the DVDs and sank down on the other side of the couch. Christina seemed willing to talk, and Megan needed a listening ear. Why not? It wasn't like today could get any worse.

"I got some bad news today. One of my piano students is pregnant—she's only seventeen. Still in high school. And I don't know why she has to go through such a trial, when a baby would be such a blessing to me." It was useless. The tears were determined to fall, splattering onto Megan's lap and leaving dark spots on her dress pants.

Christina's eyes softened. "I'm sorry. That must feel really unfair to you."

"Yeah, it does. I feel awful Sienna has to go through something this hard."

"But you're sad for yourself too?" Christina finished.

"Yes. Wow, you really get it."

A mask fell over Christina's face, and she laughed uncomfortably. "I'm trying to view the situation through your eyes. I haven't gone through nearly what you have, I'm sure."

"I'll bet that's not true. We all have our trials."

Christina nodded. "I'm sorry today's been one of yours. I don't know what you're feeling, but I can imagine what it's like to have something you want so badly just out of reach."

"I feel like no matter what I do, no matter how hard I work, things never go in our favor."

They sat in silence, but it wasn't uncomfortable like Megan expected it to be.

"We took a break from fertility treatments. Almost nine months. But we started on a new cycle of treatments yesterday. The hormone drugs make me act like a crazy person. I think that probably made my reaction today more intense than it would've been otherwise. I kept it together while she was here, but sort of exploded when she left."

Christina nodded. "Hormones can really mess you up. I've never taken fertility drugs or anything, but PMS is bad enough. I hope it works for you this time."

"Me too."

Christina rose from the couch, holding up the DVD case. "Thanks for letting us borrow *Criminology*. It's been really good for us to watch together."

Megan raised an eyebrow. "No problem. When you're finished with that season, I'll give you the next one."

Christina nodded, heading toward the front door, and Megan followed.

"I didn't even ask you about the after-school program," Megan said. "I'm sorry. I'm usually not this rude. How's that going? Co-chair still being difficult?"

"Things are improving. I think we're on the same page now."

"That's great. You know, we really should get together for a game night sometime soon. Trent and I would love to get to know you guys better."

Christina paused at the doorway. "We'd really like that."

"It's a double date. Thanks for talking to me, Christina. I actually do feel better now."

Christina blushed, making her freckles stand out. "No problem. I hope the rest of your day is better." She opened the door and stepped out on the front porch, hesitating. "You play the piano beautifully," she said. And then she was gone.

CHAPTER SIXTEEN
CHRISTINA

The day of Christina's appointment with the gynecologist dragged. She vacillated between feeling excited to find out what was holding them back and scared to death for the same reason. It felt good to be proactive, to move forward instead of standing still. She was ready to admit there was a problem and work on fixing it. But Gary? After today, what would happen?

She slung her purse over one shoulder, ready to walk out of the classroom for the day. Her cell phone rang, and she glanced at the caller ID, her stomach dropping. Gary.

Christina closed her eyes, took a deep breath, and answered. "Hey, I'm just leaving the school. Are you on your way to the doctor's?"

"Not exactly." She heard the apology in his voice. She flipped the classroom lights off harder than necessary and locked the door.

"You're not coming." It wasn't a question because Christina wasn't surprised.

"I'm really sorry, babe. Something came up, and I've got piles of paperwork to do before tomorrow."

"That's your excuse? Paperwork?" She balled her free hand into a fist, curling the other tighter around her phone. "I would really like it if you'd take an hour out of your day and go to the doctor with me."

"But you don't need me there, right? They're going to do the exact same thing whether I'm present or not. This is my job we're talking about. I'm really sorry, but I need to stay."

Christina didn't doubt he had paperwork, but he could put it off for an hour. He was lying, and they both knew it. "Fine. Once again, work comes first." Christina hung up before he could reply. It rang again, but she rejected the call.

She drove faster than she should to the doctor's office, her hands clutching the steering wheel. Christina ignored three more calls and at least two texts. She turned the rock station up uncomfortably loud, determined to stay angry and not cry. Maybe Gary wasn't ready to face their infertility, but she was. And she would do it with or without him.

Christina walked into the waiting room at the OB/GYN's office and felt her self-righteous anger and false confidences vanish. Five women, all obviously pregnant, were scattered around the room, sitting in mismatched chairs. They looked young and vibrant and glowing. Christina wanted to turn and run.

You can do this. She forced herself to walk to the reception desk and check in.

She sat as far away from the pregnant ladies as she could. One woman looked exhausted as she fought to keep her two children quiet. Another snuggled up to a man, their heads bent close as they whispered and traced circles on her belly.

Christina's heart ached. She wanted that for herself and Gary so badly. But she doubted he'd attend doctor appointments with her, even if she did get pregnant. He hadn't bothered to come today.

Christina's phone buzzed again. Her finger hovered over the "view" icon as she debated whether to read the text. The number was up to five now.

She put her phone in her purse without reading any of them.

One by one, the pregnant women were called back. As each woman left the waiting room, Christina relaxed and breathed easier. Finally it was her turn.

"Dr. Blakely wants to talk to you before the exam," the nurse told Christina, pausing outside a doorway and motioning her inside. Christina was surprised to see it was an office, with a large desk and two comfortable looking chairs in front of it. "She should be with you in a few minutes."

Christina clutched her purse strap tighter and sat down on the edge of one of the chairs. Why did Gary have to flake? Her stomach knotted with anxiety, and she wished he was there holding her hand.

She expected to wait another twenty minutes in the office, but after only five, Dr. Blakely entered. "Christina," she said with a smile, extending her hand. Christina shook it, and the doctor sat down, flipping open Christina's chart. "It's been a while. You've neglected your yearly exam."

"I've been busy," Christina said, but the excuse felt thin even to her.

"Well, I'm glad you're here now. The nurse made a notation that you're worried about infertility. Can you tell me about that?"

Christina swallowed and gave Dr. Blakely the basic rundown of her concerns. She was in the middle of answering a question about her cycle lengths when there was a knock on the door. They both looked up as a nurse stepped into the room.

"I'm sorry to interrupt, but Mr. Vincent's here," the nurse said.

Christina's mouth dropped open as the nurse left and Gary entered the room. His tie hung loosely around his neck, his suit jacket unbuttoned. Hands were buried deep in his pockets, and his face was cautiously blank. She knew he'd rather be anywhere else in the world at that moment. But he'd chosen to be here with her.

Christina's heart softened, and she forced a scowl to combat the gooey feelings of warmth. Guilt had most likely brought him here. Or maybe he didn't want to fight.

Maybe he wanted to support her, and had overcome his anxiety to do so.

Gary sank into the chair next to hers, taking her hand. She resisted pulling away, not wanting to make a scene in front of Dr. Blakely.

"Sorry I'm late," Gary said. "Please continue, Doctor."

Dr. Blakely smiled and returned to questioning Christina about her periods. Christina felt even more uncomfortable answering with Gary around, especially after their fight. She was grateful he was there. Grateful for the support. Grateful he cared.

But he should've come with her in the first place.

After another ten minutes, Dr. Blakely set down her pen. "You have classic symptoms of endometriosis."

Gary's eyebrows furrowed in confusion, as did Christina's. She had heard of endometriosis, but never thought she might have it.

"What is endometriosis?" Gary stumbled over the unfamiliar word.

Dr. Blakely grabbed a flip chart, pointing to different body parts as she spoke. "Endometriosis is when some of the uterine lining attaches itself outside the uterus. Every month the lining builds up, but when the period begins, it doesn't slough off like it should because it's outside the uterus and has nowhere to go. Instead it forms scar tissue. A lot of times this is on the fallopian tubes, which can interfere with fertility." She set the chart down. "We'll do some blood work today because it's routine, but that won't tell us if you have endometriosis or not. I'll do a physical exam as well, but we rarely find evidence that way."

"How do you find it?" Gary asked. "An ultrasound?"

"It doesn't show up there. The only way to know for sure is surgery. But let's not start worrying just yet." Dr. Blakely stood. "Let me take you to an exam room, and I'll have a nurse draw your blood."

After Christina had her blood work done, she undressed from the waist down and waited on an exam table with a papery sheet covering her.

"Christina," Gary began.

"Now is not the time," Christina said. "Why are you even here?"

"I came to be with you."

She opened her mouth to respond, but Dr. Blakely entered the room.

The exam only took a few minutes, but was surprisingly painful.

"Does that hurt?" Dr. Blakely asked in concern as she did a pap smear.

"A little," Christina admitted. *A lot.*

"You can sit up now," Dr. Blakely said. "Get dressed, and I'll meet you in my office so we can talk."

"That doesn't sound good," Gary said as she shut the door.

Christina pulled her skirt on. "Let's get back to the office so we can find out."

They only had to wait a minute or two for Dr. Blakely. "Well," she said, sitting down at her desk. "I'm ninety-five percent sure you have endometriosis."

The pronouncement took Christina's breath away. She hadn't expected to know anything definitive today. "I thought you said you can't tell through an exam."

"We usually can't, and I'm still not one hundred percent certain. Typically endometriosis isn't found on the cervix, but I think there is some on yours."

It felt like a death sentence. Would their dreams of having a family—*Christina's* dreams—be over before they'd even really begun? Would fertility treatments even work?

Maybe Gary would get his way by default.

"Since you can feel it, does that mean it's really severe?" Christina asked. Gary's icy cold fingers found hers. His face was drawn, the color drained away.

"Not necessarily," Dr. Blakely said. "Endometriosis is an odd disease. How painful a woman's periods are, for example, is not an indication of how severe the problem is. Nor is the placement of the endometriosis."

"How do you fix it?" Christina asked.

"There's no cure. Birth control can help lessen the problem, but that's not a long-term solution if you're trying to get pregnant. Sometimes I'll prescribe birth control for a few months to give the scar tissue a chance to heal, and that helps. Surgery often helps as well because I can usually clean out some of the scar tissue."

"But I was on birth control for four years," Christina said. "And you still think I might have it."

Dr. Blakely shrugged. "Like I said, it doesn't ever go away."

"So where do we go from here?" Gary asked.

"It depends on what your goal is. If you want to manage the symptoms, going back on birth control will probably help. But if your goal is to have a family, I recommend we do a semen analysis to rule out male factor infertility and get an HSG test for Christina."

It had been like pulling teeth to get Gary to agree to the appointment with the gynecologist. How on earth would Christina convince him to do a semen analysis? To let her do the HSG test? That was clearly for fertility, not her health.

"What's an HSG?" Gary asked quietly. Christina whipped around to look at him. His face was drawn, his eyes resolute.

Oh my gosh. He wanted to do the testing.

"It stands for hysterosalpingogram," Dr. Blakely said. "We shoot dye through a catheter into the uterus and watch on an x-ray machine to see if the dye spills out the fallopian tubes."

153

"And what does that tell us?" Christina asked.

"If your tubes are blocked. If they aren't, I doubt endometriosis is why you aren't getting pregnant, and maybe we just need to help you ovulate with Clomid. If they are blocked, obviously that's a problem with your reproductive health, and we'd go from there. But let's wait until we get the results of the test before worrying any more than necessary."

Back at the front desk, Gary stood silently beside Christina as she scheduled the HSG test and a follow-up appointment to discuss the results. As they walked outside, he took her hand. She pulled away, but he grabbed her hand again and held on.

"Let's go to dinner," he said. "Your pick."

"I thought you had paperwork," she said, making her tone snippy.

"It can wait."

"I'm not really hungry."

"We need to talk."

She spitefully suggested a Mexican restaurant she loved and Gary didn't, and he agreed to meet her there. It wasn't until they were seated at the table and had ordered that Gary spoke.

"I shouldn't have tried to back out of the appointment today. I'm sorry."

Tears burned behind her eyes, but she refused to give them release. "Now my worst fears have been realized. Congratulations, I'm infertile. We probably won't get a baby."

"Don't say that. I know I'm ready to be a dad, but that doesn't mean I won't ever be ready. I'm sorry for not being there for you."

The tears fell, and she let them. "You really hurt my feelings. I needed you at that appointment, and you made up some excuse so you wouldn't have to show."

"It wasn't an excuse. I do have a stack of paperwork I need to get through tonight."

"You put it off for dinner."

He shifted in his seat. "Yes."

Christina leaned back against the booth, arms folded tight across her chest. "Once again, work comes first."

"I recognized my mistake and fixed it. I'm apologizing. Doesn't that count for something?"

He was trying. She should meet him halfway. Christina released a breath. "Maybe. This is all so shocking. I don't know how to react. How to feel."

"Me either. They say ignorance is bliss."

"Oh, so you don't want to find out for sure. Then why let me schedule the HSG?"

"I do want children. And I want them with you. We can figure out the problem so we're prepared to fix it when the time comes. We're in this together. I can't promise I'll be a perfect support, but I can promise to work on it. Let's do the testing." His eyes were sincere, his voice pleading.

He was facing his fears, putting them aside for Christina and their marriage. It was time she did the same. If they were going to make this work, she had to start trusting him. "You had better mean that, Garrison. Because I can't handle this alone."

"You shouldn't have to. You won't have to. I know I have a lot of concerns over being a dad. But I'm trying to get past them. Help me be ready, Christina."

She impulsively leaned across the table and kissed him. "Okay. I'm taking a chance here, Gar. Don't you dare let me down. We're finally making progress, and I won't ruin it if you won't."

Gary half-laughed, half-sobbed. "Deal."

CHAPTER SEVENTEEN
KYRA

David and Kyra continued to pray about and discuss doing another IUI, and it felt right. When Kyra's period started four weeks after her miscarriage, she called the fertility clinic and picked up another prescription for Clomid.

Taking it felt like being pregnant, only without the baby. Last time, the side effects had caused a twinge of sadness. This time, so soon after her miscarriage, the physical reminders were agony.

The nausea showed up first, feeling exactly like first-trimester morning sickness. The hot flashes came next, and Kyra wondered if her body was trying to ovulate, or if it was being thrust into early menopause.

Her hormones were every bit as erratic as during pregnancy. Normal Kyra would never have come home from grocery shopping to find dinner dishes still in the sink and lost it. Normal Kyra wouldn't have yelled at her husband for five minutes, then left the house in an angry fit, only to return two hours later bawling.

Clomid Kyra did all those things. She had never felt so out of control in her life.

On day five, she took the final pill with relief. *No more!* she thought. *I'll feel better tomorrow.*

But it took nearly a week for the symptoms to disappear. That was new. The first time it had been almost immediate. Kyra didn't know if her hormones were still crazy from the miscarriage, or if the side effects of Clomid would increase each month she took it. The morning of her mid-cycle ultrasound, she prayed she'd never have to take it again.

Sophie sat in a chair and played quietly with her doll while Kyra perched on the exam table. They waited nearly fifteen minutes for Dr. Mendoza while Kyra bit her nails to stubs.

Dr. Mendoza finally walked into the room, and Kyra dropped her hands to the crinkly paper of the exam table.

"Hi!" Sophie said.

"Well, look at you. Did you get to come with your mommy again?" Dr. Mendoza asked.

Sophie nodded. "My baby brother went to live with God."

"I know. I'm sorry."

"Malachi doesn't have a puppy."

"Who's Malachi?" Dr. Mendoza asked.

"Sophie's friend," Kyra said. "He lives next door."

"Good to know." Dr. Mendoza sat on the stool and fiddled with the ultrasound machine. "I'm going to look in your mommy's tummy now."

Sophie nodded. "If I'm good, I get to play at the park."

"Wow, you've got a really nice mommy. Let's see how you're doing, Kyra."

Dr. Mendoza stared at the ultrasound screen. Kyra looked as well, her heart in her throat. She should be hearing her baby's heartbeat, not looking for a follicle. All she needed was one egg on her ovary, ready to drop. *Please let there be a follicle, please let there be a follicle, please let there be a—*

"You've got a beautiful follicle on your left ovary."

Kyra let out a *whoosh* of air, and her knees trembled with relief. Tears pricked at her eyes. *Thank you,* she prayed. Even though she'd responded well to Clomid last time, she'd still worried.

Dr. Mendoza moved to the right ovary and pushed some more buttons on the screen. "And you have two follicles on your right ovary ready as well."

Now Kyra wanted to cry with joy.

Dr. Mendoza removed the ultrasound probe, and Kyra sat up. "Three follicles set to release. That's fantastic. We only got two last time, didn't we? You respond well to Clomid."

"I'm three," Sophie piped up. Dr. Mendoza chuckled.

"That's great news," Kyra said, feeling more confident about spending the money on this IUI. If she'd gotten pregnant last time with two follicles, no way it wouldn't work with three.

A nurse waited for Kyra outside the room. "Give yourself the HCG trigger shot at nine p.m. tonight." She handed Kyra a brown paper sack. "Here's the container for your husband's sample. We need it at the office within thirty minutes after collection." She pulled out a pen, writing on a paper Kyra knew contained a schedule. "Make sure he's abstained from ejaculation for no more than seventy-two hours, but no less than twenty-four." It was all information Kyra had heard before, but the nurse was probably required to repeat it. "Today's Monday. We'll have your husband drop off his sample at eight in the morning on Wednesday, and we'll do the IUI at nine. Does that work for you?"

Butterflies swarmed in Kyra's stomach. She nodded without even consulting her calendar. She doubted her follicles were willing to wait.

"Mommy," Sophie whispered. Kyra squeezed Sophie's hand to let her know to be quiet for a minute longer.

"You'll start progesterone suppositories on Thursday before bed." The nurse headed over to the check-out counter. "We need to schedule an IUI for nine a.m. on Wednesday," she told the receptionist. "Do you need anything else, Kyra?"

"No, I think that will do." Three follicles!

"Great. We'll see you on Wednesday."

"Do we get to go to the park now, Mommy?" Sophie asked as they left the clinic, schedule in hand.

"Yes. You were very good at the doctor's. Thank you." It was an unseasonably warm day for March, the kind that meant spring was on the horizon and made anything seemed possible. Kyra felt more alive than she had in a month.

She wanted to call and tell David about the appointment, but knew he wouldn't be able to answer his phone. She contented herself with playing at the park with Sophie until it was time to pick him up from work. When David walked out of the building, a huge grin on his face, Kyra's heart started pounding.

"Did they hire someone?" she asked as she got out of the car to let him drive.

David leaned down, giving her an exuberant kiss. "They hired me."

"Oh my gosh!" Kyra hugged him. "Are you serious?"

"What?" Sophie asked from the back seat.

David smiled so wide Kyra feared it would split his face. "Good news, baby girl. I got a new job."

Sophie frowned. "Samantha had to go to Burginia cuz her dad got a job."

Kyra shook her head as David pulled out of the parking lot. "Daddy got a promotion. That means he still works at the same place, but he'll get paid more money now."

Sophie's concern disappeared, and she smiled. "I like today."

Kyra squeezed Sophie's leg. "Me too, Soph. I think this calls for a party."

"McDonald's!" Sophie said.

Kyra's breath hitched. Last time they'd gone to McDonald's was after the ultrasound. "Let's go to Chick-Fil-A instead." It was a more expensive fast food restaurant, but they could splurge with the promotion.

As they drove, David told Kyra all about his new job. The money wasn't fantastic, but much better than what they currently made. He'd start training for the new position immediately. While Sophie played on the slide, Kyra told David about her doctor's appointment. Ice cream and a dollar movie completed the evening. They got Sophie to bed just in time for the HCG trigger shot.

"I can't believe I got the job," David said as he watched Kyra draw the saline out of one bottle and dispense it into the bottle of powder. She swirled the contents around until the powder dissolved in the liquid.

"I'm so proud of you. They would've been idiots not to promote you." Kyra drew back the plunger, drawing all the medicine into the syringe. Then she withdrew the needle from the bottle and switched it out for the much smaller, much less intimidating needle actually used for the shot.

"This will help us out with money a lot," David said. "We can even do a few more IUIs if we budget well."

Kyra handed David the needle, then pulled up her shirt. With her eyes she drew the imaginary smiley face under her belly button, just as the nurse had directed. Kyra picked out an area without stretch marks and cleaned if off with an alcohol wipe. "We're not going to need more than one IUI. We're going to bring home a baby in nine months." She pointed to her stomach. "Do it right there. Not too fast, but not too slow either, okay?" Last time he had gone painfully slow, but she wouldn't hurt his feelings by telling him. "Try to not hit a stretch mark. The nurse said that would hurt like heck."

David nodded, swallowing hard. He took a deep breath, then plunged the needle into her stomach. Kyra felt the sting but didn't wince. He pushed the plunger down with agonizing slowness, just like last time. Her hands trembled where they held her shirt. She bit her lip, holding her breath. If she showed any sign of pain, David would feel awful.

He withdrew the needle and let out a big sigh of relief. Kyra dropped her shirt, resisting the urge to rub the injection site. "Thanks, sweetie. I don't think I could do that myself."

"Did I hurt you?"

"I didn't feel a thing," Kyra lied. She wrapped her arms around him. "I'm so proud of you. Things are turning around for us. I can feel it."

He pulled her close and nuzzled her ear. "Does that mean we can continue celebrating?"

Kyra kissed him in reply.

———•••———

Kyra woke up Wednesday feeling excited and anxious.

"What do you think?" she asked David as she brushed her hair. "I'm so nervous."

He pulled the toothbrush out of his mouth. "I think we're going to make a baby today."

"Me too. Good things are happening. It's our time. I can feel it." The Lord wouldn't ask them to suffer another loss, would He?

Kyra finished getting ready, then got Sophie up. While David took his sample to the clinic, Kyra fed Sophie breakfast.

"Why can't I come today, Mommy?" Sophie asked as she munched on cereal.

Kyra wasn't sure how to answer. They felt awkward taking Sophie to this particular appointment. "It might take a while, and we thought you'd have more fun at Mrs. Everhart's playing with Malachi."

At the doctor's office, Kyra and David waited for what felt like forever before being ushered into an exam room. Kyra waited impatiently on the exam table while David played a game on his phone. When Dr. Mendoza walked in, he stashed his phone in a pocket.

"Today's the day," Dr. Mendoza said. "How do you feel?"

"Nervous," Kyra admitted.

"Don't be. I really believe last time was an unfortunate fluke and not an indication of other problems. Your chances of success this cycle are excellent." Dr. Mendoza held an oversized plastic syringe out to them. "I need both of you to verify this is David's sample."

They both read the sticker and agreed it was, and Kyra lay on the table.

"You had an excellent sperm count again," Dr. Mendoza said conversationally as she inserted the clamps. Kyra winced, feeling like a wuss. She fought back the nerves that made her want to shiver, trying to hold perfectly still.

"How excellent?" David asked while Kyra blushed.

"Eighty-seven million," Dr. Mendoza said.

David straightened in his chair and grinned as though pleased with himself. "What's a normal sperm count?" Apparently he felt more comfortable the second time around, even if Kyra didn't.

"Anything over five million," Dr. Mendoza said. "You're even up two million from last time. I'm going to insert the catheter now." Kyra winced again, but a second later Dr. Mendoza said, "All done."

Five minutes. That's how long the procedure took. Five minutes and one thousand dollars.

Dr. Mendoza pushed a button, and the table reclined so Kyra's head lay lower than her hips. "Lie here for thirty minutes, and then you can go. I'll have a nurse knock on the door when you can get up. As far as the rest of the day, normal activity level should be fine. There's no need to stay down, although it can't hurt."

Last time Kyra had idiotically asked if the sperm would fall out when she stood. Dr. Mendoza had assured her the cervix would close and hold it all in.

"We'll schedule a blood test for two weeks from now." Dr. Mendoza patted Kyra's leg in what she probably thought a comforting manner, but it made Kyra feel more awkward and vulnerable. Did she shave this morning? Kyra couldn't even remember. What if Dr. Mendoza was repulsed by Kyra's hairy legs? Sure, she had a paper sheet covering her, but what if the hair poked through?

"Thanks, Doctor," David said as she left the room. He gave Kyra all his attention. "How do you feel? Did it hurt this time?"

"Not too bad. I'm fine."

He reached out and grasped her hand. "It's going to work, Kyra. Have faith."

With three follicles ready, it had to work. Kyra thought about what it had felt like to be pregnant with Sophie. The debilitating morning sickness of the first trimester. The first flutters. A full-term baby constantly nudging at her insides, reminding Kyra she was there.

They'd been so close last time. *Please don't let anything go wrong,* Kyra prayed. *Please let it work and let us bring home a healthy, strong baby.*

"Do you think Sophie will be upset if it's a girl?" Kyra asked. "She seems pretty set on a brother."

"I think she'll love the baby no matter what. She'll be a great sister, too. Probably even share her toys."

Kyra laughed at that.

Soon a nurse knocked on the door and told Kyra she could leave. On the drive home Kyra felt tired, and her stomach began to cramp. She knew from last time that was normal.

"Are you okay?" David asked.

"Yes, but I'm going to lie down when we get home. I need to rest."

"Of course. If your body's telling you to take it easy, that's what you'll do. We spent a lot of money on this baby, and I want to make sure it works."

"It's not a baby yet."

"No, but it will be. I can feel it."

Kyra hoped he was right.

CHAPTER EIGHTEEN
MEGAN

Megan didn't go into work the day of her mid-cycle ultrasound. Nerves made it impossible to keep up her happy face, and she wasn't in the mood for explanations to co-workers. She made some calls from home and wrote a couple of proposals, but eventually gave up on work and played the piano.

She arrived at the doctor's office a full twenty minutes early just to have a different environment to wait in. After a maddening forty-minute wait, they called her name. She then waited another fifteen minutes in an exam room, a too-small paper sheet her only covering. By the time Dr. Mendoza arrived, Megan was ready to hunt down a nurse and demand to be seen immediately.

"I'm sorry about the wait," Dr. Mendoza said as she sat down on her swivel stool. "We're running behind today. Let's take a look at those follicles."

Megan held her breath and watched the ultrasound screen as various body parts she didn't recognize panned across the monitor. After almost thirty seconds of silence, she let her breath out in a *whoosh*.

"Something's wrong," Megan said with certainty. "And you don't know how to tell me."

Dr. Mendoza withdrew the ultrasound wand. "You're right. Your follicles aren't even close to mature."

Megan had expected the worst, but it still felt like a tsunami. "Zero follicles? As in, zero?"

"I'm sorry. I'll proscribe progesterone so you'll for sure have a period this month, and we'll try injectables next month."

Injectables meant Follistim. More powerful medication meant more powerful side effects. And it meant their situation was getting more and more hopeless. Hysteria bubbled in Megan's throat, and she struggled to swallow it back.

"And what if I don't ovulate on the shots either? I ovulated on Clomid last time. Clearly things are getting worse." Despite her grapefruit and running and Metformin and everything else, PCOS was winning.

"I'm going to do everything in my power to help you, Megan. We'll pull out the big guns now."

And what was Clomid? Megan wanted to ask. Because it had felt like being run over by a truck.

She hung her head and let the tears fall. She didn't care that Dr. Mendoza looked on with sympathetic eyes. She didn't care that her bottom half was completely naked save a paper sheet that barely covered her. Nothing mattered. They'd never have a baby at this rate.

"Don't give up," Dr. Mendoza said. "Next month we'll make sure you ovulate."

Megan barely held it together as she checked out at the front desk, paying the two hundred dollars the two-minute ultrasound had cost. If there had been even one mature follicle, Megan wouldn't have cared. But there was no chance of seeing those two pink lines on the pregnancy test this month.

Somehow she drove home, despite the tears compromising her vision. She knew she should call Trent, but couldn't bring herself to pick up the phone.

Megan plopped down in front of the TV and flipped mindlessly through the channels while she cried. Trent called her once, but she hit "ignore" and kept flipping channels. She couldn't face him right now.

When Trent arrived home, Megan knew he was worried. She heard it in the cautious placement of his feet as he approached, in the tentative way he said, "Megan?"

"The IUI is canceled," she choked out.

His face blanched with pain. "What happened?"

"There weren't any follicles maturing. Dr. Mendoza said next month we'll try injectables."

His Adam's apple bobbed, and his eyes blinked rapidly. Megan knew he was fighting not to fall apart for her sake. He sat down, his arms on his knees, head down. "I'm sorry." There was nothing else to say.

Megan turned off the TV. "Why is this happening to us?" She heard the agony in her voice. "We're good people. We try to do what's right. We are ready to be parents. Why do things keep getting in our way?"

A single tear rolled down Trent's cheek. "I don't know. It feels like us against the world."

"Yeah." Megan leaned against his back, resting her head on his shoulder and wrapping her arms tightly around his waist. "I tried to stay positive this month. But we don't even have a chance."

"We'll try again next month. Injectables will work."

"No, they won't."

"Don't talk like that."

"How long until we decide enough is enough? I don't know how much longer I can take this. How much longer I can put my body through this. It's so . . ." Her voice broke. "Hard. I'm not strong enough to handle the constant disappointment."

Trent leaned his head against hers. "I'm not sure I am, either. But I keep getting the strongest impression we need to keep going. We're doing the right thing, Megan."

"I don't know if I believe that anymore. Maybe we're not meant to have kids."

"Are you saying you want to stop?" He stroked her cheek as he asked, and she knew he was genuinely interested in her answer. If she said yes, Trent would consider it.

Could she give up completely? Could they stop trying, just like that?

"I'm a freakin' nightmare on Clomid," Megan said. "How am I going to be on the FSH injections? I can't handle it. You can't handle it."

"I promise you that I can."

"I want a resolution, one way or the other. I can't keep waiting and wondering."

"I know." Trent kissed her forehead. "We need the Lord's help right now. Let's say a prayer."

Megan's first reaction was to say no. God had allowed this to happen to them, and she wasn't sure if she wanted His help. But she knew that meant she needed it the most.

The tears fell more earnestly, and she nodded. "Okay."

They closed the blinds and sank to their knees in the middle of the floor. Trent took her hands in his and pleaded with God to allow them to be parents. Then he grew silent. For nearly two minutes he didn't speak as warmth and power filled the room. It trickled through his hands, up her arms, and down her spine, like warm water cascading over her entire being.

"I know You want us to be parents," Trent said, his voice choked. "I know we're meant to have children. But we can't do it alone. We turn it over to Thee."

Megan started sobbing. Fire coursed through her veins, warming up all the parts of her soul that had grown cold as they struggled with infertility. A quiet promise burrowed into her heart.

They would have children. The Lord would allow them to be parents—she knew it.

Trent was crying too. Megan heard it in his voice. She raised a hand to her cheek to wipe away the tears, but more replaced them almost instantly. Trent closed the prayer and let go of her hands, taking a great weight with them.

Megan threw her arms around him in a hug. "We're going to be parents," she whispered, and this time she wasn't just hoping the words were true. She knew they were. She didn't know how it would happen or when. But one day they would realize their dream. "Did you feel it? The Lord knows of our struggles and desires, and He's going to help us."

"I know. I've never felt something so strongly in my life." He laughed too, burying his head in her neck. "I love you so much, Megan. There is no one I would rather go through this with."

CHAPTER NINETEEN
MEGAN

Megan was grateful for the peace Trent's powerful prayer brought since she had a piano lesson with Sienna the next day. "Hey," Megan said gently when Sienna walked inside. "How are you?"

"Dane and I met with our parents last night. They think we should let someone adopt the baby. I don't know what to do. I can't take a baby to Juilliard if I'm accepted. But I don't want to give it away." Her eyes filled with tears. "Does that make me a bad person?"

Yes. That was Megan's initial response. But she knew it wasn't the right one. Megan thought back to when she was seventeen—young, carefree, and with her own dreams of being a concert pianist. "It means you're seventeen. You have your whole life ahead of you, and a baby is a huge responsibility."

"We're going to meet with a crisis center our pastor recommended tomorrow. Just me and my mom. I guess they provide free counseling or something. Dane doesn't want anything to do with the baby, and he doesn't care what I decide.

His parents are furious with him. So am I." She laughed hollowly. "I was so stupid."

"We all make mistakes."

"Why don't you have kids yet, Megan?"

Megan thought of the prayer and clung to the peace she'd felt. "It hasn't been for lack of trying. Trent and I haven't been able to get pregnant."

Sienna let out a sob, covering her face with her hands.

Megan patted her back, alarmed. "Hey. What's wrong?"

"You must hate me. You can't have kids, and here I am, the unwed teenage mother."

Megan rubbed circles on Sienna's back. "I could never hate you."

"But doesn't it suck that I'm pregnant and you're not?"

Megan half-laughed, half-sobbed. "Yeah. It really does." Megan gave Sienna a quick hug. "Let's work on something new today. I thought we could try more contemporary pieces for a while and take a break from classical."

Sienna's eyes lit up. "Really?"

"Sure. You need to practice arranging music. What song should we do?"

The rest of the hour passed quickly. By the time Sienna left, she looked happier, and Megan certainly felt happier.

Trent's truck pull into the driveway just after Annabelle and Sienna drove away.

Megan met Trent at the mud room door with a kiss. "How was work?"

"Good. Was that Sienna?"

Megan nodded, and Trent followed her into the kitchen. "Sorry I haven't started dinner yet. I'll put the casserole in the oven."

Trent leaned against the counter as Megan preheated the oven and set the foil-covered casserole inside. "You look happy."

The statement surprised her. "I am happy. Sienna's a dream student. She's talented and eager to learn. It's a pleasure to be her teacher." Megan frowned. "I feel awful about the situation she's in with the baby."

Trent grabbed Megan around the waist and pulled her close. He nuzzled her neck, and she laughed, trying to push him away. "What are you doing?"

"I'm trying to be romantic, but you're making it difficult."

"Oh, well in that case." Megan kissed him.

A few pleasant minutes later Trent pulled away. He leaned his forehead against hers, running his fingers through her hair. "I love seeing you happy. Music is good for you."

"I wish I could teach lessons full-time." While Trent's income sufficiently supported them, it wasn't nearly enough for fertility treatments. Megan worked to support the thousands of dollars they paid a year to the RE's office.

"Then why don't you? Quit being a real estate agent and be a piano teacher."

Megan groaned, pushing Trent away. She grabbed a loaf of bread and a knife off the counter and began slicing. "We've had this discussion before. You know why."

"We don't know you wouldn't make as much money as a piano teacher."

"Yes, we do. Maybe after we have a baby—"

"It's always after we have a baby." Trent ran a hand through his hair. "I feel like we've put our entire lives on hold for a baby, and I'm sick of it. I want us to enjoy life. You can't end up like last time."

Megan stopped cutting the bread. "It's not going to be like last time."

"It certainly has been the last few weeks."

"I'm sorry. I lost myself for a while. But the prayer last night helped."

He wrapped his arms around her, and she leaned into him, breathing deeply. She caught a hint of car oil and brake fluid, and she loved it.

"You'd better stay with me this time," he said. "I need you."

"We'll get through this together. If I start falling again, you'll catch me." Megan dropped the knife and turned in his arms. "I trust you."

Trent leaned down and kissed her. It was urgent and desperate, and she kissed him back. She wanted to believe what she had said. But it was hard to stay grounded when her entire life was being overrun by something she couldn't control.

Megan hung up the phone, feeling deflated. Billing had called, apologizing for the mistake and informing her she owed an extra ninety dollars for the ultrasound she had on Monday. Talk about salt in the wound. She'd tried to hold onto the peace from the prayer, but the disappointment of a canceled IUI wasn't easy to brush off, especially when it was constantly shoved in her face.

Megan put her credit card back in her wallet and tried to forget the conversation. She shrugged into a jacket and went outside. As Christina and Megan drove to Kyra's home, this time to sort winter coats, Megan tried to act cheerful, but it was hard.

Kyra's house was one of the smallest in the neighborhood, but had a nicely kept front yard. Megan knocked on the door and plastered on a smile when she heard footsteps approaching.

"Hi, Kyra," Megan said, then tried not to wince. Too much. Time to dial back the cheer.

"Hi," Kyra said, giving her an odd look. "Come in." She looked skinny and cute as usual, in her tunic top, burnt yellow leggings, and ballet flats.

"How have you been?" Christina asked as they stepped inside.

"Good." Kyra's smile seemed tight. She sat down on a worn chair, a pile of coats in front of her. The house was sparsely decorated with carefully chosen statement pieces that Megan loved. "My house is overflowing with winter gear. We've had a good response to the drive this week."

"That's great," Christina said. "Let's sort them into gently used and more wore, and then we can sort them into coats, hats, and gloves. Thanks so much again for helping with this, ladies."

"No problem," Kyra said. "Sophie will be at that school in two years. I'm happy to help."

"And I like being involved in the community," Megan said. "So it's a win-win-win for all of us."

As they sorted winter gear, the conversation flowed easily from Sophie to David's promotion to how Christina utilized a slow cooker to simplify her life. Megan smiled a lot and commented occasionally. But mostly she brooded inside.

Did Kyra realize how lucky she was? She probably wished she had nicer furniture and a bigger house. But Megan would switch places with her in an instant. Yes, Kyra had had a miscarriage. But she'd probably announce a new pregnancy soon.

Megan had to keep going so she could have what Kyra had. She wouldn't let a few needles keep her from having a family.

"That's the last coat," Christina said.

Megan blinked. Were they finished already? Megan was really starting to lose it.

The three women loaded the boxes into Christina's car, then said their goodbyes. As soon as the car doors were shut, Christina asked, "Is everything okay? You seemed distracted."

Megan tried to hold her smile in place. "I'm fine. Why do you ask?"

"I can tell something is wrong. Come on, I'll take you out for ice cream. Just don't tell Gary it's not organic, or gluten and dairy free. I think ice cream and a listening ear can solve most of the world's problems. Or at least help us gain some perspective."

Megan didn't want to turn down Christina's overture of friendship, but she didn't want to talk about this either. She had learned a long time ago there was a fine line between being open about infertility and discussing it with fertile people. Openness was good. Discussions usually left Megan frustrated, mad, or crying. Sometimes all three. "You're probably busy. Really, I'm fine."

"I'm not busy if you aren't busy."

Megan finally nodded. "Okay. Thanks."

"Tell me what's going on," Christina said as they drove toward the shopping district of Riverton. "Is it Sienna?"

"No. I got some disappointing news this week, that's all."

"But it's about infertility, isn't it?" Christina blushed. "I'm sorry, I don't mean to pry. It's none of my business."

Megan stared at her, open-mouthed. Christina pulled into the parking lot of an ice cream parlor and got out. Megan followed, trailing Christina inside. "How did you know?"

Christina shrugged. "I imagine it weighs on your mind. How could it not?" She stepped up to the counter. "I'll have cheesecake ice cream with raspberries, and give this lady whatever she wants."

"Cake batter with brownies," Megan stuttered. Christina paid, and Megan picked up her bowl and followed Christina to a table. "People rarely talk to me about infertility. They talk at me a lot, but not to me."

Christina slid into a chair and gave Megan a sympathetic I-know-what-you're-going-through kind of smile. Did she know what Megan went through on a daily basis? Had Christina been putting up a front?

"You sound like you really understand," Megan said suspiciously.

"I don't," Christina said after a few bites of ice cream. "No one does, because no one is going through exactly what you are. But I know sometimes having someone listen is enough."

"They canceled an IUI," Megan said. She felt the tears coming, and for once she didn't fight them. "An artificial insemination. The Clomid didn't work. I'm not going to ovulate, and now we have to wait another month. And maybe it still won't work."

"That's awful."

"We've tried almost everything. IUIs, the homeopathic route. I've done acupuncture, acupressure, zone therapy, reflexology. Pretty much the only thing we haven't done is in vitro. If I knew when we'd get a baby, I wouldn't care. But I don't. Right now we're throwing money down a very large drain. And I hate it."

"I can't even imagine."

"It bugs me that I pay all this money with no guarantees. Why is it that at a fertility clinic, if I don't get what I paid for, I can't complain? If I ordered a laptop off of Amazon and all I got was a USB drive, I'd sure as heck demand a refund. But at fertility clinics you can't do that."

Christina choked on her ice cream, then started laughing. "I never thought of it that way, but you're totally right."

"Yeah," Megan said suspiciously. "It's hard because these stupid fertility drugs make me act like a crazy person."

"I wouldn't know about that. And I hope to never know. But it's so unfair that everyone else seems to get pregnant at the drop of a hat and you keep struggling."

"I couldn't agree more." Megan took a big bite of her ice cream. "I mean look at Kyra. She has this beautiful daughter, and I bet she got pregnant on the first try."

Christina shrugged. "Maybe, maybe not. She might keep her struggles quiet."

Megan scrutinized Christina. "Are you keeping something quiet?"

She laughed, but it sounded off. "Don't be ridiculous. I've told you I'm focusing on my career. I'm just suggesting maybe Kyra's life isn't as it appears."

"Do you know something you aren't telling me?"

"No. But Kyra did have the miscarriage. And Sophie's almost four, so I've wondered." She took another bite of ice cream. "It's probably nothing. I don't want to start rumors, but Kyra doesn't seem like the kind of girl who would want her kids spaced far apart."

"I do feel awful about her miscarriage. But I haven't exactly kept it a secret that I'm infertile. If Kyra is struggling, she could talk to me about it." Megan hoped her implication was clear.

"Kyra is a private person. I don't know if she'd ever say anything to anybody."

Was Christina trying to tell Megan something? Or was Megan reading too much into the situation?

Christina scraped the bottom of her ice cream bowl. "That was delicious. I know I feel better now."

Megan smiled, taking her last bite as well. "Me too. Thanks for talking to me. It's nice to know I have friends."

"I know what you mean." Christina smiled shyly. "I haven't had a real friend in a long time."

CHAPTER
TWENTY
CHRISTINA

Christina clutched Gary's hand as they entered the sterile white waiting room of the hospital. His fingers squeezed hers, the gesture both unfamiliar and comforting. Nerves still ate at her stomach, but this felt so different from her visit to the gynecologist. Gary was here, and that made all the difference.

After checking in at registration, they headed to radiology. The click of Christina's heels echoed in the empty hallway, and her fingers ached from clutching the completed registration form.

The nurse at radiology took the form and told them to have a seat. The blue plastic cushions on the chairs squeaked embarrassingly when they sat down. The nondescript artwork hanging on the blindingly white walls managed to be both modern and cold at the same time. Christina clutched at the straps of her purse. Gary put an arm around her shoulder tentatively, as though not sure what to do. Not sure what to say.

"Christina Vincent."

Her stomach flipped as they walked toward the nurse holding a folder with Christina's pre-admittance paper stapled to the front.

"Right this way," the nurse said.

Gary's hand reached for Christina's, and she clung to it gratefully. An exam table, covered in sterile white paper, stood in the center of the room. A giant machine splayed out four feet above the table, and a monitor stood to one side.

"Undress and put this hospital gown on," the nurse said, handing it to Christina. "The radiologist will be here soon."

Though Christina had undressed in front of Gary a thousand times, this time felt awkward and uncomfortable. She turned her back to him and quickly slipped into the hospital gown, then sat down on the exam table. She spread the thin paper blanket over herself, tucking it under her legs for maximum coverage. They waited in silence, her hands clutched in her lap, heart racing and breath coming in spurts.

Eventually the door opened, and a man in scrubs walked in, hand extended. "I'm Paul. I'll be doing the HSG today." He washed his hands in the sink, then pulled on plastic gloves. He returned with a long, thin tube. "I'm going to insert this catheter and push dye through it. If you'll lie down, Christina." A nurse appeared, handing Gary an apron shield and explaining he needed to wear it so he wouldn't be exposed to the radiation.

Christina lay down. her whole body trembling uncontrollably.

"Try to relax," Paul said. "It'll make this less uncomfortable. Here comes the catheter."

Christina felt pressure and sharp pinpricks of pain, but no worse than the pap smear she'd had a week ago. Her hands clutched into fists over her stomach, eyes riveted to the screen.

"Now I'm going to push the dye through," Paul continued. Black appeared on the screen. It flowed upward and seemed to stop.

Christina yelped, her fists clenching tight. Excruciating pain. Gary leaned forward as though to help, but froze. He wasn't supposed to stand too close.

"Do you need me to stop?" Paul asked.

"No," Christina gasped. Her abdomen cramped and burned as though on fire. Black spots dotted her vision, and she wondered if she'd pass out.

And then the pain lessened. The cramping was still there, still intense, but bearable now. She could breathe again.

"All done," Paul said. "Are you okay?"

Christina smiled grimly, moving to a sitting position. Gary jumped forward to help. "I'm fine." What else could she say?

Gary ran a hand through his hair. "So how did things look?"

The cramping had subsided to normal period pain, but the pit in Christina's gut told her something was wrong.

"You'll have to talk to your doctor," Paul said. "As a radiology technician I'm not qualified to read the labs for you."

"But you can tell us what you saw," Gary pressed.

Paul took off his gloves, throwing them in a nearby trash can. "Yes. I wasn't able to push any dye through the right tube. And on the left side, it didn't spill out normally. I can't tell you more than that. Your doctor will contact you in a few days with the official results."

As they left the hospital, Christina said, "It's bad, Gary. Isn't it?"

He sighed and tightened his fingers around hers. "Let's not get upset yet. That guy said himself he's not a doctor. He doesn't know what he's talking about. How they can let some tech do this sort of thing," he muttered under his breath.

Christina prayed everything would be okay.

The next few days were hard. Christina called the doctor's office the day after the HSG, but Dr. Blakely hadn't read the results yet. Christina was assured the doctor would call soon.

Trista and Christina were finalizing the curriculum for the after-school program when she got the call.

"I need to take this," Christina told Trista. "I'll just be a minute."

Trista muttered under her breath as Christina stepped into the hallway, but Christina didn't care.

"This is Christina," she said into the phone.

"Hi, Christina. This is Dr. Blakely. I'm calling with the results of your HSG test. Is now a good time?"

Her stomach fluttered. "Yes."

"I'll cut right to the chase. The results were inconclusive. Your right tube appears blocked, but it's unclear from the HSG whether or not your left tube is functioning normally."

"What does that mean?" Frustration welled in the form of tears. Why couldn't the stupid results just tell her what was going on?

"It means in order for us to fully understand what's happening, we need to do a laparoscopy. If there is endometriosis present, I'll clean out what I can, and we'll go from there."

"Surgery?" Christina whispered the word, her world spinning out of control.

"It's a small incision and easy recovery. You shouldn't have to miss more than a few days of work. I'd like to do it as soon as possible."

"Okay." Her voice was small.

"I'll transfer you over to scheduling. I'm really sorry, Christina. I know this isn't what you wanted to hear. Do you have any more questions for me?"

Christina should be bombarding Dr. Blakely with questions. But instead she said, "No." She couldn't think of a single thing to ask.

Scheduling helped Christina get everything arranged. The surgery would be in three weeks. Christina hung up the phone, dazed. She needed to talk to Gary, but his number went to voice mail.

"The results were inconclusive," Christina told the answering machine. "I'm having surgery on May ninth to try and determine what's wrong. Call me when you get a minute." It wasn't the best way to break the news, but it was all she could come up with at the moment.

Gary's Lexus was already in the garage when Christina arrived home. She got out of her car and glanced at her cell. It was only five o'clock. He opened the mud room door, clearly waiting for her.

"What did the doctor say?" he asked.

Christina slowly unbuttoned her pea coat. "What are you doing home already?"

His eyebrow rose, as though surprised she'd asked. "I couldn't stay at work once I got your message. Are you okay?"

Christina stopped unbuttoning her coat in surprise, then leaned forward and kissed Gary. "Yes. It means a lot to me that you're here."

He shuffled his feet, looking down. "Well, I did bring a few hours of work home. I hope you don't mind."

"Of course not." Gary had come home early because she needed him. He could work all night if necessary and she wouldn't complain.

Over reheated spaghetti, they talked in more detail about Dr. Blakely's phone call. Then Gary went to his office, and Christina sat down to watch TV and grade spelling tests. It was no use, though. All she could think about was her upcoming surgery. What would happen? What would they find? Would she ever be able to have children? The questions spiraled in her brain until she thought she'd throw up. She switched to a math test—much easier to grade, since all she had to do was compare numbers to the answer key.

The doorbell rang, and Christina looked up from the test in surprise. She set down her red pen and walked to the front door, peering through the peep hole. Megan stood on the front steps, smiling.

"Hi, Megan. What a pleasant surprise."

Megan held out a plate of cupcakes. "I made these tonight, and there were way too many for me and Trent. Sorry, they're not organic or anything."

Christina took the cupcakes. "They smell delicious. Thank you."

Megan nodded, peering intently at Christina. "Is everything okay?"

"Of course." Christina wanted to tell Megan about her upcoming surgery. But it was too embarrassing. Megan would know Christina had lied about not wanting kids.

Megan snorted. "Come on, Christina. You were acting strange at the ice cream parlor, and you're acting stranger now. What's going on?"

Christina fidgeted with the plastic wrap covering the cupcakes. "Just stressed about the after-school program." *Oh, yeah. And I'm having surgery. And maybe I'll never have kids.*

Megan folded her arms, rocking back on her heels. "I'm just going to say it, because wondering is driving me nuts. I swear we were having a double conversation the other day. Are you infertile?"

Christina's mouth fell open. She closed it, looking down at the plate of cupcakes. She didn't know if she should be relieved Megan knew or humiliated. "What makes you ask that?"

Megan threw up her hands. "Were we even having the same conversation the other day? If I'm wrong, tell me, and I'll bug off. But I've been infertile my entire marriage. I know a sister in the Land of IF when I see one."

Christina opened her mouth, ready to deny Megan's accusation. But then she stopped. The suspicion would always be there now. And Megan might be able to answer Christina's questions. She lowered her eyes, wanting to shy away from the prying questions, but wanting answers more. Megan would probably even understand why Christina had told a white lie to cover up the truth. "I'm having surgery in three weeks. They think I have endometriosis."

"I knew it. Why didn't you tell me?"

"I was embarrassed," Christina admitted. "I made such a big deal over not wanting kids yet."

"Okay, we're having this conversation. Spill."

Christina led Megan inside. It all came out, a tidal wave of hidden information. Nothing she said seemed to shock or surprise Megan. Her face remained impassive through it all.

"I wish you'd told me earlier," Megan said when Christina finished explaining. "We could have helped each other."

"I'm not ready for everyone to know."

"But I'm not everyone."

Christina smiled. "True. Who knows? Maybe I'm freaking out over nothing. They might not find anything during surgery." Which could be even worse. At least if they knew what the problem was, they'd know how to fix it.

"I'm wishing you all the baby dust in the world," Megan said.

Christina wrinkled her brow. "Baby dust? What the heck is that?"

Megan laughed. "It's like fairy dust for the infertile. I see it on infertility message boards all the time. It's like saying 'I hope you get pregnant' or 'good luck.'"

"Well, I'll take baby dust and fairy dust and any other kind of dust that'll give me a baby."

"Keep thinking positively. Maybe you're right, and they'll find out nothing's wrong." But Megan's eyes said she didn't believe that.

Neither did Christina.

When Megan left two hours later, Christina felt infinitely better. Relieved. She wondered why on earth she hadn't told Megan over ice cream or when Megan told her about Sienna or a dozen other times. Megan had answered Christina's questions, shared her experiences, and given Christina a glimpse into what lay ahead.

Megan empathized. She understood.

Christina didn't feel ready for the future, but she definitely felt more prepared for it. At this point, that was all she could ask.

CHAPTER TWENTY-ONE
KYRA

The two-week wait was worse this time around. Kyra wasn't just worried about getting pregnant—she was worried about giving birth to a healthy baby. From the moment they got home from the IUI, she started obsessively googling everything from "IUI + Clomid" to "early pregnancy symptoms" to "fertility after a miscarriage." Kyra wavered between being absolutely certain the IUI had worked and being convinced it hadn't.

David called on his lunch break and informed Kyra he'd be pulling another late night at the office. She got Sophie down for the night, then treated herself to a bowl of ice cream and TV time. Kyra was starting to really enjoy herself when her cell phone rang—David's number.

"Hey," she said, holding the phone between her shoulder and ear and scraping the last of the ice cream out of the bowl.

"The car won't start," David said, his voice tight with stress.

Kyra set aside the bowl and gripped the phone. "What do you mean it won't start?"

"I turn the key in the ignition and nothing. Everyone on my team has already left for the night."

Kyra bit her lip. "What should we do?"

"Isn't there someone in the neighborhood we can call?"

Kyra sighed, knowing the answer. "Cassandra. She is going to regret the day we moved in next door."

Cassandra's phone rang and rang and rang, eventually going to voice mail. Kyra hung up without leaving a message. Who else could she call? They weren't especially close to anyone nearby.

Megan and Christina. Kyra walked into the kitchen and set her ice cream bowl on the counter. Magneted to the fridge was a blue greeting card with a white daisy. Kyra had meant to throw it away after consuming the cookies, but she'd kept it for some reason. Kyra opened the card.

Kyra, I am so sorry about the miscarriage. Please let me know if there's ever anything you need. I'm here to help. Call me anytime, day or night.

—Megan Burke

She'd scrawled a phone number under her name.

Kyra flicked the card back and forth in her hand, then punched the numbers into her cell phone before she could talk herself out of it.

Megan answered the phone almost immediately. "This is Megan." The voice was professional and cool.

"Hi," Kyra said, not sure how to begin. "This is Kyra Peterson."

Megan's voice changed to warm and friendly. "I'm so glad you called. What can I do for you?"

Kyra closed her eyes and breathed a sigh of relief. Megan sounded eager to help. "My husband's stranded at work. The car won't start, and it's the only vehicle we have. I called Cassandra, but she didn't answer."

"Do you need us to get him?" Megan asked without missing a beat.

Kyra smiled, relieved Megan had made this easy. "Yes. I hate to interrupt your evening, but I didn't know who else to call."

"Don't worry about it. I'm happy to help. You know, my husband's a mechanic. Why don't you stay home with Sophie— I'm betting she's already asleep—and we'll pick up David. Trent can look at his car and tow it home if necessary."

Kyra blinked. She hadn't known Trent was a mechanic. "Th-that would be great."

"What's the address?"

"It's not far from here." Kyra rattled off directions.

"We'll leave right now," Megan said.

"Thanks. You're really saving us."

Kyra called David and let him know the plan, then reorganized the pantry to distract herself while she waited. It was ten o'clock when he finally walked through the front door, shoulders slumped.

"Well?" Kyra asked.

"Trent couldn't tell in the dark, so we towed it to his shop. He'll look at it tomorrow."

Kyra chewed her nail. "What if it's not an easy fix?"

"We'll worry about it tomorrow. I'm going to play video games for a half hour before bed. I need to unwind."

The next morning, David biked the three miles to work. Sophie and Kyra were sitting in a fort made of blankets and chairs, eating pretend tomato soup, when he called.

"Did you hear from Trent?" Kyra asked.

"Yes." She heard the defeat in David's voice. "It's bad."

"How bad?" Kyra squeaked. Sophie happily slurped imaginary soup out of a toy colander, oblivious to Kyra's stress.

"The car's totaled. The water pump busted, and a head gasket broke and that means water has been leaking into the oil." David sighed. His hair was probably a rumpled mess. "Basically, the engine has to be rebuilt—more money than the car's worth. Trent said our best bet is to sell it for parts and buy something new. Guess we need to go car shopping."

The Honda was a piece of work. But they owned it free and clear, and it got them where they needed to go. Or it had.

"We'll have to get a car loan," Kyra said, feeling sick. Even before the IUIs ate up their emergency fund, there wouldn't have been enough money for this.

"I know." She heard the despair in his voice. "Trent refused to let me pay him for his time. That's something, at least."

"That was really generous of him. I hope they know we didn't expect that."

"I'm so grateful for his help. Can you take them cookies today? We'll invite them over for dinner soon."

While Sophie slept, Kyra made a batch of chocolate chip cookies. When Sophie woke up, Kyra loaded up a plate, and they left for the Burkes.

"Why are we taking cookies?" Sophie asked as she skipped alongside Kyra. She held Sophie's hand tightly in hers, balancing the plate of cookies in the other.

"Because Mr. and Mrs. Burke looked at our car and told us what's wrong with it."

"What's wrong?"

Kyra wrinkled her nose. She barely understood the problem, and had no idea how to explain it to a three-year-old. "Something broke, and it made something else break. I think."

"Oh. Does Mrs. Burke have kids I can play with?"

"No. But we're not going to stay long anyway."

They trudged up Megan's front steps. Kyra didn't know what kind of hours real estate agents kept and had no idea if Megan would be home at three o'clock in the afternoon. But she let Sophie ring the doorbell anyway, and they waited.

It was quiet for a long time. Kyra rang the doorbell again.

"I don't think she's home," Sophie said.

"Maybe you're right." Kyra leaned down to leave the plate of cookies on the porch when she heard footsteps. She rose quickly, and the door swung open.

"Well, hello." A grin split Megan's face. "This is a pleasant surprise."

"We brought you cookies." Sophie did a little hop. "I'm Sophie. You came to my house when my baby went to live in heaven."

Kyra swallowed. Megan's eyes flicked to hers. "It's nice to see you again, Sophie."

"My mommy said you helped tell us our car breaked."

Megan laughed, opening the door wider. "That's right I guess. Can you come in for a minute?"

Kyra opened her mouth to decline, but Sophie scampered inside before Kyra got the chance.

"We won't stay long," Kyra said awkwardly, holding out the plate of cookies. "Thank you for helping us out. We really appreciate it."

"I'm glad we could help." Megan pulled a cookie out and took a bite. "These are amazing. Trent told me your car is totaled. That sucks."

"Yeah," Kyra agreed. Talk about an understatement.

"We're going to buy a pink car," Sophie yelled.

Megan laughed. "I would totally drive that."

Sophie grinned, clearly pleased with herself. "Me too."

"Probably not a pink one," Kyra said. "I'm not sure what we'll buy. We'll have to do some research first."

"Trent's an expert at cars," Megan said. "You should let us go car shopping with you. He can spot a lemon from a mile away."

Kyra nearly declined, but then reconsidered. The last thing they needed was to get ripped off, and car shopping would be difficult without a vehicle to get around in. "Are you really offering?"

"Absolutely. It'll be fun."

"Well, then thank you. We could use an expert's opinion."

CHAPTER TWENTY-TWO
KYRA

Saturday morning the Burkes pulled into Kyra and David's driveway at ten o'clock on the dot. Sophie ate a bowl of cereal at a turtle's pace while Kyra wiggled Sophie's feet into shoes.

"Sophie, they're here," Kyra said. "Please hurry."

"Who's here?" Sophie asked.

Kyra heard David welcome Megan and Trent at the front door and apologize for not being quite ready.

"Mr. and Mrs. Burke," Kyra said. "Remember? We talked about this last night."

Sophie took another huge bite, spilling milk down her chin.

"Soph, be careful." Kyra grabbed a napkin and wiped up the milk before it could dribble onto Sophie's shirt, then pulled the Velcro strap tight on one shoe. Kyra grabbed a granola bar and some fruit snacks and tossed those into her purse, which already held a collection of toys and other treats. "You have two minutes to finish eating. Then we're leaving whether you're done or not."

Sophie started shoveling food into her mouth. Kyra grabbed Sophie's bowl from her as the last bite entered her mouth and dropped it into the sink. Sophie raced to the front room and Kyra heard her ask Megan, "Are we going in your car?"

Kyra pulled Sophie's jacket off the kitchen counter and headed into the front room to rescue Megan, her giant purse flopping against her side.

"Sorry," Kyra said, hoping her stress didn't show. "We're running behind this morning. Sophie slept in."

"Not a problem," Megan said. "We've got all day."

By noon Kyra had a massive headache. At two o'clock they took a break and stopped for lunch.

"I think you should consider the Toyota in Draper," Trent said. "It's got low mileage, and the engine looks great. Or the minivan at the dealership in Sandy is a good option too."

"There's almost fifteen thousand more miles on the van. And it's three years older," Kyra said.

"The engine's in excellent condition, and it's a great price. That van will last you ten years, easy," Trent said.

"Do you think the price on the car is too steep?" David asked. Kyra heard the worry in his voice.

"I think it's reasonable," Trent said. "But it's always risky to buy from a person instead of a dealer." He turned to Megan. "I'm going to grab a drink refill. Want to come?"

"Sure," she said. Kyra smiled her thanks, and Megan nodded in understanding.

"What do you think?" Kyra asked David as soon as the Burkes were out of ear-shot.

"I want to get the minivan. I feel more comfortable buying through a dealership. And when we have another baby, we're going to outgrow a car pretty fast."

Kyra shook her head. "We've already talked about this. We need something with good gas mileage."

"I drive three miles to work. I don't think it'll make a significant difference."

"Insurance will be more on a van. We can fit in a car for a while longer. Maybe by the time a third baby's on its way—"

"Kyra." David grabbed her hand. "You could be pregnant right now. I really think we should consider the van. It's not much more than the Toyota, and it'd be the best option in the long run."

"I like green," Sophie said, taking a bite out of her cookie as though that settled things.

David smiled. "See? Sophie wants the van too."

Kyra imagined driving to Arizona for Christmas, their van piled high with presents and luggage, while Sophie watched videos on the van's built-in DVD player and the new baby slept soundly. Kyra's heart ached. "Can we afford it?" she asked.

"You tell me."

She slowly nodded. "It'll be tight, but we can make the payments, thanks to your promotion. But there won't be much left to save for fertility treatments."

"Doesn't matter; the IUI worked."

"If it did work, we're really in trouble. A baby costs money too, you know."

"We have to get a vehicle either way. Might as well pay an extra fifty bucks a month and get one that fits our family's needs."

"Okay. Let's go test drive the van again."

David grinned, rumpling Sophie's hair. "See, Soph? Mom likes the green one too."

After test driving the van one more time, they decided to buy it. Megan and Trent took Sophie over to the popcorn machine while Kyra and David waited in the office for the salesman to draw up the paperwork.

"Are we making the right decision?" Kyra asked David.

"Trent's a good negotiator. The monthly payment's squarely in our price range now. Only twenty more a month than the car would've been. We'll still have a little left over at the end of the month."

"But not enough for long-term infertility treatments. Barely enough for a baby."

"We won't need the money for treatments."

Kyra thought about Megan and Trent, who had struggled with infertility their entire marriage. How many years had they tried? How many treatments had they undergone? And they still didn't have a baby.

What if the same thing happened to Kyra and David?

Kyra should just ask her about it. Megan didn't seem like the type to get easily offended. But Kyra was the type to get easily embarrassed. Even though Megan knew about the miscarriage, she didn't know about the IUIs.

The finance officer entered the office. "I've got the paperwork right here."

Kyra swallowed back the bile. David took her hand in his.

"Everything's as we discussed," he said. Kyra's stomach knotted with every word. Soon she and David were signing the papers, the proud new owners of a minivan.

"Thank you so much for everything," Kyra told Megan as she hugged a cranky Sophie.

"It wasn't a problem," Trent said.

"We want you to come over for dinner on Monday so we can thank you properly. It's the least we can do," Kyra said.

Trent put an arm around Megan and squeezed. "I never turn down a free meal."

"It's a plan," David said.

They switched Sophie's car seat to the van, thanked the Burkes, and went home. Sophie was a bear through dinner and her bedtime routine, but she fell asleep almost immediately after they laid her down.

"Well," David said, wrapping an arm around Kyra's waist and nuzzling her neck. She scooped out generous portions of ice cream for both of them. "What do you think, little lady?"

"I think it'll be a good vehicle. I hope the payments don't come back to bite us. What if—"

"Don't even say it. The IUI worked. Everything's going to be okay."

If only Kyra was so confident.

CHAPTER TWENTY-THREE
MEGAN

I f Clomid was miserable, then Follistim was hell. It made Megan seem like a completely balanced person on Clomid.

"Megan, honey, why don't you lie down and read for a while or something?" Trent suggested one evening after dinner.

"I can't leave the dirty dishes in the sink," Megan yelled.

He grabbed a book off the kitchen counter and handed it to her. "I'll do the dishes."

Tears pricked at her eyes. "You are so sweet, Trent."

"I'll bring you some ice cream when I'm done, okay?"

Megan nodded, took the book, and walked into the living room like an obedient child. She lay on the couch, and for twenty blissful minutes lost herself in the regency romance. A sharp buzzing jolted her from the story, and she fumbled for her phone.

How are you today? Christina texted.

Follistim sucks, Megan wrote. *I am more hormonal than a sixteen-year-old girl who just found out her best friend's dating her crush. How are you? Nervous about the surgery?*

Megan flipped the phone over and reached for her book. She fumbled as she grabbed it, dropping the book to the floor. It slammed shut, effectively losing her place.

"No," Megan muttered. Tears pooled in her eyes. She sat up, grabbing the book and riffling to find her place. What had she read last? She couldn't even remember.

"Megan?" Trent stood behind the couch, a bowl of ice cream in each hand.

"I lost my place," Megan said, flipping the pages. "Christina texted me, and I dropped the book, and now I can't find where I was." She closed the book and started to cry. "Now I'll have to start all over."

"It's okay. I'll help you find your place." Trent walked around the couch, handing her a bowl of ice cream. Megan took it, wiping at her eyes with one hand. He carefully removed the book from her lap, as though worried she'd freak out again, and set it on the end table.

Megan's phone buzzed and she read the text. *I'm not too nervous.*

Megan sighed. Of course Christina wasn't nervous. She was always cool, calm, and collected.

"What's wrong?" Trent asked.

Megan took a bite of ice cream, wiping at the tears again. "I'm sorry. I shouldn't be crying. This whole thing is stupid."

Trent put an arm around her and kissed her temple. "We knew what the side effects would be."

"People always talk about how hormonal pregnancy makes you. Does that mean it's basically nine months of Follistim?"

"I don't think pregnancy will be quite this emotional. We see pregnant women all the time, and they seem fine."

"Maybe I really suck at hiding my emotions, and they're really good at it. If this is what pregnancy is like, maybe it's not worth it. What if we're awful parents?"

"You know that's fear talking. But I do agree we can't keep putting ourselves through this. If this IUI doesn't work, we should consider adoption."

Megan shook her head. "No. I'm not ready to go there."

"Some agencies have wait times of less than six months. I think the emotional aspect will be easier to handle without the hormone drugs."

"I can't talk about this right now." Megan's voice rose at the end, and she shook her head violently back and forth. "Please, I can't."

"Shhh. Eat your ice cream while we watch TV." He handed her the remote. "You pick the show."

Things calmed down over the next few days, but not by much. When it came time for Sienna's piano lesson, Megan prayed she could handle the stress. She tapped her foot nervously on the floor as Sienna played her piece, wondering if she'd talk about the baby. Knowing it was impossible to avoid the subject.

Sienna finished the piece, and Megan nodded. "Good. I can tell you practiced this week."

"I've had a lot of time. My days of hanging out seem to be over." Sienna motioned to her stomach, which was still flatter than Megan's could ever hope to be. "I spoke with a caseworker at the crisis center. She gave me a list of adoption agencies they recommend, and we talked about resources for single parenting. She was really helpful."

"That's great."

"I met with one of the agencies today. I've decided I'm going to give my baby away. Sorry, I mean *place my baby for adoption*. I'm supposed to use 'positive adoption language.'" Sienna made air quotes with her fingers.

Megan's heart tore. *Maybe you should adopt Sienna's baby.* The thought lingered at the back of her mind, but she pushed it away. She wasn't ready for adoption. Not yet.

"My caseworker Rebecca says it's not giving your baby away. It's giving your baby the best chance at a successful future."

Megan could give that baby a successful future. She swallowed hard. *Don't cry, don't cry, don't cry.* "That's true. Those couples have been waiting so long to have children, and I'm sure any one of them would be fantastic parents to your baby."

"Have you ever thought of adopting?"

Megan's stomach flipped. She chewed on her lip, not sure how to answer. "Trent's suggested it. But I'm not ready."

Sienna's face fell. "Because you don't want someone else's mistake?"

A baby was never a mistake. Megan closed her eyes, praying for composure, then placed her hand on Sienna's arm. Sienna looked up, her eyes begging for acceptance.

"Getting pregnant at seventeen probably hasn't been your finest moment. But this baby isn't a mistake. It's the answer to a couple's prayers. I've prayed for a baby every day for five years. If you place your baby, I guarantee that couple's been doing the same." Megan's voice warbled.

"You're exactly the kind of mom I want for my baby. Would you ever think about being that couple?"

Yes! Megan wanted to yell. A baby was right there. Sienna was practically offering him or her to Megan. She could stop taking Follistim. Cancel the cycle. But the sick pit in her stomach told her it wasn't the right choice.

Megan closed her eyes, praying for strength. *Let her baby be mine*, Megan begged. *I'm so tired. I want to get off this ride.*

You know her baby isn't yours, a voice whispered to her soul.

But it could be! We can do in vitro in a few years.

The baby isn't yours, the voice gently repeated.

Megan clutched her fists in frustration. *I know. But why?*

"Megan?" Sienna asked. Megan snapped back to the present. Sienna's eyes were hooded, uncertain.

Megan put a hand over her heart. "When you find the right couple for this baby, you'll know right here. I want it to be me and Trent so much. But it's not."

"I know," Sienna whispered. "I've prayed and prayed for it to be you. It'd be easier that way, I think. But the Lord keeps telling me 'no.'"

Megan's heart tore, and she sucked in air. "I'm so sorry, Sienna." *For both of us.*

"Me too."

"Your baby's family is out there. When you find them, you'll know."

Megan rushed the rest of their piano lesson, then fell apart once Sienna left. Megan called Christina and told her what happened, crying her way through the conversation.

The morning of Megan's mid-cycle ultrasound, Trent told work he'd be late.

"You don't have to go with me," Megan said as they got ready to leave. "I'm a big girl."

He leaned down and kissed her forehead. "I want to be there. We're in this together."

"Here's to hoping we have at least one follicle to call our own."

"What do you want to call our little follicle?"

"Maybe Sticky Bean," Megan said.

"It's not a very imaginative name, but all right." Trent laughed and jumped back a few steps as Megan whacked his arm. "Hey!"

"Don't insult our follicle. You might scare it."

At the clinic, Megan couldn't sit still. Her feet wiggled, fingers rapping against the paper on the exam table, making it crinkle.

"Relax," Trent said.

Megan frowned. "Easy for you to say. If I took Follistim for nothing, I'll be pissed."

"I thought we agreed to think happy thoughts."

Dr. Mendoza walked in, cutting off Megan's reply. "Good morning," Dr. Mendoza said. She sat down and pulled out the ultrasound wand. "Let's take a look-see."

Megan stared at the ultrasound screen, her body coiled with tension. "There better be good news today."

"I really hope so," Dr. Mendoza said.

Megan held her breath as Dr. Mendoza wiggled the probe around, looking at the monitor. After a minute or two, she smiled. "We hit pay dirt. You have a follicle ready on both ovaries."

Megan's entire body went limp with relief. Dr. Mendoza removed the wand, and Megan sat up.

"Do the trigger shot tonight. We'll do the IUI on Wednesday," Dr. Mendoza said. "As long as we get a high enough sperm count, I think your chances are decent this cycle."

Megan wanted to scream with happiness. But they'd been here before.

As soon as they got in the car, Trent let out a whoop. "We did it, babe." He grabbed her face and kissed her soundly.

"A follicle doesn't mean a fetus."

"We have two follicles. It's going to work."

Megan let hope peek its way in, just for a moment. "Maybe."

The feelings of anxious anticipation continued all through the next day and into their IUI appointment. As Megan lay on the exam table after the procedure, hips elevated, she couldn't help but think this might be it. For the first time in months, she let herself dream of little white booties and that new baby smell.

CHAPTER TWENTY-FOUR
CHRISTINA

Christina had never been admitted to a hospital. Sure, she'd had an x-ray once as a child. She'd had the HSG test. She'd visited people in the maternity ward. But she'd never been a patient herself.

She hadn't eaten anything for twelve hours, which didn't help the knots in her stomach. Gary had suggested the baggy lounge pants with a loose waist and cheesy t-shirt that said "2 Teach is 2 Touch a Life 4Ever."

"You want to be comfortable after the surgery," he'd reminded Christina when she pulled out a pair of jeans. "No one expects a fashion statement."

Maybe not, but Christina felt awkward and frumpy. At least Gary had dressed down too. He looked uncomfortable without his suit, which made Christina feel less alone. Seeing him in jeans and a button-down plaid shirt with the sleeves rolled halfway up his forearms was a visual reminder that today was anything but typical.

"Christina Vincent."

Another spasm seized her stomach. They rose, and Gary took her hand, loosening her fingers until they were no longer balled in a fist. They followed the nurse into a triage room. A monitor beeped distractingly a few beds over.

The nurse pulled the curtain around to form a wall between them and the empty bed beside them. "Change into the hospital gown." She handed Christina a bag. "Put all your personal items in here for your husband to hang onto. That includes all clothing and jewelry."

Christina took the bag, swallowing hard and nodding. She undressed, feeling more vulnerable by the second. If she had felt uncomfortable in her too-casual clothes, she felt downright awkward in the hospital gown. At least it tied on the side, covering her entire backside and leaving no skin exposed.

"Here." Gary knelt down beside her, a hospital sock held out as though it were Cinderella's glass slipper. Some of her tension eased at the sweet gesture. Christina let him wiggle both socks onto her feet, and then he sat down next to her. "How are you feeling?"

"Nervous," Christina admitted. She didn't know what scared her more—that they would find something or find nothing.

Gary opened his mouth to respond, but a nurse pulled back the curtain and entered. "Hi, Christina. I'm Jill. I'll be with you all through surgery, making sure you're okay. I'm going to start the IV now."

Gary rose, his hand still on Christina's shoulder. "You should lie down," he told her. The nurse nodded in agreement.

Christina let Gary pull the covers over her and tried to relax against the too-thin pillow. The nurse chattered in a friendly way as she worked, prepping Christina's arm at the elbow area for the IV. Gary asked questions, taking the role of polite patient so Christina didn't have to. His phone vibrated, emitting a faint buzz. He reached as though to pull it out. But his eye caught Christina's, and he folded his arms, leaving the phone in his pocket.

Thank you, Christina mouthed.

The needle pricked her skin. A shock of cold hit her arm and flowed outward as the saline entered her blood stream.

"I need you to sign these consent forms, and we'll get you started on some medication," Jill said.

Christina signed, barely glancing over the paperwork. Her signature looked awkward and sloppy since the IV was in her writing arm and she didn't want to bend it too much. Jill took the paperwork and left. A few minutes later she reappeared, this time with a syringe.

"This is an antibiotic." She uncapped the IV tubing and inserted the syringe. "It takes effect almost immediately. It might make you feel odd." She depressed the plunger, then threw the needle in a Sharps container and flicked the IV tubing a few times. "A lot of patients respond similarly to laughing gas."

Christina giggled. Laughing gas? Who had thought of that word? "I never act strange on laughing gas," Christina told the nurse, and giggled again. "I act totally normal."

"Told you it takes effect quickly. Dr. Blakely will stop by before we take you down to surgery, okay?" The nurse patted Christina's arm and left.

Gary's brow scrunched, and he sat forward in his chair. "Are you doing okay?"

Christina started laughing, and couldn't stop. Tears streamed out of her eyes. "What if they tell us we can't have kids? Wouldn't that be funny, Gar? All our arguments about whether or not we're ready, all our planning, and poof!" She popped her lips for the proper sound effect. "Vanished. No kids for us. The perfect Vincents would finally have a flaw." She giggled. "But we'd tell everyone we planned it that way, huh? That we wanted to focus on our careers and weren't really the parenting type. We'd lie so no one would ever figure out the truth. If you had married someone else, you'd have three kids with your fertile wife and your perfect sperm. You aren't the problem. Or maybe you'd be happy, because your other wife wouldn't want kids."

"Shhh, Christina. Don't talk. The medication is making you loopy."

"Maybe it's making me honest. What if they can't find anything wrong? What then, Gar?" Christina shivered, her teeth chattering as she laughed. The saline and whatever medication they'd given her pulsed through her blood, cool and invasive. "I've never had a problem I couldn't fix. Guess I've finally met my match."

Gary's brows were still furrowed in concern when Dr. Blakely appeared. "How are you feeling, Christina?"

Christina laughed. "I feel fine."

"The medication's making her act strange," Gary said. Why did he sound like he was apologizing?

"That's not uncommon." Dr. Blakely sat down on a chair near Gary and Christina. "I want to go over what to expect."

Christina tuned Dr. Blakely and Gary out, instead focusing on the whir of machines and the beep of the monitor from a few beds over. Soon Gary kissed her goodbye, and she was wheeled down the hallway and into the operating room. They lifted her onto a cold, white table. A bright light directly above hurt her eyes, and she squinted. Someone laid a warm blanket over her, and her shivering lessened.

"We'll try to warm you up," Jill said. "The anesthesiologist is right here."

"Hi, Christina," a man said. He put a mask over her mouth. "Count backward from one hundred for me, okay?"

Christina closed her eyes and started counting. "One hundred, ninety-nine, ninety-eight, ninety-seven . . ."

Darkness.

CHAPTER
TWENTY-FIVE
CHRISTINA

Christina heard the pulsing of her heartbeat on the monitor first. Her limbs felt heavy, and she struggled to open her eyes. No luck. She gave up and let herself drift.

Next she heard the shuffle of feet and soft voices. "She should be waking up soon."

"Thank you." That was Gary. Chair legs slid across linoleum as he sat down.

A hand gently squeezed hers. Only then was Christina aware of something clipped to her index finger. For her pulse, she realized. That's where the beeping came from. "I'm here, Christina," Gary said quietly. "You're out of surgery, and you're fine." A kiss brushed her temple. "I love you. Rest for a few more minutes, then try to wake up so we can go home."

Christina tried to wake up. She became more aware of her surroundings. Shoes dragged by in the hallway. The florescent lighting of the recovery area burned through her lids. A click that sounded like texting sounded near her head. Christina's midsection felt strangely deadened and heavy, but she could tell moving would probably hurt a lot.

What happened? Christina wanted to scream. *What did they find?* She struggled harder to open her eyes and managed to flutter them. She tried again and this time kept her eyes open.

"Hey, babe." Gary's smile, small and sad. He glanced at his cell phone, then put it in his pocket.

"Hi," Christina croaked. Her mouth felt full of cotton, and she needed a drink badly.

Gary seemed to read her thoughts and brought a mug with a straw to her lips. After sipping deeply, she tried talking again. "What did the doctor say?" Her throat still sounded raspy, but at least he could hear her.

Gary patted her hand. "Let's not get into that right now. How do you feel?"

"Fine. What happened?"

Gary frowned, and his shoulders hunched forward. "It wasn't good news. Dr. Blakely found a lot of endometriosis, and it's causing some problems." He patted her hand again. "But don't worry. We'll figure it out. You focus on recovering quickly, okay?"

Christina opened her mouth to demand more answers, but Dr. Blakely entered the curtained-off room, clipboard clasped in both hands. "Hi, Christina. How are you feeling?"

"Fine."

She walked over to a monitor and wrote down a reading. "Can you rate your pain on a scale of one to ten?"

What did it matter? Christina didn't care about the pain. She cared about answers. "A four or five. Gary said I have endometriosis."

Dr. Blakely didn't get flustered, just nodded. She flipped a page on Christina's chart and turned it around. Christina drew back. The pictures were disgusting, a mass of tissue that looked unnatural.

"That's your right fallopian tube." Dr. Blakely pointed to the first picture. "And that's your left. That's part of your uterus." She flipped the chart closed. "I'm not going to sugar coat it. You have stage four endometriosis. Your fallopian tubes and the outside of your uterus are covered in scar tissue."

Christina couldn't process what Dr. Blakely said. "Did you get it off?" Christina felt stupid for asking the question but couldn't think of anything else to say.

Dr. Blakely shook her head. "It's everywhere. It's blocking both of your fallopian tubes—the right side one hundred percent, the left side about ninety-five percent. It's actually attaching your tubes to your ovaries so they can't move to catch an egg. If I tried to remove the scar tissue, you'd lose your tubes. I cleaned off what I could, but the bulk of it's still there."

Blocked tubes. Hard to comprehend in her drug-induced state, but it sounded bad. Gary's hand held steadfastly to Christina's, comforting and begging for comfort.

"Where do we go from here?" Christina's voice sounded higher and more raspy than ever. Her hands shook, her thin grasp on composure disappearing.

Dr. Blakely looked at her sadly. "I'm afraid at this point that in vitro is really your only option. I'm sorry."

Christina couldn't focus after that. Dr. Blakely mentioned if she did get pregnant, it would help lessen the endometriosis since she would go nine months without a period. That, even though the chances of getting pregnant naturally were less than one percent, if it did happen she needed to have an ultrasound at six weeks since there was a ninety-nine percent chance it'd be a tubal pregnancy. Dr. Blakely said in vitro was more affordable than ever, and they shouldn't be discouraged. This didn't mean they'd never have a baby.

Christina didn't care what Dr. Blakely said. It felt like the end of the world. She turned her head into the pillow, letting the tears leak out.

She was twenty-seven years old. Twenty-seven, and already her prospects of ever being a mother were grim. Her shoulders shook, and she struggled to control them. How could she be here, hearing these things? *Life wasn't supposed to be like this,* Christina prayed angrily. *We were being responsible! We were trying to do things the right way. We didn't know.* A sob caught in her throat, begging for release. How could they have known? If they'd tried to get pregnant sooner, would it have made a difference?

Dr. Blakely left, and Christina's tears slowed to a trickle, then disappeared entirely. "I'm sorry," Gary said.

"I want to go home."

Two hours later they let Christina leave. Home. She had always imagined that would one day mean three or four children. What if now home only meant a too-clean house and quiet rooms? Would she ever hear the echo of laughter through her hallways? Would she ever scold her kids for not picking up their toys?

Gary would never agree to something as invasive as in vitro.

Christina sat on the edge of the bed. Gary pulled out his phone, and her heart dropped. He was withdrawing. But he pushed a few buttons, then stuck it back into his pocket. He helped her into pajamas, then pulled the covers over her as she lay down.

"Do you want to watch TV or anything?" Gary asked.

Christina shook her head. "I want to sleep."

He nodded, and she closed her eyes. After a few minutes, she heard him walk out of the room.

What was he thinking? Did he wish he picked a different wife? She couldn't stop the thoughts from flooding her mind. He hadn't known she was broken when they got married. If he had, would it have changed things?

My fault, Christina thought as she drifted off to sleep. *My fault, my fault, my fault* . . .

CHAPTER TWENTY-SIX
CHRISTINA

Christina woke up at six the next morning, her incision on fire and abdomen throbbing. "Gary," she whispered hoarsely.

He jerked awake. "What is it?"

"I need some pain meds."

He rubbed his eyes and rose. "Sure." A few minutes later he returned with a white pill and glass of water. Gary helped Christina sit up. Every movement brought tears to her eyes. She bit her lip to keep from gasping. She took the pill and then lay down with Gary's help.

"Is there anything I can get you?" he asked.

Christina shook her head. Her eyes watered, tears trembling to be set free. Her shoulders shook, making her stomach ache. The burn of repressed sobs clung to the back of her throat.

Gary flipped on a lamp. "Want to talk about it?"

No. "Why did this happen? We saved ourselves for marriage. Obtained college degrees. We did everything right! So why is God punishing us?"

"He's not punishing us." It sounded like he was trying to convince himself. "This is our trial. We'll meet with that fertility specialist Dr. Blakely recommended and do in vitro."

"You can barely stand the thought of a baby. How on earth will you handle fertility treatments?"

Gary drew away, and she heard the hurt in his voice. "We're in this together. If you hurt, I hurt. Don't think I'm unaffected by this. I do want kids. I never realized how much until—" He broke off abruptly, his Adam's apple bobbing.

Was he crying? She stared at the lone tear trickling down Gary's cheek. Had she ever seen him cry?

"I never realized how much I want children until I was told it might not be possible. I regret every negative thought I've ever had about having a baby. I would take them all back if I could. I feel like this is my fault. I made this happen by not wanting one." His shoulders shook. Christina reached out and massaged his back, alarmed. "I'm so sorry. I never meant for this to happen."

"It's no one's fault." Her own shoulders shook, and Christina struggled to control the sobs. Each movement sent pain shooting through her midsection. "Where do we go from here?"

They sat there and cried until sunlight peeked through the blinds and spilled across the room in horizontal stripes. Eventually she fell asleep, but it wasn't restful.

A while later she felt Gary's hand on her arm. "Christina, Megan's here to see you. She brought dinner."

Christina opened her eyes. "Dinner?"

"Yeah."

Christina blinked, struggling to sit up. Gary quickly moved to help, situating pillows behind her back so she'd be comfortable. "That's nice of her," Christina said.

"She wants to talk to you for a minute. Is that okay?"

Christina didn't feel like visiting, but she nodded. "How do I look?"

Gary smoothed a few curls behind her ear, then leaned down and kissed her. "Beautiful."

When Megan appeared, her smile was full of complete understanding. "I told Gary we'd talked before your surgery," she said. She sat down in a chair Gary had brought from the kitchen. "I hope that's okay."

"Of course." Had Gary been upset Christina had shared such intimate secrets?

"He told me what the doctor found." Megan said the words carefully, her eyes probing Christina's for some signal as to where to go from there.

"Gary told you?" Christina couldn't imagine him sharing personal details about their lives.

"He's really worried about you." Megan set her purse on the floor and leaned on the edge of bed, her face in her hand, elbow propped on the mattress. "Apparently Trent mentioned we were struggling with infertility when you guys helped us move in, and Gary thought maybe I could help."

Christina looked away, not wanting to cry in front of Megan. Christina didn't want to cry at all. She was sick of tears. Sick of feeling miserable. Would it never end?

"It's important to talk about it. If you keep it all inside, it will eat you up. Your entire life will be consumed by infertility until there is nothing left." Megan paused, and the next words were so quiet Christina almost didn't hear them. "I know. I've been there."

Christina laughed, then winced at the pain. "You never keep things bottled up."

Megan's eyes widened, and she burst into giggles. "I didn't expect that to come out of your mouth."

Christina blushed. "Sorry. Can we blame it on the pain meds and forget I ever said that?"

Megan shook her head, her blonde curls flipping back and forth. "No way, it's too funny." Her smile dropped, and she sobered. "But you were right to call me on it. There was a time when we kept quiet about our infertility. I let it overtake my life. I couldn't sleep. I couldn't stop eating and gained tons of weight. I didn't want to play the piano or read a book. Infertility was all I could think about. Having a baby consumed my entire life until there was nothing left."

Christina stared in amazement. She couldn't imagine this strong, vivacious woman ever being that broken.

"It got so bad I had to go on anti-depressants. Trent and I went to counseling, and that's where we learned the importance of openness. We may have taken it to an extreme, but it's saved us."

"How?" Surely letting people know their uncomfortable secret wouldn't help anything.

"Because it forces you to admit to it." Megan grabbed Christina's hand. "You need to accept it. Infertility is a part of you now. It always will be. Even when you have a baby—and one day you *will* have a baby—it's always going to be there, trying to take over everything good in your life and remind you of the bad."

"How did this happen?" Christina's anguished words pierced the air. "In vitro is our only option. My endometriosis is so far advanced they can't do anything about it. I don't know what to do."

Megan leaned back and extended her legs, slouching in the chair and folding her arms across her stomach. She looked perfectly relaxed, as though she had nothing better to do than sit and talk. "An RE can help you create a plan. That's code for reproductive endocrinologist, an infertility specialist. I've liked mine, and I'd be happy to give you her name and information. There aren't many in the area."

"Not yet. I need time to process what's happened."

"It takes years to process." The words were gentle, but with a hint of steel. "My philosophy is it's better to take action while processing than miss your window of opportunity."

"I—I can't. I can't even think about it."

"Tell me how you feel," Megan said.

Christina shook her head. "I can't—"

"Does it make you feel like less of a woman? Do you feel like you've failed Gary?"

"Stop." Christina covered her face with her hands. Her stomach screamed, but she couldn't stop the shivers wracking her body.

"Do you feel like your body is broken? Does it make you view yourself differently?"

"I feel like a failure!" The words were out of Christina's mouth before she consciously thought them, but she instantly knew they were true. She wiped at her cheeks, the cool wet tears trickling down her fingers.

"How have you failed?"

Christina leaned against the pillows and took slow deep breaths, trying to relax the muscle spasms in her midsection. "In church they always tell us that women were put on this earth to be wives and mothers." The words were slow, painful, and heartbreakingly true. "I've had the importance of motherhood drilled into my brain my entire life. It's our purpose for being here, right?"

Megan said nothing, but kept her gaze steady and reassuring, and her posture relaxed. It was easy to open up to her. She was someone Christina could trust.

"I feel like the Lord has failed me." Christina winced as she said the words. Stand back, lightning might strike. "He's commanded us to multiply and replenish the earth. But He's given me this disease that's making it nearly impossible for me to obey Him. How is that fair? How is that just?"

Megan shrugged. "I don't know."

"Am I being completely ridiculous?"

Megan smiled and shook her head. "No. I've had the exact same thoughts."

"How do you do it, year after year? We've only been dealing with this for a few months, and already I feel like I'm breaking."

"It goes in waves. We've been at the edge many times. But even though it feels like God's deserted you—given us this impossible task to accomplish—He hasn't." Megan swallowed, and tears brimmed in her eyes. "I've felt His hand guiding us on this journey. And even though I have no idea why we've had so many disappointments or why He hasn't given us a baby yet, I know it's in His hands, and everything is going according to plan. Maybe not my plan, but He knows what He's doing." Megan grabbed Christina's hand. "Don't let infertility define you. You are not just someone who is infertile. You're also a wife and a teacher and a neighbor." Megan laughed, her voice shaky. "And you have the makings of a really great best friend."

Christina smiled, squeezing Megan's hand. "I haven't had a best friend in years. But visiting me today seems like a best friend thing to do. Thank you for coming."

"Anytime. We're in this together. You can talk to me about anything, no matter how awkward or embarrassing. We're sisters in the Land of IF now."

"The same goes for you. We can be infertile friends."

Megan laughed, standing. "I like the sound of that. But we can be friends outside of infertility, too. I should let you sleep. You need to heal so you can get to work on getting pregnant." She winked.

"Thanks for dinner."

"Anytime." Megan paused, her hand on the door. "I'm sorry you're going through this. I wouldn't wish infertility on my worst enemy. But you are an answer to my prayers. I am so glad to have a friend that understands. Get better, okay? Physically I mean. The emotional stuff takes a while."

"How long?"

"I'll let you know when I get there."

CHAPTER TWENTY-SEVEN
KYRA

Am I pregnant? The phrase repeated in Kyra's head like a broken record for days. Every pregnancy symptom in the book, real or imagined, manifested itself after their IUI. She couldn't get through Tuesday without an afternoon nap. She unloaded the dishwasher, and her stomach growled and gurgled from bloating. She folded laundry, then curled into a ball on the floor and cried when she realized a crayon had gotten in with the load. *This is a good thing,* Kyra reminded herself. *Last time you didn't really have any symptoms. Maybe this means the pregnancy's viable.*

If she was even pregnant. It could all be in her head.

Two days, Kyra reminded herself as she helped Sophie dress. Two days, and she'd know for sure.

"What're we gonna do today, Mommy?" Sophie asked as Kyra helped her put on socks.

"We're going to drop Daddy off at work and go to the store."

Sophie frowned. "Does that mean we have to hurry?"

"Yes. We don't want Daddy to be late."

At the store Kyra grabbed a cart and strapped Sophie in. Toothpaste, bar soap, and deodorant all were checked off the list and tossed in the cart. Kyra headed for the lotion.

And that's when she passed it. The family planning rack. There, on the top row, sat boxes of home pregnancy tests, neatly lined up and screaming Kyra's name. Without consciously deciding to, she brought the cart to a stop.

She didn't need one. The blood pregnancy test in two days would be accurate enough.

But Kyra needed to see those two pink lines for herself.

"This isn't lotion," Sophie said, startling Kyra out of her thoughts.

Before Kyra could argue with herself, she grabbed a box of two—the cheapest brand on the shelf—and threw it into the cart. "We're going there now."

Kyra wouldn't take a test, she told herself as they finished shopping. Not unless the blood test came back positive. Then she'd take it to post the obligatory "We're pregnant!" photo on social media.

At home, Kyra got Sophie down for a nap, then unpacked the groceries. She put a block of cheese in the fridge, a bunch of bananas in a basket, and moved on to another bag. The pregnancy tests stared up at her. She set them deliberately aside.

The tests bored holes into her as she unloaded bags and put away items. Kyra put a jar of peanut butter in the pantry— the very last item—and wadded up the plastic bags to throw into the recycling bin. What would it hurt to take a test right now? She drummed her fingers on the counter, staring at the box. *Results five days before your missed period!* it said in large red letters on the front.

She grabbed the box and headed to the bathroom.

If it was negative, that didn't mean she wasn't pregnant.

She started the stop-watch on her phone. Two minutes. An eternity.

A negative result could mean her HCG levels weren't concentrated enough in her urine since she was taking the test mid-day. She should've waited for morning like the box recommended. Or it could mean they weren't high enough yet to show up on the test.

The timer on her phone beeped. Kyra took a deep breath. A negative result didn't mean anything. A negative result didn't mean anything. A negative—

One pink line. Not even a hint of a second one.

She threw the test into the trash in disgust.

The morning of Kyra's HCG test she woke up feeling bloated, nauseated, and definitely pregnant.

"We come here a lot now," Sophie said as they waited at the clinic. She swung her feet back and forth and held onto the seat of her chair. "It's kind of boring."

"I know." Kyra reached into her purse and withdrew a coloring book and crayons. "Want to color?"

"No, that's boring." Sophie sighed dramatically. "Maybe I can play with your phone or something."

Kyra hid a smile. "Here you go." Sophie could find which game she wanted without Kyra's help.

A few minutes later they were called back. "Do you faint?" the nurse asked as they walked to the phlebotomy room.

Kyra sank into the chair the nurse indicated while Sophie sat on the one next to Kyra. "I never have before. Why?"

"I've had three ladies pass out on me this morning." The nurse shook her head as she prepared the needle. "I haven't had anyone faint in months, and then three today. And it's not even nine o'clock."

"I'll be fine." Hopefully. How traumatized would Sophie be if Kyra collapsed?

The nurse wrapped a tourniquet around Kyra's left forearm. She pumped her fist a few times as instructed, and the nurse inserted the needle.

"Mommy, is she hurting you?" Sophie asked, her eyes wide as she stared at the vial filling with blood.

Kyra shook her head, forcing a smile. It did hurt, but she wasn't going to let Sophie know. "I'm fine, baby girl. Don't look, okay?"

"Why does she need blood?"

"They're going to test it to see if there's a baby in my tummy."

Sophie's lips pursed. "Do you think there is?"

Kyra wanted to say yes. She felt like the answer was yes, whatever that negative home pregnancy test had said. But what if she was wrong? She didn't want to disappoint Sophie. Again. "I guess we'll find out."

Kyra didn't faint. After the clinic, she and Sophie went to the mall for a needed distraction. They were on their way home when the phone rang. Kyra glanced down, surprised to see the clinic's phone number. Already? It wasn't even two o'clock, and they'd told her they'd call between three and five. Kyra answered the phone, her other hand clutching the steering wheel. "Hello?"

"Hi, Mrs. Peterson. I have the results of your HCG test." The nurse paused. "It's negative. I'm so sorry."

Negative.

No baby.

A sucker punch to the gut.

Kyra stopped for a red light. Why hadn't she pulled over to take this call? "Are you sure?"

"Yes. Stop taking the progesterone. When your period starts, give us a call and we'll send in a prescription for Clomid and try another IUI."

"But I have all the pregnancy symptoms." Kyra's voice sounded choked. The light turned green, and she followed traffic forward.

The nurse's voice was soft and compassionate. "Progesterone can mimic pregnancy symptoms. I'm really sorry, Mrs. Peterson."

Kyra vaguely remembered them mentioning that before the first IUI. She'd forgotten. The disappointment crushed her.

"Thank you for calling," Kyra said and hung up. She returned both hands to the steering wheel and held it until her fingers throbbed. Focus on the drive. Focus on the road.

"Who was that, Mommy?" Sophie asked.

Kyra cleared her throat, trying to hide the tears. "The doctor's office."

"Is there a baby in your tummy?"

Tears blurred Kyra's vision, and she blinked. "Not this time."

Sophie's voice sounded cheerful and unconcerned. "That's okay. My baby brother is coming pretty soon I think."

If only Kyra were so optimistic. She had been optimistic, and look where it had gotten her.

At home, Kyra turned on a movie for Sophie. Then she went to her room and shut the door.

No baby. Their last-chance IUI hadn't worked. Why? David's sperm count had been higher this time. They'd had one more follicle. She lay down on the bed and sobbed. Ten minutes. She would allow herself ten minutes to cry before going back to Sophie.

Twelve minutes later, Kyra dried her tears and headed into the family room. Sophie sat on the floor, her eyes glued to the TV screen. Kyra lay down on the couch, wanting to be near Sophie. At least she still had her daughter. It helped, but only a little.

Sophie crawled up on the couch and patted Kyra's cheeks, frowning. "Are you sad, Mommy?"

Kyra nodded. "Thank you for noticing. That's very polite."

"Why are you sad?"

"Because there's not a baby in my tummy."

"But he's coming soon." Sophie shrugged as though that settled things. "I'm happy."

"How do you know a baby brother is coming?"

Sophie shrugged again. "I just do." She snuggled up against Kyra's side and focused on the TV. Kyra wrapped her arms around Sophie and held tight.

They cuddled and watched TV until it was time to pick David up from work.

"How about we stop at the park on the way home?" Kyra said.

"Yay!" Sophie ran off to find her jacket. Kyra grabbed her purse, and they left.

David was waiting when they arrived. "Hey." He kissed Kyra as she got out of the car to let him drive. "I'm sorry I didn't call earlier. I had meetings all day. How did the appointment go?" His voice, bright with hope, broke Kyra's heart.

She shook her head, the devastation washing over her again. "It didn't work."

His face blanched. "Are they sure?"

She nodded.

David stood there, then leaned down and kissed her once more. "We can talk about this at home."

"I promised Sophie we'd go to the park," Kyra said as they climbed into the van.

"Yeah," Sophie said from the back. "Mommy said we can go to the big park."

"Well, let's get going," David said.

It was an especially warm April day. They told Sophie to stay in sight and sat down on a bench to watch her play.

"I'm so sorry, Kyra," David said. "I really thought it would work."

"Me too." A tear fell, and she wiped it away. "I feel like we missed out on our last shot."

"Why do you say that?"

"We said we had enough money for one more IUI, and it didn't work."

"I have the promotion now. I think we can squeeze in another attempt."

"But we have the van payment too." A van with extra space they didn't need. "That's eating up almost all of our available resources." Why hadn't they bought a car?

"The fertility clinic told us we could apply for a loan. Maybe we should set up a consultation with their financial representative."

"Do we really want to go into debt for another disappointment?" Kyra's voice was high pitched, her nerves frayed. David leaned forward to hug her, and she crumpled against him. "I'm serious, David."

"We owe ourselves another shot. Are you willing to try again?"

The hole in her heart had doubled in size. "What if it doesn't work again? We had three follicles this time. Three— one more than last time. And none of them worked."

"We're not going to do this. We'll stay optimistic and hopeful. We can swing one more try if we apply for the loan. I'm not ready to give up."

"I can't jump into another cycle right now. I need a month to think about things."

"Kyra—"

"I'm not saying no. I'm saying give me a month."

He nodded reluctantly. David kissed her temple, then sighed. "I'm so sorry, Kyr. So, so sorry."

"Me too."

Two days later, her period started. It hurt worse than the phone call from the clinic. Kyra locked herself in the bedroom and organized their closet, leaving David to get Sophie ready for bed. How could something hurt this badly?

But she knew how. Three little follicles had matured and ovulated. They had been right there, ready to fertilize. Losing them meant losing three possibilities. Three chances at a miracle.

Kyra wondered how many more chances they would get.

CHAPTER
TWENTY-EIGHT
CHRISTINA

Christina had expected the fertility clinic to be different than her obstetrician's office. It wasn't. Doctors' office couches, nondescript paintings, friendly staff. The two were identical, unless you considered the patients. None of the women here were pregnant, at least that she could tell.

One week. Christina couldn't believe it had only been a week since her surgery. She fidgeted with her purse strap as she listened to Dr. Mendoza confirm Dr. Blakely's diagnosis. Gary sat in the chair next to her, his expression carefully blank.

"Your endometriosis is quite severe," Dr. Mendoza said, "and unfortunately there's nothing we can do to unblock your tubes without damaging them. The fact they're attached to the ovaries is also a problem. It makes it practically impossible for the tubes to catch an egg. Sometimes the stretching of the uterus during pregnancy will pull scar tissue away and make the tubes usable again, but for now we have to bypass them. And the only way to do that is in vitro."

"What exactly is involved in IVF?" Christina asked. Did she want to know?

"The first step in the process is to suppress your natural cycle," Dr. Mendoza said. "You'll administer daily injections of Lupron for ten days. Then we do an ultrasound and perform a blood test to check your estrogen levels. If we successfully suppressed your cycle, we can move on to the next step— boosting your egg supply. That means twelve days of injections of Lupron, along with Follistim. About day five of Follistim, we do another ultrasound to make sure there are enough follicles developing to continue the cycle."

Christina's mind reeled. "So almost an entire month of daily shots?"

Dr. Mendoza nodded. "Thirty-six hours before we go in for the egg retrieval, you give yourself another injection. This time it's an HCG shot to trigger ovulation."

Christina gave up calculating how many shots she'd be administering to herself. No way Gary would be around to do it. "Then what?"

"You come into the office, and we retrieve the eggs." Dr. Mendoza pulled out a chart and pointed. "We use an ultrasound to guide the whole process. A tube is inserted up through your vagina, and that's used to guide a needle into your ovary to retrieve the eggs."

Christina flinched, and Gary took her hand in a comforting gesture. "Am I awake for this?"

"We sedate you. My patients tell me it's not too painful." Dr. Mendoza smiled sympathetically. "Then you start taking more injections to help prepare your uterine lining for implantation. After the egg retrieval, we collect a sperm sample. The eggs and sperm are mixed and closely monitored in our laboratory for about eighteen hours. We take the eggs that have fertilized and incubate them in our laboratory for another one to two days."

Christina's mind spun with the complexity of the procedure. "And after that, you put them back in me and freeze the rest?"

Dr. Mendoza nodded. "We pick the best two to implant, again using an ultrasound and catheter. Strict bed rest is encouraged for two days afterward. You'll start daily injections of progesterone at that point. Two weeks later, we do a blood pregnancy test to see if it worked."

Christina had never known IVF was so involved. There were so many places along the way where things could go wrong. So many opportunities for failure.

"That's really intense," Gary said. His gaze flicked to Christina. "Maybe we should wait."

Christina knew what that meant. He wasn't ready for this.

Dr. Mendoza spoke up. "I don't want to frighten you, but endometriosis is something that progresses over time. The longer you wait, the less chance you'll have of success."

Christina's stomach tightened. Gary was already backpedaling, and now they had a ticking time bomb on their hands.

They talked with Dr. Mendoza for another hour, weighing the risks and benefits. Eventually Gary and Christina looked at each other. They'd run out of questions to ask.

"Most patients need time to process this," Dr. Mendoza said. "When you're ready, call us, and we'll get the ball rolling."

Christina barely registered the walk to the car. "Well?" she asked Gary when they climbed inside.

"The whole thing is so involved."

Christina's chest tightened. "We have to do it. Now. It's our only chance." Her throat caught on the word. "I'm ready to be a mom, Gary."

He sighed, pulling onto the main road and heading toward home. "That's like six weeks of daily hormone injections. More if we get pregnant. Are you ready for six weeks of hormone injections?"

"Yes! I'll give them to myself. You won't have to do a thing."

"Can we handle the disappointment if it doesn't work? I'm not ready to see you go through that."

Christina threw up her hands. "It's not like I'm thrilled right now. At least we'll know we gave it our best attempt."

"I want a child. But I've got to be honest. I'm not ready for this."

"You heard the doctor. It's now or never." Christina slammed a hand on the dashboard. "Dang it, Gar. I thought we were past this. You told me you'd be there for me, that we'd be in it together. Was that just talk?"

"Of course not." His voice was quiet, soothing. Contemplative. "But what if we go to all this effort to have a baby, and I screw up our kid?"

Christina opened her mouth to respond, then shut it, a new terror gripping her heart. "I don't know. What if we do screw him up?"

"Are you serious?"

"Well, you're kind of freaking me out right now. I've never been a parent before. It scares me too. But not enough to give up. I want a baby. *Your* baby."

He reached out and took her hand. "Me too."

"You're willing to try?"

He nodded slowly, hesitantly. "I couldn't live with myself if I made us wait, and we never had a child. Money isn't an issue, so whenever you feel ready."

"I'm ready now."

They were quiet the rest of the way home, but Christina felt the nervous bubbles in her stomach. They were really going to do this. She had never imagined she would one day have to turn to in vitro, but now that they were here, she was okay with it. The needles and procedures and hormones didn't scare her. But the thought of never being a mother did.

It's going to work, Christina told herself. *Have faith.*

CHAPTER TWENTY-NINE
MEGAN

Megan's cell phone rang, a shotgun in the quiet kitchen. She jumped and yanked the phone out of her pocket, putting the last gallon of milk in the refrigerator door as she did so. The number of the fertility clinic flashed across the screen. "Hello?" She clutched the phone, closing her eyes tight and praying for all she was worth.

"Hi, this is Natalie from the Center for Infertility and Reproductive Medicine. Is this Megan?"

Megan nodded, then realized Natalie couldn't see her and forced herself to speak. "Yes." *Please let it be positive.*

"I'm calling with the results of your HCG test."

Please let it be positive.

"It's negative. I'm sorry, Megan."

Negative. "Really?" Her legs trembled beneath her.

"Dr. Mendoza would like to schedule a consultation to discuss where to go from here."

Megan made the appointment and hung up, then clutched the phone to her chest. She leaned against the fridge and slid to the floor, sobbing.

Negative.

Empty. A dark void had engulfed Megan's heart and swallowed her whole. Trent and Megan sat in Dr. Mendoza's office, hands clasped. Trent's eyes were suspiciously red—had been for two days now. He'd taken the news as hard as she had.

The door clicked open. Dr. Mendoza gave them a sympathetic smile and sat down at her desk. *Stop smiling!* Megan wanted to scream. She didn't want the doctor's pity.

She's trying to help you, Megan reminded herself. She didn't hate Dr. Mendoza. It was the hormones talking. It always took a few weeks to get them out of Megan's system.

"I'd say it's good to see you, but I'd hoped we wouldn't have to have this conversation." Dr. Mendoza leaned forward, arms on the desk, fingers clasped together. "How are you doing?"

Megan didn't want to start crying. Again. "We're disappointed. Where do we go from here?"

Dr. Mendoza pulled out her reading glasses and opened their file. "In vitro."

Megan's heart plummeted. Trent looked as devastated as she felt. They had known that was where they were headed, but to actually hear it said aloud . . .

"We're at that point?" Megan's voice was barely a whisper.

"I'm afraid so. You've done six IUIs, and last cycle we had near perfect circumstances."

Megan's hands shook, and she held her back rigid, trying to keep the shivers from overtaking her body.

"What are our chances with IVF?" Trent asked.

"About fifty percent a cycle, so significantly higher than an insemination."

"And if it doesn't work?" Megan didn't want to ask the question, but she had to know.

"We can try again."

Megan brought a trembling hand to her face and tucked a lock of hair behind her ear. "How much does one round of in vitro cost?"

"We can set up a meeting with one of our financial advisers to get a more accurate number, but it will probably be somewhere in the neighborhood of twenty thousand dollars for a fresh cycle."

Megan gulped. Twenty thousand dollars. For one attempt.

"If we're able to freeze eggs, it would cost about five thousand dollars next time. But let's not get ahead of ourselves. IVF works best if you minimize stress. We know there's a link between stress and infertility. And we know it's impossible to relax and not worry about IVF. That's why it's important to get rid of any stresses you can eliminate. Now, I'm sure you have some questions."

They left the doctor's office in a daze. Megan's whole world had imploded. In vitro. In the beginning, she'd honestly never considered they'd have to go to such lengths to have a child.

At home, Trent took Megan's hand and led her to their patio. He pulled her onto the porch swing, and she curled up against his side. They sat there in silence, rocking.

"What are you thinking about?" Trent asked quietly.

"I'm thinking about our wedding day, and how I never imagined life would take us here. I can't believe we're to this point."

He slowly stroked her hair. "You want to do it though, right? In vitro, I mean."

Megan shook her head and felt his arms tense in response. "No. I am sick and tired of the hormones and treatments and appointments and drugs. I want to stop." Trent opened his mouth, and Megan put a finger to his lips. "But I want a baby more. So no, I don't want to do IVF. But I'm willing to give it a try."

His grip relaxed, and he rested his chin on her head. "You don't have to put yourself through this. We can adopt. Sienna—"

"You know that baby's not ours. And I want to give pregnancy every chance."

He nodded, accepting her words. "Then you should cut back at work. Relax and spend more time with the piano."

Megan put her feet down to stop the movement of the swing. "That makes no sense at all. Did you hear how much IVF costs? We need my income now more than ever."

Trent pulled her against him, setting the swing in motion again. "We need to minimize stress so we only have to do it once. My income is enough for our day-to-day expenses. I'm not suggesting you quit, just cut back. We have enough in savings to offset the difference." He hugged her tight. "You need to take it easy. Take on a few more piano students if you're worried about money. At least that doesn't stress you out. I need my wife."

Megan didn't like it, but she couldn't argue with his logic. She did feel tired. She was ready for a break.

The next day, she told her boss she was going to part-time.

"Hey." Megan opened the door wider to let Sienna inside. "How've you been this week?"

Sienna stepped inside, looking dazed. "Juilliard's accepted me for fall semester."

"Sienna, that's great!" Megan laughed, pulling her into a hug. "I'm so proud of you."

Sienna hunched her shoulders and started to cry. "They've accepted me for fall semester. And I can't go until after the baby's born."

"You'll just have to defer a semester. This is Juilliard we're talking about." Megan patted Sienna's hand. "You'll figure it out."

"My mom and I have spent all week on the phone with them. They won't let me defer. I'll have to reapply next year."

"Oh, Sienna." Megan wrapped an arm around her and guided her to the piano bench. Juilliard. Every musician's dream. Gone, just like that. "I'm so sorry."

Sienna looked down, tracing circles on her barely showing stomach. "It's a boy. We found out yesterday."

A boy. Megan blinked. An actual human being. Someone who would grow up to love football and eat entire pizzas and graduate college. "That's . . . great." It sounded lame, but it didn't feel like a congratulations-type moment.

"He was wiggling and jumping around like crazy on the ultrasound. And all I could think was, 'He's the reason I don't get to go to Juilliard.' I want to slap myself for being so selfish."

Megan didn't know what to say. "Maybe Juilliard is still a possibility. You got in once. You can get in again. Let's start practicing for next year's audition, okay?"

Sienna nodded and started to play.

CHAPTER THIRTY
CHRISTINA

Sunday dinners with Elauna and Alexander were as unavoidable as taxes. Christina and Gary had dodged them for two weeks, citing Christina's surgery as the reason, but now they were out of excuses and on the front doorstep with a plate of brownies and a carton of ice cream.

Elauna flung open the door and held out her arms, waiting for Gary's hug. "Hello, darling. I was beginning to think you'd forgotten us."

"Of course not, Mom. We've been busy."

"Oh yes, the surgery. How are you feeling, Christina? It's lucky they were able to remove your appendix before it burst."

Appendicitis—that was the "surgery" they said Christina had. She held out the brownies to Elauna. "I'm feeling better. We brought brownies and ice cream for dessert."

Elauna raised her eyebrows. "Are they one of those mixes?"

Christina was more than a little insulted. "Of course not. I made them from scratch." With all natural and organic ingredients. They were even vegan.

Elauna took the pan, frowning. "Pity." She headed toward the kitchen. "One of the partners brought us the most divine brownies last week. He said his daughter made them from a mix. So simple, and so yummy."

"Unbelievable," Christina muttered.

"Be nice," Gary whispered. "We'll eat and leave, okay?"

"There's a package on the couch for you, dears," Elauna said from the kitchen.

Christina's eyes met Gary's in horror. "But they haven't gone anywhere," she said.

Elauna reappeared in the front entryway. "Well, I can buy things from around here too, Christina."

"I didn't mean—"

Alexander appeared and thrust a box at Gary. "Here. Just open the darn thing so your mother will stop throwing a tantrum."

"I wasn't throwing a tantrum," Elauna insisted.

Gary opened the box, clearly desperate to distract Christina and Elauna from their argument. He lifted the lid and pulled out a stuffed bear.

"It's the Jazz Bear," Elauna said. "The firm had a suite for the last home game, and we decided to go. It was fabulous. The Jazz Bear was so entertaining. I simply had to buy it for your baby."

Christina gritted her teeth. "That's so thoughtful. Except we don't have a baby."

Elauna raised an eyebrow, calling over her shoulder as Christina and Gary trailed her into the living room and took their seats. "I'm aware. I know you like saving those Hispanic children or whatever it is you do at that job of yours. But you need to make my boy a father."

"Mother, it's not just Christina's decision—" Gary began.

"I'm sixty-two years old. I would like to see my grandchildren before I wither away and die."

"Mother—"

Elauna turned in her seat to face Christina, lips pursed. "I know Gary wants to be more established, but you can talk him into a child. You two need to stop this career nonsense and focus on what's really impor—"

"We're infertile!" Christina screamed.

Elauna's mouth fell open mid-word. Alexander closed his newspaper and set it aside. Gary looked like he'd been stunned by a Taser gun. But he nodded, encouraging her to go on.

"We're infertile," Christina repeated, quieter now. "That's what my surgery was for, not appendicitis. We won't have children unless we do in vitro."

Elauna blinked. "That seems like a premature conclusion. How long have you been trying? All I hear about is how you're not ready yet."

"We've been trying for more than a year," Gary said, taking Christina's hand in his.

"You can't be trying hard enough."

Alexander snorted. "Elauna, really. There's only one way to make a baby. I don't think they're doing it wrong."

Christina's face burned. Where was a cave to crawl into when she needed one?

"You need a second opinion," Elauna said. "This is too important to trust to any old doctor."

"We already got one," Gary said. "And if we want children, it's not going to happen the old fashioned way."

Elauna shook her head. "You can't honestly be considering one of those test tube babies. If you have enough faith—"

"IVF is a medical miracle," Christina interrupted. "If we end up having a baby that way, it will be no less amazing than if we got pregnant on our own."

"But you grow your baby in a test tube." Elauna stood, shaking with anger. "It's unethical. Do you know what they do with the babies you don't want? They kill them. You can't do it. I won't let you."

Gary stood as well. "It's not your decision."

"If you prayed harder, were more faithful—"

"That is enough!" Gary turned to Christina. "We're leaving."

Christina should've been surprised that Gary was finally— *finally*—standing up to Elauna. But she was too busy trying not to tear Elauna to shreds. They left the room, Gary's hand at Christina's back.

Elauna's heels clicked on the marble floor behind them, and Christina heard the shuffle of Alexander's slippered feet.

"We need to discuss this, Gary," Elauna said. "You shouldn't make such a rash decision without first consulting your parents. Maybe if you talk to the pastor—"

Gary whirled around. His eyes blazed with fury. "This isn't happening because we lack faith. Christina is a good woman. She is a good wife." He took Christina's hand, pulling her to him. "We're good people. God isn't punishing us. This is just our trial right now." He turned to Christina. "Wait right here, and I'll grab the dessert. Since it isn't a mix, Mother and Father won't miss it."

Elauna followed Gary to the kitchen. "You're being ridiculous. Dinner's all ready. We can discuss this while we eat."

Gary reappeared with the pan of brownies in one hand and ice cream in the other. He motioned for Christina to open the door. "This isn't an issue we need to discuss with you. When you are ready to apologize for your behavior, we'll be more than happy to return to your home."

"Garrison Alexander Vincent!" Christina heard the hysteria and fury in Elauna's voice, but Gary ignored it. Christina opened the car door and got inside while Gary put the brownies and ice cream on the back seat. Elauna was still yelling at them as they drove away.

"I can't believe you did that," Christina said. "Thank you."

Gary's jaw clenched. "She had no right to insult us. No right to question our judgment."

"I know. You defended me, and I appreciate it. I know it's hard for you to go against your mother."

His gaze flicked to Christina, then to the road. "I'm trying to be a good husband. When Mother started talking back there, I suddenly knew we were doing the right thing. Call it a return to teenage rebellion if you want, but we're on the right path." His hands flexed on the steering wheel. "I'm still scared. I'm still uncertain. But I'm in this one hundred percent now. We're where we're supposed to be."

CHAPTER THIRTY-ONE
KYRA

"Make sure you mind Mrs. Everhart and be a sweet girl," Kyra told Sophie as they walked across the lawn to Cassandra's.

"Where are you going?"

"Daddy and I have an appointment."

"For what?"

Kyra's fingernail found its way into her mouth. They were meeting with the financial adviser at the fertility clinic. If Kyra told Sophie, she might let it slip. And then Cassandra would know they were having problems, both in the fertility and financial arena. "Some adult stuff."

"Oh."

They trudged up the stairs to Cassandra's front door, and Sophie rang the bell. Kyra heard the pounding of little footsteps, and then the door flew open. Cassandra opened her mouth, presumably to say hello, but Malachi jumped forward. His corkscrew curls stood up wildly on his head, and he grinned. "We're going to play with bubbles."

"Yay!" Sophie said. She moved to run inside, but Kyra grabbed her arm.

"What are you going to do?" Kyra asked.

"Obey Malachi's mom," Sophie said.

Kyra nodded and gave Sophie a kiss on the cheek. "Good girl. I love you." Sophie disappeared into the house. "Thanks for watching her again," Kyra told Cassandra.

"No problem. I hope everything goes well at the doctor's."

Kyra tried to keep her face impassive. "I'm sure it will."

"I hope David doesn't need surgery," Cassandra said.

A white lie. David's carpal tunnel had been acting up over the last few days—an occupational hazard of being a computer programmer. Kyra hoped her guilt didn't show. "We should be back in a couple of hours."

"No rush. Malachi loves having someone his age to play with."

David waited for Kyra in the car, eighties music blaring from the radio. He sang along to the radio, oblivious to her distress.

"What if we don't qualify?" Kyra asked.

David stopped singing. "For a loan?"

"We have a lot of debt."

"Yeah, but it's not like it's credit card debt. We qualified for the van."

"I guess." Kyra chewed on the end of her fingernail.

"IUI isn't too expensive. It's not like we're financing in vitro."

At the fertility clinic they checked in at the front desk. But instead of staying in the waiting room, a nurse ushered them downstairs to the financial planner's office. Two mismatched filing cabinets stood against the far wall. A long folding table supported a printer and fax machine. Post-it notes were stuck all over the wall behind the computer.

"Diane, your two o'clock is here," the nurse said.

A woman looked up from her computer. Her long gray hair fell nearly halfway down her back in a braid. Chunky turquoise jewelry adorned her ears, fingers, and throat. "Thanks, Leanne." As the nurse left, Diane rose, leaning across the desk to shake each of their hands as they made introductions.

"So, tell me your situation," Diane said.

David and Kyra explained their infertility diagnosis, the medical procedures they needed, and their financial situation.

"Give me a few minutes to crunch some numbers," Diane said when they finished.

"Of course." David leaned back in his chair. Kyra went back to gnawing on her nail, and Diane used the ten key. The fax machine beeped, and papers started slowly printing. A desk fan whirred quietly. Diane's fingernails clicked on the keyboard.

"We don't qualify, do we?" Kyra asked five minutes later.

Diane looked up. "Oh, I've worked with tighter budgets and a lot worse credit scores than this. I'm confident they'll be able to qualify you for a loan, no problem."

Kyra relaxed against her chair, some of the tension easing from her back and shoulders.

Diane turned back to the computer. "I'm giving you estimates for a monthly loan payment with a few different APRs and terms. Just a few more minutes, I'm almost done." She pushed a button and spun around in her chair to grab a paper from the printer. She placed it on the desk in front of them. "Of course, you still have to meet with the loan company, but I work closely with them, and my numbers are usually only off a few dollars, if anything." She explained the table to them. There were different loan amounts, interest rates, and terms in each box, but it gave Kyra and David a good idea of what they were getting into.

"Once you meet with the loan officer, it takes a few weeks to get approved," Diane said. "But the clinic won't make you wait. You can start treatments for your upcoming cycle, and the loan will retro-pay for anything from the point of application on."

"What if we aren't approved?" Kyra asked.

"You will be. Don't worry. But if you aren't, the clinic will work out a repayment plan. Just know they won't let you move forward with treatments until your balance is paid from the previous cycle." Diane pulled a business card from the top desk drawer and handed it to Kyra. "Here's the number for the loan officer. Tell him you've spoken with me, and he'll get you in right away."

They both shook Diane's hand and thanked her for her help.

"Good luck," Diane said. "I hope you get pregnant soon."

Me too, Kyra thought. They smiled and left the office.

"Well?" Kyra asked David as they got in the van.

"I think we should get the loan. We can afford one of the lower payment amounts with longer terms."

"Which begs the question, how big of a loan do we take out? We have no idea how many IUIs this will take."

"Dr. Mendoza said for most couples it happens within the first three IUIs."

"We've already done two."

"Yeah, and I think we should give ourselves two more."

"So a two thousand dollar loan." Kyra looked down at the paper Diane had printed off, locating the column with that amount and going across to the monthly payment. It would be tight, especially with the van payment.

But they could make it work.

"And what if we aren't successful in two IUIs?" Kyra asked.

"We'll take out another loan. But we won't have to. It's going to work."

Another two thousand dollars spent on fertility treatments. Kyra's stomach roiled at the thought. She hated debt. But she couldn't put a price tag on the joy Sophie brought them. So how could she put a price tag on their future children? Once they had the baby—once they held that sweet child in their arms—none of it would matter.

"Let's make the appointment with the loan officer," Kyra said. "I want to keep trying."

When they got home, Kyra walked over to Cassandra's to pick up Sophie. "How was she?" Kyra asked as she helped Sophie put on her shoes.

"Great," Cassandra said. "I barely noticed she was here. How did the doctor appointment go? Will David need surgery?"

Kyra lowered her head, focusing on the buckle on Sophie's shoe. "No surgery."

"Oh, that's a relief."

"Yeah." Time to redirect the conversation. Kyra really hated lying. "Thanks again. Please let me know if I can return the favor."

A few days later, they met with the loan officer and were approved. By the time Kyra started Clomid, the financing had come through. The first bill for the van came a few days later.

The IUI will work, Kyra told herself as she made the payment for the van online. *The loan is worth it. We're doing the right thing. The IUI will work. Please, let it work.*

CHAPTER THIRTY-TWO
CHRISTINA

Christina couldn't help but feel sad as she looked around her classroom. All twenty-eight students were spread around the room, enjoying the laid-back atmosphere of the last day of school. Some sat in the reading nook, lounging on bean bag chairs with a book in hand. Others were in the discovery corner playing game or doing crossword puzzles on the floor. Excited chatter filled the room.

After today, she'd no longer be their teacher, and they'd no longer be her students. The bulletin boards were empty, stripped of all her hard work. The counters had been scrubbed. Student desks gaped empty and black, pushed into one corner of the room.

Christina would miss this class. It never ceased to amaze her how much her students grew in the course of a school year. What had started out as an incredibly rambunctious set of six-year-olds were now a group of seven-year-olds possessing considerably more self-control.

Christina looked at the clock on the wall. Only a half hour left of school. She rang the bell on her desk, and within seconds the noise level dropped considerably. "I need everyone to put away their books and games and meet me at the rug. We're going to read one last story together. Clap if you understand."

Scattered claps sounded, and the students scurried to put away their things and gather at the rug. After five minutes of prodding them to hurry, Christina sat down. From the easel she picked up the book she always read on the last day of school— *Oh, the Places You'll Go* by Dr. Seuss.

Christina struggled to keep back the tears as she read. The last day of school was always hard, but she'd started Lupron injections a few days ago, and her hormones were going nuts. The students laughed at the funny rhymes and offered commentary, mostly using their reader questions to guide the discussion. Christina smiled in pride. At the first of the year, they hadn't even known what reader questions were. Now they asked them without prodding.

Twenty minutes later Christina closed the book, holding it in her lap. "I am going to miss each and every one of you," she said. It was mostly true. There were one or two she definitely wouldn't miss. "It has been a pleasure to teach you this year. I know you will do great things in the second grade."

"We'll miss you too, Mrs. Vincent," a little boy called from the back.

"Yeah, you're the bestest teacher ever," another student agreed. "Can we come back and visit you?"

A needle stabbed her heart. "Of course. I would love that."

Christina had officially renewed her contract last month and would be at Riverside Elementary School for at least another year. She loved her job, but wished she'd be home with a baby instead. At least she wouldn't have to worry about the after-school program next year. She and Trista had been able to put aside their differences, and the district had granted funding. But Christina had declined co-chairing it again. Hopefully she would need the time for doctor appointments and baby shopping.

The bell rang, and kids bustled around the classroom, gathering their backpacks and hugging Christina as they ran out the door. The noise level in the hallway grew, the excitement and energy of the students permeating every brick of the school.

Christina looked around the room and laughed. Books and games littered the floor. In the excitement of summer, items had been forgotten. She walked over to the reading corner and picked a book off the floor. After thirty minutes of straightening, the noise in the hallway had died down to the eerie quiet of summer.

"Are you as sad as I am?"

Christina wasn't surprised to see Stacey, watery-eyed and smiling. Christina picked up another book. "Yes. The last day is always hard."

Stacey waved a hand in front of her face. "This is ridiculous. I shouldn't be sad. I'll be back next year."

"You've decided to come back after having the baby?"

"Yes. My mom's going to watch her while I teach. We can't do without the money."

"I'm sorry," Christina said, and she really meant it. "I know you wanted to stay home."

"T.J. graduates in April. Maybe next year will be my last."

"Yeah." Maybe it would be Christina's, too.

Stacey smiled, crouching down to help Christina pick up the books. "Maybe you'll have a baby soon. And we can both quit and hang out together with our babies." Stacey laughed. "T.J. says I need to find some 'mom' friends because my other friends won't want to hang out with me once I pop. You're not going to ignore me once I have this kid, are you? I swear I won't become boring when I'm a mom. I would be so sad if you stopped talking to me because you've always helped me so much."

"I won't ignore you. Promise."

Stacey wrapped her arms around Christina's shoulders in an awkward side hug. Christina froze, feeling the tiny bulge of Stacey's stomach press against her side. Stacey let Christina go, not seeming to notice she hadn't returned the embrace. "I'm going to miss seeing you every day. Let's get together this summer, okay?"

Christina smiled at Stacey. Not a chance.

It took another hour to straighten up the classroom, but soon Christina ran out of things to do. She looked around the room, then turned off the lights and shut the door. Summer vacation had officially begun.

She was surprised to see Gary's Lexus already in their garage when she arrived home.

He waited inside, a glass of sparkling cider in one hand. "Surprise!"

"What's this?" Christina took the glass uncertainly.

Gary grinned, taking her briefcase and setting it on the floor. "We're celebrating your last day of school." He took her hand, leading her into the kitchen. "C'mon, I ordered a gluten-free cake from that specialty bakery you like."

"Shouldn't you be at work?"

"I decided to take off early. Are you surprised?"

Christina leaned forward and kissed him. "Very."

"I've got a full night planned. We're going to dinner at your favorite restaurant, then catching a chick-flick marathon. I thought we could see those two new romantic comedies you've been eying."

Her heart swelled with love. This was how Gary had been when they were first married. She'd missed him. He had his faults, and they had their difficulties. But he was a good man. "Sounds fabulous." Christina clinked her glass against his. "To a night of relaxation."

He grinned, and they both drank.

Christina held her breath as Dr. Mendoza inserted the ultrasound probe. The doctor looked at the screen, and Christina's fingers curled into a fist. All their hopes, all their dreams, hinged on these few brief moments. Her stomach ached from the constant needles and swollen softball-sized ovaries. If this didn't work, she wasn't sure she had it in her to try again.

Dr. Mendoza removed the probe. "Everything looks great, Christina. You should be ready for the egg retrieval the day after tomorrow."

Christina sighed in relief. "Will there be enough eggs to freeze?"

"We won't know until we see how many fertilize, but I think the odds are in your favor. Give yourself the HCG trigger shot in four hours."

Christina called Gary on her way home. "Everything looks great. The egg retrieval's Wednesday at eight o'clock in the morning."

"I'll let work know I need to take a personal day," Gary said.

Her heart fluttered with happiness. Six months ago, she would've had to beg Gary to take the day off. Now she didn't even have to ask.

Christina was more scared the morning of the egg retrieval than she had been the day of surgery. Gary squeezed her hand as they drove to the clinic.

"Everything's going to go great," he assured her.

"I hope there's enough to freeze."

"You don't think it'll work this time?"

Christina wondered how to reply. Even if it did work, at some point they'd want another baby. "I think it will work. And I think in four or five years, we might want to do it again."

Gary swallowed hard, then nodded. "I've always wanted one of each."

Christina couldn't believe he was thinking that far ahead. "Me too."

At the clinic, she changed into a gown. The nurse started an IV and sedated Christina. By the time Dr. Mendoza arrived, Christina's thoughts were all cloudy, and she struggled to stay awake. Gary held her hand.

"We're going to start the procedure now," Dr. Mendoza said. Her voice sounded far away.

"Okay," Christina mumbled.

She felt dull pricks of pain, and her thoughts drifted as though on waves.

"They're all done, Christina," Gary said. His hand squeezed hers. "You did great."

"How many?"

"They extracted fifteen eggs. Dr. Mendoza said you need to rest for a few hours before we can go home."

Christina nodded and fell asleep. A few hours later, she woke up to Gary's hand on her arm. "Dr. Mendoza is here to talk to us."

Christina tried to focus on Dr. Mendoza, but her eyes kept sliding shut.

"You did well, Christina. Fifteen eggs is a good number," Dr. Mendoza said.

"How many do you think will fertilize?" Christina's words came out slow and labored.

"Hopefully all of them. But sometimes we lose a few. We'll call you in two days and let you know. Start your new medication tonight to help thicken that uterine lining, okay?" Dr. Mendoza turned to Gary. "When she feels ready, help her get dressed, and you can go home. She needs to rest today."

Christina floated in and out of sleep for the rest of the day. The following day, Gary returned to work. Christina still felt tired, so she mostly watched TV and lay in bed.

It was late afternoon when the call came from Dr. Mendoza's office. "Twelve eggs fertilized," the nurse told Christina cheerfully. "We're all ready for you tomorrow at nine o'clock."

Twelve fertilized. They'd have ten to freeze. Christina was excited and scared and happy and terrified.

That night she was a nervous wreck. At midnight, they gave up trying to sleep and went to a late night movie at the theater.

They were tired, but anxious when they arrived at the clinic the next morning.

"It's an exciting day," Dr. Mendoza said. She motioned for Christina to lean back on the exam table. "This shouldn't be nearly as bad as the egg retrieval. I'm going to insert the catheter very slowly to minimize uterine cramping, then insert the eggs. You need complete bed rest for two days, and I don't want you doing anything strenuous until we know if you're pregnant or not."

"Okay," Christina said.

"Here we go."

Christina closed her eyes and prayed it would work.

CHAPTER
THIRTY-THREE
KYRA

Kyra knocked on Cassandra's door, glancing at her watch. Malachi had come over an hour ago asking if Sophie could play, and Kyra had agreed. Her HCG test later that day had her jumpy with nerves, and the reprieve from Sophie's chatter had been welcome.

Cassandra opened the door, and Kyra smiled. "Hi. I'm here for Sophie."

Kyra heard a squeal. Sophie ran around the corner, Malachi close on her heels. Sophie skidded to a halt, then ran in the opposite direction. "Sophie!" Kyra called. "Come back. We're going to be late."

"Oh, do you have an appointment?" Cassandra asked.

"Just a quick one." She hoped Cassandra wouldn't ask here. "Sophie!"

Sophie peeked around the corner, a pout on her lips. "I don't want to go. The doctor's office is boring."

Kyra closed her eyes. Why had Sophie mentioned their destination?

Cassandra's brow creased. "Is something wrong?"

Kyra wracked her brain for a believable explanation. "Oh no. Just some follow-up blood work after the miscarriage."

"Three months later?"

How did Kyra respond to that? Avoid the question. Kyra shrugged. "Come put your shoes on," she told Sophie.

"Why don't you leave her here?" Cassandra said. "She and Malachi are having fun, and you won't have to worry about her at your appointment."

"Yeah!" Sophie said, running off with Malachi before Kyra could protest.

"Are you sure?" Kyra asked. "You've watched her so much lately."

"Really, it's not a problem. She keeps Malachi entertained, so it's actually easier to get things done when she's around."

Kyra glanced at her watch again. She didn't have time to argue. "Thanks. I won't be gone long."

Kyra drove to the office and had her blood drawn without incident. "We'll call you before six tonight," the nurse told her. Kyra paid the receptionist and opened the door to the waiting room. She hoped Sophie wasn't being a nuisance. Kyra would insist Malachi come over tomorrow for a play date to return the favor.

"Kyra?"

She froze. Oh no. No, no, no. Kyra knew that voice. Slowly, she turned around. Nestled together on the couch were Megan and Trent Burke.

Kyra should've known they'd use this fertility clinic. It was one of only a few in the county, and by far the most reputable. Well, she couldn't exactly avoid them now.

"Hi," Kyra said awkwardly, walking over to them. "Um, how are you guys doing?"

"Great," Megan said. "We're having our egg retrieval today." While visiting at church last month, Megan had mentioned they were doing in vitro. Kyra knew Christina was as well.

"Oh, good luck. I hope everything goes well." An incredibly awkward pause. "I should go pick up Sophie."

"Wait!" Megan stood. "Why didn't you tell me you were struggling with infertility?"

Kyra's shoulders sagged. "I don't know." Because it was embarrassing. Because it felt insignificant in light of Megan's five-year struggle.

"How long have you been coming here?"

"About six months." Kyra debated whether to say more. "I just had the HCG draw. For our third IUI."

"I had no idea."

"We haven't told anyone."

"The miscarriage?"

Kyra nodded.

Megan sucked in a breath. "I'm such an idiot. All these months talking to you, and I never knew."

"It's not anywhere near as traumatic as in vitro, I'm sure. You and Christina—"

Megan cut her off. "Infertility hurts. No matter what."

"Megan." They both turned to see a nurse holding a clipboard, waiting expectantly.

"I have to go," Megan said. "But I want to talk more. I hope the IUI worked."

"Thanks. And good luck."

Megan nodded, and she and Trent followed the nurse. Kyra quickly left.

As she climbed into the van, Kyra wondered how she should feel about this. Megan knew, and she would tell Christina. Should Kyra be upset? Pretend nothing had happened?

Relief. That was what Kyra felt. Her heart felt lighter. Megan knew now. And she understood.

Kyra started the van, flipping the A/C to high as her phone started ringing. She looked at the screen, surprised to see Cassandra's number. She never called when she had Sophie.

"Hey," Kyra said uneasily. "Is everything okay?"

"Don't freak out," Cassandra said. Kyra's breathing quickened. "Sophie's going to be fine, but there was an accident. My oldest is watching my kids, and I'm taking her to the pediatrician's now."

"Oh my gosh." Kyra slammed her car into reverse and backed out of her parking spot, turning left toward the pediatrician's. "What's the matter?"

"I think she broke her wrist. You use South Jordan Pediatrics too, right?"

"Yes, I'll meet you there."

Kyra parked at nearly a forty-five degree angle, taking up two entire parking spaces, and ran into the doctor's office. Sophie's pitiful sobs filled the building. Cassandra stood at the check-in counter holding Sophie. Her head rested on Cassandra's shoulder and tears streamed down her cheeks.

"Mommy!" Sophie said, wailing even louder.

Kyra ran over, and Sophie reached out to her with one arm. The other she held close against her chest, and the wrist seemed to hang unnaturally. Kyra took Sophie into her arms, careful of her wrist.

"Are you the mother?" the nurse asked.

Kyra nodded.

"We can take you back now."

Kyra turned to thank Cassandra, but she shook her head. "Oh no, I'm coming with you." Since Cassandra knew all the details, Kyra didn't argue.

"What happened?" Kyra asked. But Dr. Brighton entered the exam room before she could answer.

"What's the matter here?" Dr. Brighton asked.

"I think she broke her wrist," Kyra said.

The doctor groaned. "Oh no. Sophie, how did you do that?"

Sophie clung to Kyra and whimpered.

"I was babysitting," Cassandra admitted. "I was in the restroom and heard a crash, and came out to find her screaming on the floor." She flicked guilt-filled eyes to Kyra. "Malachi said they were playing Superman, and Sophie jumped off the kitchen counter."

"Uh-oh, that's not good," Dr. Brighton said. "Sophie, can I look at your arm?"

Sophie whimpered, but allowed him to extend it. He barely touched her wrist, and she drew back with a scream.

"It's definitely a break," Dr. Brighton said. Sophie clung to Kyra. "Let's get some x-rays to determine the extent of the damage. If it's severe enough, she might need surgery to set it."

Kyra gulped, looking down at Sophie's swollen wrist. It looked horrible. How much was this going to cost? Would it mean they couldn't take out another loan if they need to? Kyra guiltily shoved the thought aside. Sophie came first.

They were taken to a back room that held the x-ray machine.

"Sit on this chair and hold her. We only need her arm on the table," the nurse said. The nurse and Kyra helped Sophie into a lead apron. "Before I forget, is there any chance you could be pregnant?"

Kyra's heart thumped in her chest. She glanced at Cassandra, then at the nurse. "Yes."

"No problem," the nurse said, grabbing another lead apron off a hook. "You need to wear this."

Kyra quickly put on the apron, avoiding eye contact with Cassandra, and cradled Sophie close. Kyra tried to sit, but Sophie screamed and clung to her with her one good arm.

"Shhh," Kyra said. "It's all right. I'm going to sit here on this chair, and you can sit on my lap."

Eventually, with Cassandra and the nurse's help, they managed to get Sophie's arm under the x-ray machine. Then they were led to the exam room and told the doctor would be there shortly. When Dr. Brighton walked in, he held three films. He placed them on the flat whiteboard and flipped on the light to read the scans.

"Broken," he said.

Kyra pulled Sophie tighter, but relaxed her hold when Sophie whimpered.

The doctor pointed to the white line across Sophie's wrist. "The good news is it doesn't need surgery. We'll set and splint it for now, then cast it in a few days when the swelling goes down."

The tears streamed down Kyra's face as they set Sophie's wrist, and she screamed in pain. Kyra held her close and prayed the doctor would work quickly. Sophie mercifully fell asleep against Kyra's chest as they wrapped her arm.

"I've faxed the prescription for her pain medication," Dr. Brighton said as they walked out of the exam room. "I'll see her in three days to cast it."

"How long will she have the cast?" Kyra asked.

"About six weeks."

Six weeks. An eternity.

"I'm so sorry," Cassandra said as they left the office. "I don't even know what to say."

"It could've happened to anyone," Kyra said. "Don't beat yourself up. Thank you for all your help."

"Call me if you need anything." Kyra knew Cassandra wanted to ask if she was pregnant—she could tell by the way Cassandra's eyes flicked to Kyra's flat stomach—but she was too polite to ask.

Kyra slowly put Sophie in her car seat, trying not to jostle her. Her face was red and tear streaked, and she mercifully stayed sleeping. "I'm sorry," Kyra whispered. "I should have been there."

It wasn't Cassandra's fault Sophie fell. She couldn't keep an eye on all four of her children plus Sophie every single moment. This was Kyra's fault. If she would've been there, it wouldn't have happened.

Kyra called David on the drive home and explained the situation. "They set it, but she can't get a cast until the swelling goes down."

"I'm coming right home."

"How?"

"I'll ask a co-worker to drive me, or I'll jog. Do you need anything?"

"Just the prescription from the pharmacy." It was on his way.

Kyra drove slowly, making sure to avoid potholes and make her stops and starts smooth and easy. She had just laid Sophie in bed when David appeared in the doorway, the medicine bottle and plastic syringe in hand.

Kyra measured out the proper dose of medication. Sophie woke up enough to swallow, then promptly fell back asleep. David kissed her gently on the forehead and they left the room.

Kyra shut the door, and David opened his arms. She fell into them, hiding her head in his shoulder.

"Let's go downstairs so we don't wake up Sophie," he said. "Then you can tell me what happened."

David led Kyra into the kitchen and made her hot chocolate—Kyra's comfort drink, even in June. "What happened?" he asked as he set a glass of milk in the microwave to heat.

Kyra explained why Sophie was at Cassandra's. "We're so consumed with getting another baby, I wasn't there for the one we already have." Her shoulders shook, and she put a hand to her mouth to hold back the sobs. "If I hadn't been at the doctor, maybe—"

"Don't say that. It wasn't your fault, and it wasn't Cassandra's. These things happen. The important thing is Sophie's fine."

"She's not fine. She's going to be in a cast for six weeks."

David placed the cup of hot chocolate in front of Kyra. "Drink."

She brought the cup to her lips and sipped. It was the perfect temperature, not too hot and not too cold. "I should have been there," Kyra repeated.

"What's this really about?"

She wrapped her hands around the mug, letting the warmth seep through her. "I feel like my energy is so devoured by the miscarriage and getting pregnant that I can't even be a good mom to Sophie."

"You're a great mom."

"Not lately. I've been snippy and cross and short on patience."

"I haven't noticed."

"Sophie wanted to stay at Cassandra's. And I wanted to be alone. So I let Cassandra convince me to leave her, and Sophie got hurt."

"Sophie will be fine."

"It could've been so much worse. She almost needed" —Kyra choked on the word— "surgery."

David sat on the stool next to hers. "Hopefully the IUI worked, and you won't spend much time at the clinic anymore. Have you gotten a call from the doctor yet?"

Kyra hadn't even thought about the blood test since Sophie's accident. She checked her phone for a voice mail and found one from the clinic.

Negative.

She clutched at her chest, her heart pounding. Her vision blurred, and she hung up the phone.

"Well?" David asked.

Kyra shook her head. "I can't," she gasped. David pulled her close, stroking her hair. "I can't do this again." She struggled for breath.

"Shhh. We don't need to talk about this right now. We can take a month off. Kyra, breathe. You're scaring me."

"I—" A rustle on the baby monitor cut off Kyra's words, followed by Sophie's ear-splitting wail.

Kyra shook her head to clear the black spots in her vision and ran up the stairs. David was right behind her.

"Kyra, go lie down. I've got this," he said.

She sent him a withering glare. "I've been gone quite enough today. I'm going to comfort my daughter now." And she opened Sophie's door.

CHAPTER THIRTY-FOUR
MEGAN

"That was weird," Megan told Trent as they waited in the exam room for Dr. Mendoza.

"What?"

She gave an exasperated sigh. "Kyra! Here. At the fertility clinic."

He leaned forward and gave Megan a kiss. "What I'm concerned about right now is everything going well with the egg retrieval."

Megan's stomach clenched. "That's why I keep bringing up Kyra—to keep my mind off of things."

Dr. Mendoza walked in, and a nurse followed behind her.

"Ready, Megan?" Dr. Mendoza asked as the nurse prepped Megan's arm for the IV.

"Ready as I'll ever be," Megan said.

"Your sperm count wasn't fantastic, but adequate," Dr. Mendoza told Trent as the nurse worked. "Four-point-seven million. I would've liked to see it over five million, but we can work with this."

A shudder of relief coursed through Megan as Trent's shoulders visibly relaxed. They'd been so concerned the whole cycle would have to be canceled because the sperm count wouldn't be high enough.

"I still think we should do ICSI," Dr. Mendoza continued. "To give this cycle the best chance."

ICSI. Intracytoplasmic sperm injection. Instead of throwing Trent's sperm in a petri dish with Megan's eggs, they'd carefully pick out the best sperm, and inject one directly into each egg. Of course, it would cost more money. But it was worth it after coming this far.

"Let's do it," Megan said. "Whatever gives us the best odds."

"Of course," Dr. Mendoza said. "Let's get started."

Megan took a deep breath and gave Trent a reassuring smile. This would work. It had to.

———◆◆◆———

"Hey, Christina." Megan lay flat on the couch, resting today at Trent's insistence, and held the cell phone against her ear.

"Hey, Meg. How did the egg retrieval go? I thought about you all day yesterday."

"It went good. We retrieved five eggs. They're using ICSI on all of them."

"That's great."

They had hoped for more eggs, but were thrilled they'd gotten any. "You'll never believe who I saw at the fertility clinic."

"Who?"

"Kyra."

"Are you serious?"

Megan shifted, trying to find a more comfortable position. "I know. Why would she keep that a secret from us? We could've been helping her the last three months."

"Maybe she didn't want us to know."

That Megan couldn't comprehend. "Why?"

"I know you don't see it this way, but it's embarrassing for a lot of women. We're really good friends, and I still didn't tell you until my surgery."

"Yeah, and that was silly of you."

"All I'm saying is I understand where Kyra's coming from. She's actually why I'm calling. Did you know Sophie broke her arm?"

"I had no idea." It must've happened after she saw Kyra at the clinic. "Is everything okay?"

"Yeah. She'll be in a cast for six weeks but doesn't need surgery."

"That's got to be stressful for Kyra, especially on top of everything else. Maybe we should take her out for a girl's night. Dinner, a movie, the whole thing."

"Sounds fun," Christina agreed.

"I can do it next weekend, after the egg transfer and bed rest."

"I'll call her and let you know."

Fifteen minutes later, Christina called Megan back. "Girls' night next Friday. Seven o'clock. I'll drive."

"See you then." Megan wondered how that night would play out.

———•••———

Megan wasn't sure why she was so nervous for their girls' night out.

"You're preening way more than you do for a date," Trent said with a pout.

"It's been a long time since I went out with friends. Don't be jealous." Megan winked.

"What's the plan?"

"Dinner first, then maybe a movie. We'll see how the evening goes."

"Just take care of yourself," he said gruffly. "It's only been a week since the transfer."

And seven days until they found out if it worked—tomorrow for Christina. Like Megan could forget.

Christina waited for Megan in her driveway, and a few moments later they pulled up to Kyra's. The front door opened, and Kyra stepped outside. Megan saw tiny Sophie waving goodbye at the door, her arm overwhelmed by a pink cast, while David stood protectively beside her.

"Hi," Kyra said as she climbed into the backseat.

"You ready for an awesome night?" Megan asked.

Kyra smiled, but it seemed unsure. "Of course."

Christina rolled her eyes. "Megan seems to think we're all sixteen and going to spend the night talking about boys."

Megan made a *psh* sound. "You say that like it's a bad thing. I'm eternally sixteen at heart."

They made polite small talk during the drive and while waiting for their food at the restaurant. Once the waitress left,

Christina and Kyra dug into their meals. Megan sighed and did the same. Were they going to make light conversation all evening?

Maybe Megan should follow Christina's advice and pretend she'd never seen Kyra at the fertility clinic.

They were halfway done with their food when Megan set down her fork. She wasn't Christina. "Are we seriously going to avoid this topic all evening?"

Kyra looked like a deer in the headlights, and Christina frowned.

"We don't need to talk about it," Christina said. "Not if Kyra doesn't want to."

"Yes, we do." Megan locked eyes with Kyra. "I know you're hurting from the miscarriage. I know you're mad and angry and upset." Megan shook her head, the tears burning. "Christina and I are mad too. I am so sick and tired of everyone acting like infertility is a subject to be avoided. It hurts, and it sucks, and not talking about it makes everything worse. You knew I was struggling with infertility, and you knew Christina was. And yet you never said anything. That hurt."

"Not everyone wants to talk about it," Christina said, casting a glance at Kyra.

"Yes, some of us like to hold things in until we explode at our in-laws." Megan gave Christina a pointed glance.

Christina opened her mouth to retort, but Kyra broke in. "Megan's right. It does make it worse not to talk about it. I'm sorry I never said anything. I was . . . embarrassed. They can't even tell me why I can't get pregnant. And I felt insignificant. IUI pales in comparison to in vitro."

"Your problems aren't less significant," Megan said. "I am so sorry you felt that way."

"Infertility hurts, no matter the cause," Christina said quietly.

"Aren't you mad?" Megan asked them. "Mad at infertility?"

"Yeah," Kyra said. "I'm furious it's so hard for me to get pregnant. I'm furious about the miscarriage. Why did God give me a baby, then take it away? And I'm furious infertility made me be at the doctor's when Sophie broke her arm instead of home, keeping her safe." Her voice caught on the last word. "I feel like I'm so busy trying to figure out how to get the next kid I can't even focus on the one I have, and I don't know how to make it stop. Because I can't stop thinking about it. Every second of every day it's on my mind." Her eyes shimmered with tears, her voice raw with emotion. "I'm tired of not talking about it. Of pretending like it doesn't hurt. It sucks. I hate it, and I'm bitter, and I don't care."

Silence. Christina looked shocked at Kyra's outburst, but Megan wasn't. She'd been infertile long enough to know it had probably been a long time coming.

What did shock Megan was Christina's reply. "I'm mad too," Christina said. "I'm so mad I can't even see straight. And sometimes I think this whole thing is my fault. Gary and I focused on our careers, and maybe we lost our window of opportunity. Truthfully, I feel like I don't deserve to be a mom. I chose teaching over motherhood, and now I'm getting what I deserve."

"Don't say that." Kyra looked shocked. "You're going to be an excellent mother."

Christina shrugged. "You don't know that. No one does. The whole thing is a crap shoot."

"I don't even want to be optimistic that IVF worked, because I can't handle the hurt if it didn't," Megan admitted. "Why do teenage girls get pregnant in the back of cars every day, but women who are ready for children can't? It's like they're accidentally blessed with what I've prayed and begged for without any results."

"It must be so hard to teach Sienna," Kyra said.

"It was," Megan said. "I used to be so jealous of girls like her. But the last few months I've watched Sienna, and I think, 'How is this fair to anyone?' She's having such a hard time, and my heart hurts every time I see her. I can't be jealous. I definitely can't hate her. Her entire future has changed because of one error in judgment."

Christina nodded. "I think in vitro worked. For both of us." She turned to Kyra. "And you'll get pregnant soon."

"Our last IUI failed," Kyra said. "We met with Dr. Mendoza, and she wants us to do one more before moving on to in vitro. Sometimes I feel like we're throwing money down a really large drain."

The waitress appeared then. "Can I get you some dessert?" she asked.

Megan usually passed on dessert at restaurants, but this called for chocolate. She pointed to a chocolate brownie heart attack on the menu. "Bring us three of these. We're all in serious crisis mode."

The waitress paused, then took the dessert menu from Megan. "I'm sorry to hear that. I hope it's nothing to do with your meal."

"We're infertile," Megan said. "All of us. And I don't think the food's to blame."

The waitress's mouth dropped open, and then she walked away without saying a word. Kyra burst into laughter, and Christina shook her head.

By the time dinner ended, they were all laughing and crying and complaining about their infertility.

"I think we need to have a bonfire," Megan said as they all stood to leave. "My house. Let's forget the movie and go buy the fixings for s'mores."

"We just had dessert," Christina said.

Megan shrugged. "So what? We'll have an impromptu infertility funeral."

Christina's eyebrows rose. "A funeral? Really? That's a little . . ."

"It's perfect," Kyra said.

"I was going to say morbid," Christina said.

"I'm serious. Let's do it for all the babies we haven't had. For all the dreams that have been broken. For everything we've given up."

"Okay." Christina glanced back and forth between Kyra and Megan. "I think you're crazy, but I'm in."

They stopped at the store and bought graham crackers, marshmallows, and chocolate. Trent was surprised when they all walked through the front door. He reached for the remote, muting ESPN.

"You ladies are home early."

"We're going out back for a bonfire," Megan said. "It's a funeral for our infertility."

Trent didn't even raise an eyebrow. He nodded as though that made perfect sense and unmuted the TV. "Don't burn yourself. Call me if you need a Boy Scout."

They didn't need a Boy Scout, and in no time they had the fire blazing.

"What now?" Christina asked, staring into the flames.

Megan thought about this. How were they supposed to heal from this kind of hurt and pain? "I think it's time we accept ourselves for who we are," Megan said.

Christina snorted.

"I'm serious!" Megan turned to Kyra. "Kyra, you have a child. How did you feel about yourself when you had Sophie?"

Kyra looked surprised at the question. "Good, I guess. I mean, I never really thought about it before. I finally had a clear purpose in life. When they laid Sophie in my arms for the first time, I couldn't believe God had trusted me with this perfect little human. That out of all the women in the world He could have sent Sophie to, He chose me." She clutched her hands together in her lap. "When we didn't get pregnant again right away, it felt like the Lord took back His trust. Like I hadn't done a good job with Sophie, and He wasn't sure if I should have another chance. But we got pregnant, and I thought, 'Wow, He does trust us.' When we had the miscarriage, it felt like some big cosmic joke."

Christina and Megan didn't say a word. Megan had always wondered if God didn't trust her enough, if that was why she had PCOS. But somewhere in the back of her mind, she'd rationalized that she'd never had children, so how could He possibly not trust her with one? But Kyra's fear was so raw and real.

The fire crackled, the only sound between them. Kyra hung her head and sobbed. Her whole body convulsed with the movement. Megan sat next to her on the bench, placing an arm around her shaking shoulders.

"He must not trust me." Kyra's words were muffled. "Because He took away our baby, our second chance. And I don't know if I'll ever get another child."

Megan looked at Christina across the firelight, helpless.

"That's the most ridiculous thing I've ever heard," Christina said. Her words were harsh, and Megan winced. Christina's voice softened. "It's ridiculous, because I've never seen a better mother than you."

Kyra wiped at her eyes. "You're just saying that."

"No, I'm not. I see a lot of parents through teaching. A lot of really, really bad parents. And I can assure you that you're not one of them."

"Sophie broke her arm."

"Yeah. And it was an accident. I've met parents who purposely broke their child's arm. You try, Kyra. You make mistakes, but you try."

"I have an idea," Megan said. "I'll be right back." She returned a few minutes later with a notebook and pen for each of them. "Write everything you hate about infertility on here. Everything that's unfair and unjust and hurtful. Write down all the bad thoughts and feelings you have."

"And then what?" Kyra asked.

Megan smiled. "We'll toss it into the fire and burn it. Tonight we're starting fresh, ladies. We are not our infertility. This isn't a punishment. It's just life. And we are going to stop living like victims and start choosing how to think and feel and act about this. We are strong, independent women. We're more than this."

For the next fifteen minutes they were quiet. Megan hunched over her notebook, barely able to read what she wrote in the dim glow of the fire. Tears streamed down her face as she wrote. *I hate feeling like my body is broken. I hate feeling like I've failed Trent. I hate that I am left out of so many conversations because I don't have kids. I hate feeling sad. I hate not being in control of the situation.*

On and on Megan wrote. Eventually she ran out of things to say. She stopped and looked up. Christina and Kyra were both waiting patiently.

"Well?" Megan asked.

"I'm ready to burn this thing," Christina said.

They all stood and walked to the fire.

"On the count of three?" Megan asked. They nodded. "One . . . two . . . three!"

They threw their pages on the fire. Flames licked at the paper. Megan watched in fascination as the fire curled around the edges, turning it to ash.

I am enough for Trent, even if we never have children. I can still live a fulfilling and happy life, even if I'm never a mother. The Lord has given me this trial because He knows I'm strong enough to handle it. Megan listed off every positive thing she could think of until the notebooks were completely consumed by flames. Flecks of ash rose into the air, disappearing into the night sky.

"Well?" Megan looked between Christina and Kyra.

"I feel better," Christina said.

"Lighter," Kyra added.

"Maybe IVF worked," Megan said.

"I think it's going to work. For both of you." Kyra was quiet for a moment. "Sophie keeps telling me her baby brother is on the way. I'm going to start believing her."

"To positivity," Megan said. "Who wants a s'more?"

CHAPTER
THIRTY-FIVE
CHRISTINA

Christina had never been so nervous for a blood test. As the nurse prepared the needle, then inserted it into the vein in her arm, she felt nothing but panic.

The nurse slapped a label on the vial of blood and told Christina she'd get a phone call before the end of the day with the results.

All day to think, and no work to keep her mind off things. Back at home, Christina looked around her perfectly clean and orderly house. There were no dishes in the sink. No laundry to be washed. Nothing at all to distract her.

She walked resolutely to the pantry and pulled out the stepstool. Behind the bins of xylitol and gluten-free flour was her secret stash. She selected a can of chocolate fudge frosting. She had at least four hours of shows on her DVR. Today seemed like a good day for laziness and indulging.

She watched all four hours of unrealistic dating scenarios and miraculous weight loss transformations. Then she watched another hour of mindless sitcom reruns. She was debating between two movies when the telephone rang. Her hand shook, and she frantically tried to push the talk button on the cell phone.

"Hello?" she squeaked. "Yeah, this is Christina."

"I have the results of your HCG test."

Christina clutched at the phone, her emotions as taught as a wire.

"Congratulations, Mrs. Vincent. You're pregnant."

The wire broke. Christina dropped her head into her hands with a sob.

After she hung up the telephone, she sat there in stunned silence, the tears flowing. Images flickered on the TV, the sound muted and silent. She stared at the screen, blurry through her tears, unable to comprehend what she'd been told.

Pregnant. Christina put a hand to her stomach and felt it flutter. She knew it wasn't the baby—just nerves—but she laughed anyway. Pregnant!

She really shouldn't have eaten that whole jar of frosting.

Pregnant. She was having a baby.

Christina grabbed her purse. She had to deliver this kind of news to Gary in person. Would he be happy? He'd come a long way, but she still didn't know what to expect.

She walked into the law office thirty minutes later.

"Hello, Mrs. Vincent," the receptionist said. "I absolutely love that shirt on you. You're positively glowing."

The pregnancy glow. It was already happening. To Christina. She had the pregnancy glow.

"Thank you." Butterflies of excitement and nerves swarmed in her stomach. "I'm heading up to Mr. Vincent's office."

The receptionist nodded and picked up the phone. "I'll let him know you are on your way."

"No need. I want to surprise him."

The receptionist paused, then set the phone in its cradle. "Okay. Go right on up."

Did she just wink at Christina? What did it matter? They were having a baby! Christina hoped Gary would be happy. She hoped this moment wouldn't be ruined.

She waited impatiently for the elevator, forcing herself not to bounce from foot to foot. As she rode up to the fifth floor, she prayed she wouldn't run into Gary's father. Christina hadn't seen him since that last disastrous dinner. Did Alexander and Elauna even know they'd done IVF? Would they accept and love Gary and Christina's child?

Alexander was nowhere to be seen. Luck was on Christina's side—again. Was this really happening to her, or was it a fantastic dream?

Gary's office door stood open. His back was toward the door, head bent and phone pressed to his ear as he sat on the edge of his desk. Christina slipped into his office, closing the door quietly. His eyebrow lifted when he saw her. He knew. He had to.

And he was going to be as excited as she was.

"Daniel, something has come up. Can I call you later? Yeah. Okay. Mmm hmm. Thank you." He hung up. "Well?" Christina heard the hope, fear, and worry wrapped in that one simple word.

"You're going to be a daddy. We're having a baby."

Gary let out a whoop, grabbing her up in a bear hug. She laughed.

"We're pregnant?" he asked, as though he couldn't believe it either.

"We're pregnant."

Gary buried his head in her neck. Christina clung to him, tears streaking down her face. After all their marriage had suffered the last five months, they were finally having a baby.

"I'm taking you out to celebrate." Gary's voice was gruff, working to hide his emotion.

Christina laughed, wiping her eyes. "Right now? It's only three o'clock."

He shrugged and pulled his suit coat off the back of his chair, then slipped it on. Typical Gary. Even in ninety-degree weather, he was always the professional. "I think I can take off early for this."

They went to dinner at their favorite restaurant. They laughed and talked as they hadn't since their dating days. "I can't believe it," they kept saying. "I can't believe this is happening."

They were on their way home when Christina got the text from Megan. *Well?*

Christina showed it to Gary. "Can we go over there and tell them?" she asked as they pulled into their driveway. "Looks like they're home."

Gary grinned. "If you want to tell them first, before our parents or anyone else, be my guest."

Christina hadn't thought about it like that. Did she want Megan to know before her own mother? If Megan wasn't pregnant, would their friendship survive? "We've been through this together. And she's still waiting to find out. I think I owe it to her to let her know."

Megan threw open the door before Christina even knocked. She took one look at Christina and shrieked. "You're pregnant!" Megan hollered over her shoulder. "Trent, get your butt in here."

Relief coursed through Christina. She should've known Megan would react like this. Christina feared her grin would split her cheeks. Megan pulled Gary and Christina inside, hugging them both. Trent appeared and offered his congratulations as well. They laughed and talked, and the excitement swelled around Christina, filling the whole house.

It was almost an hour before they got home.

"I have something for you," Gary said, tugging her upstairs.

In their bedroom he ducked into the closet, reappearing with a box in his hand. Christina took the box from him, and he motioned for her to sit down on the bed.

"When did you get this?" she asked.

He shrugged. "I guess it was right after your surgery. I saw it at a boutique while I was out with a client. Open it."

Christina eagerly unwrapped the gift. She lifted the lid to find a porcelain statue of a mother in a rocking chair, holding a baby. She let out a gasp. "Gary, it's beautiful."

He turned the figurine over to reveal a turnkey. He twisted it, and the statue started playing a lullaby—"All Through the Night." He placed it back in Christina's hand. "I saw it and knew it had to be yours."

The tears gushed, and she leaned forward to hug him. In that moment, everything was absolutely perfect.

CHAPTER THIRTY-SIX
KYRA

The bonfire with Megan and Christina left Kyra freer and more optimistic than she had been since the first IUI. When Christina called a few days later with the news she was pregnant, Kyra was thrilled. An infertility survivor. It gave her hope she'd have her own happy ending.

Taking Clomid for the fourth time wasn't as challenging as the others. Maybe it was because Kyra knew what to anticipate and was therefore better prepared to handle the side effects.

Today would be their fourth IUI. She could hardly believe they were to this point again. If this didn't work, they'd have to take out another loan to continue. But should they? Maybe all the failed attempts were the Lord's way of telling them they weren't supposed to have more children. Did she want to keep putting her body through this?

"I'm sorry I can't be there today," David apologized as he got ready for work. "I have to attend this meeting."

"It's okay," Kyra lied. "It's not like we haven't done this before." Wouldn't it be ironic if she ended up getting pregnant on the one IUI David wasn't present for? It did hurt that he wouldn't be there, but she knew it couldn't be helped.

After dropping David's sample at the clinic, Kyra left David at work.

"Where are we going now?" Sophie asked from the back seat.

"Mrs. Burke's. Remember, she's going to babysit you." It had felt so good to be honest about why Kyra needed a sitter.

"Are you going to the doctor again?"

Kyra glanced in the rear view mirror at Sophie. "Yes."

"Is my baby brother coming soon?"

Kyra pulled into the Burke's driveway. "I hope so."

She got Sophie out of the van, and they walked up the front steps to Megan's. She opened the door before Kyra even had a chance to knock.

"I saw you pull up," Megan said. "Come in."

"Thanks for watching her," Kyra told Megan as they stepped inside.

"No problem. I've got crayons and movies and all sorts of fun things. We'll be fine."

"Mommy says you play the piano," Sophie said. "I want to learn."

Megan laughed. "We can do that too, although it might be hard with your cast." Her voice turned serious. "Good luck, Kyra. I've been praying every night it will work this time."

"Thanks." Kyra swallowed back her emotion. They needed it.

At the doctor's office, Kyra flipped through a magazine until a nurse called her back. The procedure went just as the others—flawlessly. It was another textbook perfect cycle, with three follicles and a sperm count of ninety million. The only difference was David's absence. After the procedure, Kyra lay on the exam table for the required thirty minutes, her eyes squeezed shut as she prayed.

We spent all this money, and took out that loan, Kyra reminded the Lord. *We've put all our trust in You. We're doing our part, but we need a miracle to make this happen.*

The door opened. "You can get dressed now, Kyra," the nurse told her. Kyra nodded, and soon left the clinic to begin her two-week wait.

She pulled up to Megan's at the same time as a red Suburban. A teenage girl climbed out of the driver's side, her stomach poking out. Sienna. It must be her.

Should Kyra wait until Sienna went inside, then go herself? No, that would be awkward. Should Kyra walk beside Sienna but not say anything? No, that would be weird too.

Kyra got out of the car. They both headed toward the front door. Sienna smiled uncomfortably.

"Hi," Kyra said. "I'm Kyra."

"Sienna," she replied.

"You must be one of Megan's piano students."

Sienna nodded, but said nothing.

"I live a few blocks away. She's babysitting my daughter."

"Oh."

Kyra forced herself to keep smiling, and Sienna rang the doorbell. A moment later the door opened.

"Mommy!" Sophie launched herself at Kyra's legs.

"Hey, baby girl." Kyra leaned down and hugged Sophie, then looked up at Megan. "Was she good?"

"A perfect angel," Megan said. "Hey, Sienna. Go start on your scales. I'll be there in a minute."

"I learned a scale. And I did it with only one hand." Sophie turned to Sienna. "Do you know scales?"

Sienna smiled, showing signs of loosening up for the first time. "I do."

"Can I play you my scale?" Sophie asked. "I worked really hard."

"Sophie, Mrs. Burke needs us to leave so she can teach Sienna," Kyra said.

"It's fine." Sienna smiled at Sophie. "I would love to hear a scale."

"I did promise her she could play it for you," Megan said.

"If you're sure." Kyra stepped inside, and Megan shut the door.

Sophie pranced over to the piano bench, climbing up on it and placing her one good hand on the keyboard. She started playing a scale, hitting a few wrong notes but mostly getting them right.

If they weren't paying for fertility treatments, Sophie could take piano lessons. The thought came unbidden, and Kyra quickly pushed it away. Sophie played the last note, and Kyra clapped loudly.

"Great job, sweetie." Kyra leaned down and kissed her head.

"You're a natural," Sienna said.

Sophie turned on the bench to face them, beaming. "I can't play with this arm cuz it's broke."

"I can see that," Sienna said. "How did you break it?"

"I flied like Superman." Sophie thrust her arms out, flapping them like wings. "But I felled."

"Ouch." Sienna scrunched up her nose.

"That was really good, Soph, but we need to go now," Kyra said. "Go put on your shoes."

"Okay. Bye." Sophie waved at Sienna and ran to the front door.

"Start working on your scales," Megan told Sienna. "I'll be back."

Kyra followed Megan to the entryway and bent down to help Sophie with her shoes. Music swelled, filling the house with its rich notes, which radiated emotion. "Those are scales?" Kyra asked.

Megan laughed. "Hard to believe, huh? That girl is going to do amazing things. Juilliard wants her."

"Impressive." Kyra's eyes flicked to Sienna. Her back curved as she bent over the piano keys, coaxing the scales into a beautiful crescendo. What would she do at Juilliard with a child? "Thanks again for watching Sophie."

"Anytime." Megan smiled at Sophie. "We're good buds."

"Megan's my friend," Sophie said.

Kyra laughed. "We'll let you get back to Sienna." She sobered. "Have you heard anything yet?"

"Friday."

"You'll let me know?"

Megan smiled. "Only if you let me know."

"It's a deal." Hopefully they would both have good news.

CHAPTER THIRTY-SEVEN
MEGAN

A fifty percent chance of success. That was all Megan could think about as she paced the house, waiting for the call telling her whether their twenty thousand dollars had been worth it. The thought of that much money made her ill.

Christina was on the positive side of that statistic. Did that mean Megan would be on the negative?

A fifty-fifty shot. A fifty percent chance her dreams would come true. A fifty percent chance they'd be shattered.

Trent wrapped his arms around her. "How are you doing?" he asked. He'd taken the day off work so they could be together.

Megan opened her mouth to respond, but the phone rang. She looked down at the cell, buzzing in her hands. Trent released her, and she answered with a shaking finger, putting it on speaker. "Hello?"

"Congratulations." The word was barely out of the nurse's mouth before Trent and Megan screamed and hugged each other, jumping up and down.

The nurse laughed. "You're pregnant!"

"Oh, thank you." Megan sank onto the couch and began to cry. "Thank you so much for calling."

Trent took the phone from Megan and finished the call, then wrapped his arms around her as she bawled.

"Two thousand seventy-two days," Megan choked. "Almost six years. That's how long it took us to get here."

Trent kissed her deeply. "And it was worth every day to get to this point."

She cradled her stomach with her hands. "Yes, it was."

They went shopping for baby clothes. They didn't buy anything, but it felt amazing to look, knowing they'd buy these items soon. They went to dinner and discussed baby names and which room they would convert into the nursery. Then they stopped at the Vincents to tell them they'd been successful too.

Christina hugged Megan tight. "We're pregnant," she said. "Both of us. Can you believe it?"

Megan shook her head, laughing. "No. I really can't."

Two thousand seventy-two days. Two thousand seventy-two times she'd woken up without being a mother. But never again.

It had been two weeks since the positive pregnancy test, and today Megan would finally see her baby. After nearly six years of waiting, hoping, and praying, it was happening.

Trent squeezed Megan's hand as Dr. Mendoza inserted the ultrasound probe. An image of Megan's uterus popped up on the screen, all fuzzy lines and unclear images.

"Where is it?" Megan asked anxiously. "Where's my baby?" Dr. Mendoza pointed to a dot on the screen. "Here. There's the yolk sack." She outlined it with her finger.

Trent and Megan stared in awe. "There it is," Trent said. "We did it, Meg."

"Can we hear the heartbeat?" Megan asked.

"No heartbeat yet." Dr. Mendoza drew lines on the screen, measuring the baby. "You're right on target, though. Baby's measuring at six weeks four days."

No heartbeat. Megan's chest tightened. That didn't sound good. "Why isn't there a heartbeat?"

"Don't worry. It's common not to hear one this early." She withdrew the probe and Megan sat up. Dr. Mendoza cleared her throat. "I don't want you to get your hopes up, but there might be another yolk sack."

Another yolk sack. Another . . .

"Twins?" Megan's heart skipped a beat. Two babies. Twins. "What do you mean 'might'?" Trent asked.

"It's too early to tell for sure. Come back in two weeks, and we'll know. We'll hear the heartbeat then, too. Everything looks great. Congratulations, you two."

"Twins," Megan said as soon as they were in the car. "Can you believe it? We might have two babies."

Trent had a huge smile on his face. "Isn't it great? I really hope it's two, but I'm happy either way."

Megan laughed, then frowned. "But Trent, what if it is two?" Double the diapers. Double the feedings. Double the everything. She was only one person. How would she take care of both of them? She'd seen how harried Sienna's mother always was. "What if it's not two?" How was it possible she'd already latched onto the idea of twins? Already longed for there to be two children? She'd learn to do things in doubles quickly enough. After all the pain and anguish of their years of infertility, Megan loved the idea, despite the added hardships she knew it would bring.

She had met Sienna's brothers, after all.

Trent squeezed Megan's hand. "We'll take things as they come. For now, let's be happy we're pregnant. We will love those babies, no matter if there's one or twelve."

"Twelve!"

Trent laughed. "Relax. Dr. Mendoza only mentioned two babies. I think we're in the clear."

The next two weeks were incredibly long, in more ways than one. Megan got sicker. And sicker. And sicker. She cut back her hours at work to practically nothing. Puking during house showings wasn't a great selling point. Christina was sick as well, and they spent a lot of time together, watching TV and being blissfully miserable.

The thought of twins nagged at the back of Megan's mind, but by the time their second doctor's appointment rolled around, she had convinced herself it wasn't happening. She was thrilled to have one. No matter the number, they were blessed.

Trent took off work to go to the appointment with her. In the exam room Megan hopped onto the table.

"Are you ready to hear that heartbeat?" Dr. Mendoza asked.

"You have no idea how ready." Megan watched the screen anxiously, and soon her uterus appeared. The white blob was bigger than last time. "Wow, baby's really grown. How does she look?"

"She?" Trent asked. "That could be our son you're talking about."

Dr. Mendoza peered at the screen intently.

"Everything's fine, right?" Megan asked. "The baby's okay?"

"I can't believe it." Dr. Mendoza laughed and grabbed a pen out of her coat pocket to point at the screen.

Twins. Megan's heart sat somewhere in the region of her throat. Oh my gosh. It was happening.

"Here's the baby." Dr. Mendoza pointed to a tiny flicker in the middle of the blob and pushed a button. Sound filled the room, the thu-thump, thu-thump, thu-thump of a heartbeat. Megan's breath caught. It was more beautiful than any piano concerto. "One hundred sixty-seven beats per minute. A good heartbeat." Dr. Mendoza pointed to the screen again. "And here's another baby." A slightly faster sound filled the room. "One hundred seventy-two beats per minute for that one."

Megan stared at Trent. "Twins," he breathed. Megan shook her head in thrilled disbelief.

"And this is the third baby right here." Megan whipped her head around to stare at Dr. Mendoza as a third sound filled the room. "One hundred fifty-nine beats per minute. Congratulations. You're having triplets."

For perhaps the first time in Megan's life, she was speechless. "Triplets?" She stared hard at the screen. It all looked like one big white jelly-bean to her.

"Three babies?" Trent repeated. "Where?"

"But we only put in two eggs," Megan said.

Dr. Mendoza pushed a button on the screen to freeze the pane and withdrew the ultrasound probe. Megan leaned forward, and Trent peered over her shoulder.

"Here's Baby A," Dr. Mendoza said. "Here's the fetus, and right here is the outline of the sack. Here's Baby B, and here's Baby C." Dr. Mendoza pointed to the first baby. "This baby—Baby A—is a fraternal triplet. These two, however—Baby B and Baby C—are identical twins. One of the eggs split."

The image disappeared from the screen. Megan opened her mouth to protest, but Dr. Mendoza pulled off a long string of photos and handed them to her. Megan stared down at the three little dots, distinct in her mind now that they'd been pointed out. Three people were inside of her. Triplets. Three babies. Three.

"I'm so happy for you both," Dr. Mendoza said. Was that a tear in her eye? "Moments like this make my job worth it. Get dressed, then meet me in my office. I'm sure you have lots of questions, and we'll get to all of them."

Megan should have lots of questions, but her mind froze. She was stunned, unable to wrap her head around what she just heard. "Triplets," she whispered as she dressed.

Trent shook his head. His smile was so wide Megan worried it would split his face. "An instant family."

So many of their friends who had married at the same time as them were on their third child. Now they were going to catch up all at once. It was exhilarating and overwhelming.

Dr. Mendoza was already in her office when they arrived. "Sit down. Let's talk." Trent and Megan nodded mutely and sat. "You seem in shock. How are you feeling?"

"Excited," Trent said at the same time Megan said, "Scared witless."

"Both perfectly normal reactions," Dr. Mendoza said. "What are you scared about, Megan?"

What wasn't she scared about? "The pregnancy. Getting all three babies here safely. The logistics of taking care of them. I'm scared to let myself be excited, in case something goes wrong."

"I'll do everything in my power to make sure all three babies are born healthy and strong," Dr. Mendoza said. "I'm referring you to the best perinatologist in the state. That's an obstetrician who specializes in high-risk pregnancies." She scribbled on a paper. "Do you have a regular OB/GYN?"

"Not since we moved," Megan said.

"Dr. Johnson is amazing. You'll meet with both Dr. Johnson and the perinatologist, Dr. Hansen, for the rest of your pregnancy. We'll get you in to both of them before the end of the week. But I can already tell you what they'll both recommend—that you quit working immediately. The health of your babies will depend on lots of rest, eating well, and taking it easy."

Trent took Megan's hand in his. "Megan will turn in her notice today."

This was all happening so fast. No more selling houses? Not that she'd miss it. "What about teaching piano lessons?" Megan asked. "I have three students depending on me."

"You'll have to ask Dr. Johnson and Dr. Hansen about that," Dr. Mendoza said. "But I'm guessing they won't have any objections."

Megan would stop teaching if she had to. It would be worth it for the babies. She would do anything for her children.

Triplets. Three babies.

Their lives had been turned upside down.

CHAPTER THIRTY-EIGHT
CHRISTINA

At six weeks on the dot, Christina started throwing up. She woke up Sunday morning, got out of bed, and ran for the bathroom.

"Are you okay?" Gary asked when she reemerged.

Christina couldn't stop the grin that spread across her face. This tangible evidence of the child inside had her bursting with joy. "I'm really pregnant." She hugged Gary tight.

Over the next week, Christina gained a new sympathy for Stacey. Christina's stomach ached from the constant heaving, and she quickly learned what smells and foods to avoid. But nothing could lessen her joy. Every time she threw up, she said a prayer of gratitude. The pregnancy books said morning sickness was a sign the baby was growing healthy and strong.

At six weeks, they also had their first ultrasound. They couldn't hear a heartbeat, and the baby looked like a little blob. But Gary and Christina were in love. At seven and a half weeks, they had another ultrasound. Christina spent the morning lying flat on the couch, the TV on with the volume low, hoping she could make it through the appointment without embarrassing herself. It took nearly two hours to get ready for the day since she had to stop frequently to get her nausea under control.

At the clinic, Gary helped her to a chair in the waiting room. She closed her eyes and tried to think happy thoughts while he checked in. *You'll see your baby soon,* Christina reminded herself. *Don't throw up now.*

A nurse led them to an exam room, and Christina undressed and sat on the table. Her stomach roiled, but mostly from excitement.

"You two are positively glowing," Dr. Mendoza said. "How are you feeling, Christina?"

"She's been throwing up constantly," Gary said. "Should we be worried?"

"No. It's part of pregnancy. I'll write a prescription for something that should help. Now let's see that baby."

Dr. Mendoza inserted the ultrasound wand, and Christina's uterus popped up on the screen. There, in the middle of it all, was a tiny white blob that looked like a jelly-bean. Christina gasped as the bean wiggled around. Her hand went to her throat as she stared in awe at their baby. Gary's hand found hers.

"There's your baby." Dr. Mendoza pointed at the screen. A sound filled the room. Thu-thump. Thu-thump. Thu-thump.

And Christina's whole world changed. Her baby became real.

"One hundred sixty-eight beats per minute, and measuring right on schedule. You've got a strong baby here."

Christina couldn't stop grinning for the rest of the day.

"Are you sure you want to tell them?" Christina asked Gary. For the first time in two months they were having Sunday dinner with the Vincents. A few days after the fight, Alexander and Elauna had sent a fruit basket as some sort of apology, but Christina had insisted she wasn't going back to their house, and Gary had agreed.

"We're going to have to tell them at some point." They'd called Christina's parents in France the night before, and they had been thrilled. "I think it's time, don't you?"

"I guess. But if they call our child a 'test tube baby,' I'll go all crazy hormonal lady on them." Or maybe she'd throw up all over Elauna's Persian rugs.

Gary laughed. "Fair enough."

The second they walked through the front door, the smell of cinnamon and Elauna's perfume hit Christina and made her nauseous.

"Are you okay, Christina?" Gary asked. Elauna and Alexander were staring at Christina like she had three heads.

Christina shook her head, bolting past them for the bathroom. She barely made it to the toilet before throwing up.

She splashed cool water on her face and patted it dry, her entire body flush. They'd never believe she was anything but pregnant now. She wasn't sure she was ready for that conversation, but she needed to be.

Gary rose and came to her side when she entered the living room. "Feeling better?"

"I guess you ignored us and went and made one of those test tube babies," Elauna said. She sat on the couch with her feet crossed, hands in her lap, and nose so high Christina hoped Elauna's neck would snap in two.

"Is this true, Gary?" Alexander looked back and forth between the two of them. "Are you expecting?"

"Surprise," Gary said.

Elauna's eyes widened. "I'm really going to be a grandma?"

"You're going to be a grandma," Gary confirmed.

"If you think you can love a 'test tube baby.'" Christina couldn't keep the bite from her voice.

Elauna sprung out of her chair. "Oh my goodness. This is so exciting." She turned to Alexander. "Did you hear him? We're going to be grandparents!"

"I heard, Elauna." Alexander grasped Gary's hand and slapped him on the back. "Congratulations, kids."

Elauna flung her arms around Gary's neck. "My friends will be thrilled. No one needs to ever know it's one of those test tube babies."

"Okay, we're setting some guidelines right now," Christina said, looking to Gary for support. He nodded, pulled away from his mother, and led Christina to a chair.

"Guidelines?" Elauna sniffed. "I don't think being a grandparent is difficult."

"You've shown some insensitivity in the past toward Christina," Gary said.

"I never—"

"Sit down, Elauna." Alexander took his own seat. "Let the boy talk."

"You won't refer to your grandchild as a test tube baby," Gary said. "This child is a miracle, and deserves all the love in the world, no matter his or her manner of conception."

"I would never mention that to the baby." Elauna seemed horrified at the thought. "The child doesn't need to know, as far as I'm concerned."

"That will be up to me and Christina to decide. Do you understand?"

Elauna leapt up, pulling Gary into another hug. "Of course. I'm so pleased." She motioned to Christina, who joined them in their embrace. "Today you've made me the happiest mother in the world." She pulled back, waving a hand in front of her eyes as though to ward off tears. "I need to buy a stuffed animal. What should I get?"

"The baby already has ninety stuffed animals," Christina reminded her.

"But this is special."

Christina laughed. For the first time, Elauna's obsession didn't bother her.

CHAPTER THIRTY-NINE
KYRA

Kyra's hands shook as she shoved the phone in her pocket. Their fourth IUI hadn't worked. And the loan money was gone.

"Mommy, here." Sophie held out a handful of mail.

Kyra took the mail, her hands still shaking. She should tell David. He needed to know. "Did you and Daddy go to the mailbox?"

"Yes. I saw a big dog, and I wasn't even scared. It was on a leash, and I got to pet it."

"That's great, sweetie."

"I'm going outside. Daddy said I can go swimming." Sophie disappeared out the back door.

No baby. Another failed IUI. Money down the drain.

Kyra flipped through the mail, trying to regain her composure before telling David. Three credit card applications, an advertisement for window cleaning, and a bill from the pediatrician's office. She sucked in a breath, slowly opened the envelope, and withdrew the statement. The dollar amount started up at her, mocking her with all those zeros.

When would they catch a break? A tear slipped down Kyra's cheek. How could they keep paying for student loans, unexpected medical bills, life, and fertility treatments?

Maybe Kyra could work from home. Take on a few kids to babysit. Sell her inherited curio cabinet, the only piece of furniture they owned worth anything substantial.

It wasn't supposed to be like this. She should be worrying about how to pay for a delivery, not how to pay to get pregnant.

They'd make it work. If they took out another loan and sold a few pieces of furniture, they'd be okay. Who really needed a dining room table? Or a couch?

Kyra wandered into the backyard. David sat in a chair, laughing as Sophie splashed water at him from the wading pool. Kyra shut the sliding glass door, the noise echoing in the small yard. David's face paled, and he walked over to her.

"It didn't work?"

Kyra shook her head. "They want us to come in and discuss our options on Monday."

David squeezed his eyes shut, then pulled her into his arms. "It'll be okay. We'll figure this out."

"Mommy, look."

Kyra wiped quickly at her eyes, pulling from David's embrace.

Sophie stopped, frowning. "Why are you crying?"

"I'm sad right now, Soph."

"Is it because the baby went away?"

David and Kyra glanced at each other. He was fighting tears, too.

"Yes." Kyra brushed back Sophie's hair. "I'm happy to be your mommy, though."

"You shouldn't be sad," Sophie said.

"Why not?" David asked.

Sophie furrowed her brows as though that was a stupid question. "I already told you—God said my baby brother is coming really soon. Remember?"

"I guess I forgot," Kyra said. "Tell me again. How did He tell you that, sweetie?"

Sophie sighed like it was obvious. "Mo-om. He said to not be sad, that my baby brother is coming soon and we just gots to be paytents. What does paytents mean?"

The warmth, practically a fire, encompassed Kyra's whole being. "Do you mean patient?"

Sophie nodded. "Yeah, that."

There was no way Sophie would come up with that word on her own. *Be still, my daughter.* The voice was deep in her soul, quiet and calm. Her arms broke out in goosebumps, and she shivered. *It is in my hands. All is well.*

David's eyes glistened with tears. He reached out a hand, squeezing Kyra's. Everything would be okay. They just needed to have patience.

Four IUIs. Six months ago, David and Kyra had said they could afford one. Now they sat in Dr. Mendoza's office, discussing their options.

"I think it's time we try IVF," Dr. Mendoza said. "We've done three IUIs since your miscarriage. The odds are no longer in our favor."

Kyra felt physically sick. In vitro. The procedure itself didn't scare her. Much. But the money . . .

Well, that was terrifying.

"There's a much higher success rate with in vitro," Dr. Mendoza reminded them. "Fifty percent."

Pregnancy success rate. Once those words had filled Kyra with hope, but now she knew all too well a pregnancy didn't necessarily mean a baby. "And how many of those women miscarry?" Kyra asked.

"About ten percent, the same rate as in unassisted pregnancies." Dr. Mendoza leaned forward, her hands on the desk. "Kyra, I know this has been hard for you. But my goal is to get you a baby. I would rather you spend your money on one in vitro attempt with a high likelihood of success than on ten IUIs we know probably won't work."

Kyra hung her head, and the tears burned. Megan and Christina got pregnant with IVF. Maybe it could happen for her, too. But could they make it work financially?

"And if we can't afford in vitro?" Kyra asked.

"We offer payment programs and loan options. There are a number of grants available, but most give preference to childless couples. At this point, I think you're really looking at three options."

Three. Kyra clung to that. One of those options had to be affordable, right?

"Okay, let's hear it," David said.

Dr. Mendoza ticked them off on her fingers. "You can try in vitro. You can adopt. Or you can be thankful for the beautiful little girl you have, and decide to leave it at that."

Kyra remembered holding Sophie for the first time, and the way her whole world had changed. She thought of Sophie's insistence that her baby brother was coming. The third option was not a choice. Not for Kyra. But in vitro versus adoption . . .

She didn't care about the pregnancy. Not anymore. All she wanted was the baby.

"Is adoption less expensive?" Kyra asked.

Dr. Mendoza chewed on her lip as though considering. "Adoption through foster care definitely is—maybe two thousand dollars, and the state reimburses most of that cost. But the goal of foster care is to reunite children with their biological parents, so there's always that risk. With a reputable adoption agency, you're almost guaranteed a baby. Plus you get a tax credit that helps financially, at least some."

Adoption. Kyra had never considered it before.

Be still, my daughter. It is in my hands. All is well. The same warmth she'd felt when Sophie told her about a baby brother spread through her heart. Adoption. It was worth considering.

"Let's at least find out our options for in vitro," David said. "Is Diane the one we would discuss that with?"

"Yes. I'll see if she's free."

They spent two hours with Diane, going over every possible option. The results were disheartening. Best case scenario, they were looking at twelve thousand dollars. Worst case, it would cost more than twenty thousand.

The moment they got into the car, Kyra started to bawl. "Twenty thousand dollars!" she shouted at David. Their emergency fund was gone, and they were living paycheck to paycheck. They were nearly twenty-five thousand dollars in debt, between the student loans, medical bills, and the loans for IUI. That didn't include the van payment. They couldn't sell enough possessions to come up with twenty thousand dollars, and Kyra knew they couldn't afford the monthly payment on that hefty a loan. "How are we going to come up with that kind of money?"

If only that debt was cash in the bank. Then they wouldn't be having this conversation.

David put the car in reverse and backed out of the parking lot. He wiped at his eyes with the back of his hand. "I don't know."

"Could we get a loan for twenty thousand dollars? Even if we wanted to?"

"Probably. Heck, we get credit card applications in the mail every day. But they'd have an insane interest rate."

"We couldn't afford the payments." Kyra was bawling again, barely able to speak through her tears.

David glanced over at her. "Hey, we're going to figure this out."

"Twenty thousand dollars!" Then, more quietly: "Maybe it's time to consider other options."

David swerved into the parking lot of a department store. He came to a stop in an empty stall near the back and turned off the car. "Are you saying you don't want to try anymore? I'm not ready to quit."

"Me either. I'm saying I think we should try adoption."

"You're really serious about this."

"If we get a baby, who cares how it comes? Let's at least consider it. It might be less expensive."

"It might be more."

"It would be less physically taxing. When Dr. Mendoza mentioned it . . ." Kyra pointed to her heart. "I felt it right here."

"Adoption," David said.

"Yes."

He took off his glasses and rubbed his eyes, then replaced them. His thumb twitched as though itching for a game controller.

Kyra took his hand in hers. "A baby is a baby. Does it matter how our family is made?"

"No. I just want all this behind us."

"Let's go home. While I make dinner, you can call the pastor and get information on the crisis center I've heard about in church. I know they sometimes help facilitate adoptions." Kyra pulled down the sun visor, making sure her makeup was intact. She didn't want to worry Sophie, to make her ask what was wrong.

At home, David went inside while Kyra picked Sophie up from Cassandra's. Sophie bounced with excitement, eager to tell Kyra about her adventures with Malachi. Kyra listened with half an ear while preparing dinner.

David came in as Kyra began setting the table. "I just got off the phone with the crisis center."

Kyra paused, then set a cup on the table. "And?"

"Dr. Mendoza is right. Most agencies are around thirty thousand dollars. But the crisis center can help us find ways to save money with a recommendation from our pastor. They help lots of couples adopt for a third of that amount."

All is well. The words whispered to Kyra's heart again. This is what they were meant to do. They just needed to be patient and wait.

"Soph, finish setting the table. I'm going to talk to Daddy in the other room."

David followed Kyra into the living room. "I made us an appointment for next Tuesday. If we find a birth mother, we could do a private adoption through an attorney inexpensively. And there are grants we may qualify for. The crisis center knows the most inexpensive agencies for something called a home study—I guess we have to get one of those and they're pricey?—and the most reputable attorneys. It doesn't cost anything to meet and find out our options. What do you think?"

Warmth poured through Kyra's veins. This was what they needed to do. "I want to go to that meeting."

David pulled Kyra into a hug. "Me too."

Adoption. The thought of leaving fertility treatments behind—of pursuing a different path—was like a breath of fresh air.

<hr />

Chelsea, the caseworker David and Kyra met with at crisis center, wore a flowing multicolored-skirt and blouse. She couldn't be much older than Kyra. Her office resembled the pastor's—same familiar dark wood desk and black office chair, the blue and maroon floral love seat. There was even a picture of Christ in the Garden of Gethsemane on one wall.

"I'm so glad you made an appointment," Chelsea said, flipping through a filing cabinet and pulling out brochures. "We get a lot of birth mothers in here, but not many people realize we can help adoptive couples, too."

"That's what we're hoping," Kyra said. "There's no way we can afford the thirty thousand dollar price tag a lot of agencies have."

Chelsea nodded, spreading open a brochure open. "Not many couples can. That's why we partner with outside agencies to help keep the costs down." She pointed to the brochure, where agencies were listed. "What we've found is that the couples who experienced successful placements are usually the ones who take control and find their own baby. A lot of couples don't advertise themselves because it's uncomfortable." She opened another brochure. "But there's a lot you can do to gain visibility—pass-along cards, a blog, spreading the news on social media. You can even place ads in newspapers. As for the money, a lot of couples choose to run online campaigns to raise the funds. You can do yard sales, bake sales, anything really. You'll be surprised how much money you can make just by selling things around your house."

Chelsea continued talking, walking Kyra and David through the basic legal process they could expect. She discussed foster care, private adoptions, and adoption agencies. For over an hour she patiently answered their questions and helped them explore all their options.

"Here's my phone number and email address," Chelsea said, handing them a business card. "If you have any other questions or concerns, let me know. I'm here to help however I can."

"What do you think?" David asked as they got into the car.

Kyra pointed to an adoption agency in the brochure, one that Chelsea said was affordable and great to work with. "I want to work with this adoption agency. It's still a lot of money, but it feels right." Kyra held a fist to her heart. "I know if we get our name out there, we'll find our baby. I'll babysit to earn money. We'll start an online campaign. We'll do a yard sale. We can come up with the funds."

David squeezed her hand. "It'd cost about the same to do the cheapest in vitro option."

Kyra pointed to the brochure. "But this is the right choice. Don't you feel it?"

"Yeah. I do."

"We're really doing this. We're going to adopt?"

"Yeah. We're going to adopt."

THREE
MONTHS
LATER

CHAPTER FORTY
MEGAN

Megan was sure her brain would rot before she gave birth. Nineteen weeks pregnant with triplets meant she measured thirty weeks. She was convinced she felt at least as bad, if not worse, than most women in the third trimester.

Life had become a series of doctor appointments. Megan had already been hospitalized once for a kidney infection, and was on modified bed rest, which meant she spent all day sitting or lying down. At least she'd been able to keep teaching her three piano students.

She pushed herself off the couch with a groan. Sienna would be here any minute, and it would take Megan at least that long to waddle to the living room.

Sure enough, the doorbell rang. "Coming," Megan called, wincing as one of the babies pushed against her rib cage. With three babies, it felt like a circus in her belly, even if Dr. Johnson claimed their movements were small.

"Come in," Megan told Sienna. She was eight months pregnant now, but her baby bump still looked smaller than Megan's.

"Hi, Megan. How are you feeling?"

"Big. How about you?"

"Ginormous." Sienna walked over to the piano bench without a hint of a waddle. "Just trying to get everything ready for Pennsylvania. I can't believe I'll be moving in a few months." Sienna had decided to attend the University of Liberal Arts in Philadelphia. She'd start in January, and reapply for Juilliard in a year.

"And what about the baby?" Megan asked. "Have you found a family for him yet?"

Sienna's eyes were pained. "No, and I've been through all those profiles a hundred times." She put a hand on her belly. "We're running out of time. He's due in four weeks."

"Keep praying. You'll find his family."

"I wish you could take my baby, Megan."

Megan's heart wrenched. She wished so badly she could ease some of Sienna's burden. Megan placed a hand on her belly. "I'm going to have three babies in a few months. You know I'm not your baby's mother."

"I know. But I want you to be." Sienna's voice clogged with tears. "It's less scary if it's you. I know you'd love him and raise him well. I know you'd let me be Aunt Sienna."

"When you find the right family, you'll feel the same way about them."

Sienna reached into her piano bag and pulled out a folded sheet of paper. "My caseworker emailed me last night. This family was just approved for adoption." She unfolded the paper, stared at it for a moment, and handed it to Megan. "I think you know them."

Megan took the paper, her heart in her throat. She already knew who it would be. Along the top of the paper it said *Kyra and David* in all caps. A family photo Megan recognized from the fireplace mantle in Kyra's home took up the majority of the page, followed by a letter that began *Dear Birth Mother.*

Megan had read that letter. Kyra had asked her to proofread it a few weeks ago.

"I recognized the little girl," Sienna said. "You babysat her a few months ago."

"Yes." Megan handed the paper to Sienna.

Her eyes filled with tears. "When I saw them, I started crying. I've never cried over any other profile. My mom said that was God telling me this family might be the one."

Megan's heart pounded, and she barely dared breathe. She sent a quick prayer heavenward: *Don't let me ruin this for Kyra.* She'd thought of telling Sienna about Kyra before, of course. But she hadn't wanted to overstep her bounds. The choice needed to be Sienna's.

"Is this my baby's family, Megan?"

"Only you can know for sure."

Sienna wiped away the tears with the back of her hand. "That little girl. That adorable little girl." She touched her heart. "Every time I look at her, it gets me right here. But now everything seems real. And I don't know how I can give my baby away." Her shoulders shook. "The problem is, I know I can't keep him, either."

"Sienna." Megan scooted onto the piano bench, wrapping Sienna in her arms. Their bellies stuck out in front, both their bums barely fitting on the bench. "I'm sorry."

Sienna cried harder. "Are they good people, Megan? Will they love my baby?"

Megan's throat caught, and she nodded. "So much. They've been waiting for a baby for a long time. And Sophie." Megan let out a strangled laugh. "Well, she's wanted a baby brother for a while now."

Sienna sniffed, pulling back. Megan returned to her own seat. "Do you think they would still let me see my baby? Send me pictures and stuff?"

"You'd have to talk to them about it. But they've said they'd like an open adoption." Megan motioned to the paper, clutched in Sienna's hand. "You should meet with them."

"I don't want to get their hopes up. What if I change my mind?"

"You won't," Megan said with certainty.

"No." Sienna's voice was unbearably sad. "I won't."

"And you'll love Kyra, David, and Sophie."

"I know."

"Call your caseworker. Have her set up an appointment."

"Can we meet here?"

Megan almost said yes, but thought better of it. "You need to find neutral territory. This can't be about me and our friendship. It has to be about what's right for your baby, and if you want an open adoption, you need to foster that relationship outside of ours."

"Why do you always have to be right?" Sienna smiled, but it was forced. "Can I call my caseworker before I chicken out?"

"Sure."

Five minutes later, Sienna hung up. "She's going to contact them and get back to me." Sienna straightened the paper with

Kyra and David's photo, then put it back in her music bag. "Sorry, I didn't mean to hijack our lesson. What should I play first?"

CHAPTER FORTY-ONE
CHRISTINA

"Okay, class, pencils down," Christina instructed, shifting in her chair uncomfortably. She felt a small kick and placed her hand on her stomach with a smile. Twenty weeks pregnant. Halfway there.

Pencils hit desks with a clatter. Groans of excitement and frustration filled the room. Christina shifted in her seat again, wincing at the tight pain in her back. She had woken up feeling under the weather and felt steadily worse as the morning progressed.

"Switch papers, and we'll correct the test," Christina told her students. "Do it quickly, please. Lunch is in fifteen minutes." Another sharp pain. She gasped involuntarily.

"Mrs. Vincent?" a student asked. "Aren't you going to write the words on the board?"

Christina smiled tightly and stood, then sat back down with a yelp. The pain was becoming more intense by the second.

Panic clutched at her—something was wrong. A little foot kicked again, soothing her nerves. No, everything was okay. The baby was moving. She probably had another urinary tract infection. The last one had laid her flat in bed for three days. She'd call the doctor during lunch and see what he said.

Christina tried to stand again, but couldn't. "Change of plans," she told the class. "Someone from each table bring me your spelling tests, and we'll correct them after lunch. Tommy, can you turn on the TV and push play?" She'd planned to watch the educational kids show after lunch as a lead-in to their science lesson, but she needed a breather.

Tommy started the episode, and the kids were mostly quiet. Christina sat at her desk, forcing herself to drink water as the pain grew worse and worse. She glanced at the clock with tears in her eyes. Ten minutes until lunch. Instead of calling the doctor, she would go in.

Christina called the front office. "Hi, Linda," she said, her voice low so she wouldn't disturb the students. "Can you find someone to cover my class for the rest of the day?"

"Of course," she said. "Is everything okay?"

Christina glanced at the clock. Only five minutes to go. "I'm sick. But after I get a prescription from the doctor, I'll be fine. Thanks, Linda."

"Sure thing, sweetie. Get feeling better."

Christina hung up. Two minutes until lunch. "Tommy, can you push stop? We'll finish the show after lunch. Everyone line up by the door." Someone flipped on the lights, and the room erupted in movement as students grabbed their coats and lunches. Christina remained seated at her desk, relaying instructions. "Candice, can you give everyone a squirt of hand sanitizer? Looks like Danielle is the line leader today." Normally

Christina would walk the students to lunch, but today she didn't know if she could even walk to her car. The bell rang, and she silently prayed the students would clear the room quickly.

Christina opened up the bottom desk drawer with her foot. She leaned over with a groan and grabbed her purse as the last student left. The trek to her car could best be described as a hobble. The baby kicked, increasing her pain. It took every ounce of willpower she had to drive to the doctor's office and waddle across the parking lot.

"I think I have a UTI," Christina told the receptionist. "Is there any way I can be seen?"

The receptionist looked up from her computer screen and her eyes widened. "Are you okay? You don't look well."

"I don't feel well." Black spots flicked across Christina's vision, and she swayed.

The receptionist was around the counter in an instant. "You're white as a sheet. Let me help you to an exam room. I'll have the doctor come in immediately."

Christina nodded, tears pricking her eyes in gratitude. She'd get a prescription, then go home and sleep. She'd feel much better tomorrow. Or in a few days, at least.

They passed a nurse in the hallway. She ran over and grasped Christina's other side. "Honey, you look like you're going to pass out."

"I . . . have really bad . . . back pains." Christina's words came in spurts.

"Get the doctor," the nurse instructed the receptionist. "Quickly, please. It's Christina, right?" Christina nodded, her lips pursed in pain. "How many weeks along are you? About twenty?"

"I'll be . . . twenty-one . . . tomorrow."

Dr. Blakely arrived. "What's the matter?" she asked as the nurse helped Christina onto the exam table. Christina relayed her problem between gasps. This was much worse than last time. Would she have to be hospitalized, like Megan was for her kidney infection?

"How long has this been going on?" Dr. Blakely asked.

"Since . . . this morning." Christina's hand went to her stomach, and she hunched over as another wave of pain overcame her. "Is the baby . . . okay?"

"Let's see."

Christina lay back on the table and lifted her shirt. Dr. Blakely put the Doppler monitor on her stomach, and the sound of the baby's heartbeat flooded the room. Tears trickled out of Christina's eyes, a combination of relief and pain.

"I think . . . it's another . . . UTI," Christina managed to say. "I had one . . . a few weeks ago."

Dr. Blakely put the monitor away, and Christina pulled her shirt down. "I think you're in labor. We need to get you to the hospital right away."

"Labor? But I'm only" —Christina gasped in pain— "twenty weeks."

Too soon.

Too soon.

Too soon.

"Annie, call the hospital and have them send an ambulance. Then call Dr. Henderson and let him know she's on her way. He's on call at the hospital today."

The nurse nodded and left the room.

"I can't . . . be in labor." Tears streamed down Christina's face, and she clutched the edge of the exam table.

"If we hurry, we might be able to stop it," Dr. Blakely said. "You'll be on bed rest for the rest of your pregnancy, probably hospitalized, but first we need to get these contractions to stop."

A few minutes later Christina heard a siren, and Dr. Blakely helped her stand. A nurse brought in a wheelchair. The waiting room was full of people with wide, curious stares, but Christina didn't care. Two EMTs were already pulling a stretcher out of the ambulance, and they raced toward her.

The trip to the hospital was a blur. An EMT took Christina's blood pressure and started an IV. At the hospital they were met by Dr. Henderson and raced up to labor and delivery. Nurses swarmed around her, and two monitors were hooked to Christina's stomach.

"Heartbeat one sixty-seven," a nurse told Dr. Henderson. "Contractions three minutes apart."

"Start a magnesium drip," Dr. Henderson said. "Christina, you're definitely in labor. The magnesium sulfate will make you feel horrible, but it'll hopefully stop the contractions."

"What if you can't stop them?" Christina asked, her voice high with panic.

"Let's not think about that."

"Gary." Christina gasped as another pain—what she now knew to be a contraction—overcame her body. "I need my husband."

The doctor nodded at a nurse, who hurried out of the room saying, "I'll call him."

Christina knew Gary was in Provo for a client meeting. It would take him at least an hour to get to her. An entire hour of pure, unadulterated fear.

That hour was a blur. Doctors and nurses swarmed around Christina, but despite their best efforts, they couldn't make the contractions stop. They got harder and harder, and Christina felt the overwhelming need to push.

"No!" she screamed, clenching the bed rails. Her vision blurred from the magnesium—a muscle relaxant—and she fought the urge to throw up. "It's too soon."

Gary rushed into the room, and Christina sobbed in relief.

"They can't make it stop," she said. He grabbed her hand, looking at the doctor for confirmation.

Dr. Henderson's eyes locked on Christina's. "This will be the hardest thing you have ever done, but I need you to push."

Christina turned her head into Gary's shoulder and sobbed. Their baby's heartbeat, strong and steady on the monitor, pounded in her ears.

"It's too soon." Christina stared up at Gary, and his eyes were wide and haunted. She wanted to stay in that moment forever, holding onto her baby. As soon as she pushed, it would be all over.

Another contraction hit, hard and painful. Christina's breath caught.

"Now," Dr. Henderson said. "Christina, push!"

It was impossible to fight the pressing need. Gary gripped her hand, and she bore down.

Beep beep beep. The heartbeat, strong and clear.

Christina gritted her teeth and gave a mighty push.

Beeeeeeeepppppppp. The heart monitor flat lined.

CHAPTER FORTY-TWO
CHRISTINA

There was no mad rush to save their baby's life. A nurse took the infant and placed it on the scales.

"What is it?" Christina gasped. She and Gary had decided they wanted to be surprised, and hadn't found out the gender at their ultrasound. Had that really only been last week?

"It's a girl," Dr. Henderson said.

A daughter. Christina held a hand to her mouth.

The nurse came over, a bundle tinier than Christina thought possible cradled in her arms. "Would you like to hold her?"

Christina nodded, holding out her arms. The nurse gave her the bundle of blankets, so light Christina could almost imagine their baby wasn't inside. Could pretend she was still pregnant.

"Thirteen ounces," the nurse said. "Eleven inches long."

Christina looked at her baby's face, and the tears fell harder. The baby was so tiny, so perfect. She pulled back the blanket, counting all ten fingers and toes. She had Christina's nose and Gary's chin.

"She's beautiful," Gary said, his words choked.

"I'm so sorry," the nurse said, and Christina saw tears glisten in her eyes. "We'll clean her up, and you can have family come and say their goodbyes if you'd like."

"No," Christina said quickly. This moment didn't belong to anyone else. "I don't want anyone else here. Can I hold her a while longer?"

The nurse nodded, and soon they were alone. Just Christina, Gary, and their daughter's tiny body.

"Why couldn't you stay with us, little one?" Christina whispered, stroking the baby's head. "We worked so hard for you."

"Can I hold her?" Gary asked. Christina nodded and transferred the baby, overwhelmed by blankets, into his arms. He started to sob—great, wracking sounds that ripped through her. Sounds Christina had never heard from her husband before.

"I'm sorry," he whispered. "I'm sorry for waiting so long for you. I'm so sorry."

A nurse came in a while later. Christina stood, sore but determined, and she and Gary helped bathe their baby girl. The nurse gave them a tiny gown to dress her in. A photographer arrived, somber but professional, and took the first—and only—family photos they'd ever have with their little girl.

Then they took her away. The grief counselor arrived, and then the doctor.

"What happened?" Christina asked Dr. Henderson. "Why did I go into labor?"

"I believe you have what we call an incompetent cervix. It can't stand the pressure of a baby, and once the fetus gets too big, your cervix starts to dilate and you go into labor."

Christina hung her head. It was her fault. Her body's fault.

"What do we do now?" Gary asked.

"When you're ready, we can discuss it in more detail. But basically, the next time you get pregnant, we'll perform a surgery at about fifteen weeks and sew the cervix closed. It's called a cerclage." He placed a hand gently on her arm. "You did nothing wrong, Christina. Unfortunately, the only way to diagnose this problem is when something like this happens."

"If I'd come in this morning, could you have stopped labor?" Christina didn't want to ask, but the question haunted her.

Dr. Henderson's eyes were hooded. "There's no way we can speculate over that. I am so sorry for your loss."

But Christina had her answer in his eyes. If she had come in earlier, she might still be pregnant. Might still be listening to the *beep beep beep* of her baby's heartbeat.

Might not be mourning the loss of her only child. Her firstborn. The daughter they'd gone through hell and back to conceive.

"I want to go home," Christina said. "When can we leave?"

"As soon as you feel up to it," Dr. Henderson said. "We can keep you overnight for observation if you'd like."

"I'm ready to go."

"I'll have a nurse bring in the discharge papers."

Two hours later, Gary pulled into their garage and helped Christina from the car. She walked slowly up the stairs and into the mud room. The house felt empty. So frighteningly silent. She started to cry again.

Gary's arms held her tight. "Let's get you upstairs. You need to rest."

"We need to let people know," Christina choked out.

"I'll take care of it."

"I'm sorry, Gary." Christina sobbed, turning in his arms. She caught his gaze, begging for understanding. "I had no idea I was in labor. If I had known . . ."

"Shhh." He put his finger to her lips. "Don't you dare blame yourself. It isn't your fault."

"It hurts so bad."

"I know. I want her back, too."

"Grace. She should have a name, and I want it to be Grace."

CHAPTER
FORTY-THREE
KYRA

"Can I help make dinner?" Sophie asked Kyra, wandering into the kitchen. Sophie had turned into quite the helper. The last three months she'd thrown herself into the adoption. While Kyra tracked down documents and filled out paperwork, Sophie had patiently practiced changing diapers on her baby doll. She'd helped Kyra organize the yard sale to earn money, and then put on her adorable smile and helped sell most of the items. She'd eagerly offered input on the scrapbook Kyra had made for the expectant mothers to look through.

Last week, their profile went online with the agency the crisis center had recommended. Now it was a waiting game.

"Of course you can help, baby girl," Kyra said.

Sophie frowned. "I'm not your baby anymore, Mommy."

Kyra's heart cracked. Sophie had turned four right before Halloween, and all traces of toddler were disappearing. "No, I guess you aren't."

"Can I squish the potatoes?"

"Sure." Kyra helped Sophie onto a chair and handed her the potato masher. "Let me know when you're finished, and I'll get the beaters."

The telephone rang and Kyra fished it from her pocket. The number for their caseworker, Molly, scrolled across the screen.

Kyra's heart stuttered, then started pounding. She scrambled to answer the phone. "Hello?"

"Are you sitting down, Kyra?" Molly asked.

A birth mother was interested. That had to be it. "No, I'm making dinner. What's up?"

"Another caseworker called me. She has a birth mother delivering in a few weeks, and she wants to meet you and David as soon as possible."

Kyra nearly dropped the phone. "Are you serious?"

"I wouldn't joke about this. Her name is Sienna. She said she knows Megan. Do you know who she's talking about?"

Sienna. Megan's piano student. The girl Megan talked of with such fondness. The girl Kyra had bumped into a few months ago when picking up Sophie. And she was with the same agency as them. "Yes, I know Megan. When can we meet Sienna?"

"Friday afternoon, here at the office. Her mother will be with her."

"What time?" David could cancel whatever was going on at work for this. He'd have to. This could be it. Kyra's heart galloped in her chest.

They ironed out the details, and Kyra hung up.

"Mommy, are the potatoes squished enough?" Sophie asked.

"Keep squishing. I've got to call Daddy." David would be thrilled.

———◆◆◆———

Kyra's fingers dug into David's arm as they waited in the conference room for Sienna and her mother to arrive.

"Why are you nervous?" David asked, prying Kyra's hand from his arm. He laced his fingers through hers. "You said you've met her before."

"Only briefly. And not like this."

"Well, she obviously liked you enough to set up this appointment."

Kyra had been analyzing that first meeting in excruciating detail. Had she been friendly? Positive? Cheerful? Knowing she'd met Sienna before almost made Kyra more nervous.

The door swung open and Molly walked in. Kyra's hands felt clammy, and she wiped them discreetly on her jeans as they stood. If this went well, they could walk away with a baby.

A rustle at the door had Kyra's stomach jumping. In walked Sienna. She hadn't changed much since Kyra last saw her, other than the size of her stomach. Sienna had the same long blonde hair, the same scared blue eyes. Kyra couldn't imagine how hard this must be for her. Kyra's heart leapt and fell in her chest with each breath she took. She wanted to run and hug Sienna. Wanted to stay frozen so that she couldn't ruin this. Two other women followed Sienna into the room, presumably her mother and caseworker.

"Thanks for coming today," Molly said.

Like they would've refused the introduction. Sienna was considering giving them her baby. They would meet her whenever and wherever she wanted.

"I'm Rebecca, Sienna's caseworker," the woman holding a file folder said. "This is Annabelle, Sienna's mother. And this is Sienna."

Kyra smiled, hoping it said "I'm happy to meet you" and not "Give me your baby. I'm desperate." Kyra held her hand out to both of them and prayed they didn't notice how it shook. "I'm Kyra, and this is David." David held his hand out as well.

"We've met before," Sienna said. "At Megan's."

So she did remember. Of course she remembered. Kyra should've mentioned it first. Did Sienna think Kyra was trying to hide her relationship with Megan? Kyra needed to calm down. All she could do was be herself.

"We'll leave you to talk," Molly said. "Rebecca and I will be in our offices if you need anything."

They left, the door clicking shut behind them. Silence fell over the room like a suffocating blanket. What were they supposed to do now? Kyra should've asked Molly. She didn't want to blow this. "Thank you so much for meeting with us," Kyra said finally.

"Megan said your little girl wants a baby brother." Sienna's hand dropped to her stomach. "Is that true?"

Kyra mouth fell open, but she closed it quickly. Obviously Megan and Sienna had talked about this at length. Kyra admired Megan for keeping Sienna's confidence. "She prays for one every night."

"When Rebecca sent your profile, I recognized Sophie in the photo." Tears filled Sienna's eyes. "Your profile is the only one that's ever made me cry. I think I knew you were his family almost immediately."

Kyra's heart pounded. Did she just say what Kyra thought she'd said? Kyra had expected a polite interview. But it sounded like Sienna had already made her decision.

"Do you mean . . ." Kyra trailed off, unable to finish that sentence.

Sienna looked away. Annabelle's arm went around her daughter's shoulders. "Sienna's been trying to find a family for months. She's poured over every file."

"No one's ever felt right," Sienna said. "Until you."

A baby. Was this really happening? David's eyes were wide with shock.

"Wow," he said. "We're honored."

Sienna's hand went to her belly. "I know he'd be your baby, not mine. But it would be nice to be Aunt Sienna. To come to his birthday parties and send him Christmas presents. I don't want to confuse him or be the mom." Her voice choked. "I just want to know he's okay. Megan said you're interested in an open adoption."

Kyra glanced at David. He nodded. They'd discussed this in detail.

"We want our baby to know the wonderful person who gave him life," Kyra said. "We're happy to have you as Aunt Sienna."

Sienna wiped away the tears running down her cheeks. "Do you play the piano?"

Kyra's heart hammered. Would this be a deal breaker? "No, but Sophie is begging for lessons."

"I'm moving to Pennsylvania in January to study music, and I've composed a lullaby for the baby. I was hoping if I put it on a CD, you'd play it for him every night before bed."

Tears filled Kyra's eyes. Sienna loved her baby so much. "Of course. We'd be honored."

"I'm not considering any other families right now. I don't want you to worry. You're it." Sienna leaned forward, placing her elbows on the conference table. "You know Megan pretty well, huh?"

"She goes to my church, and we've worked together on a book and coat drive. I consider her a dear friend."

"Megan helped me realize it was okay to place my baby for adoption." Sienna glanced over at Annabelle. "Mom and Dad kept telling me I should, but Megan's the one who helped me make a decision. Every time I looked at profiles, I kept thinking of her, and what a great mom she'll be. And I wanted someone like that for my baby."

"Megan's a wonderful person," Kyra said, not sure where Sienna was going with this.

"If you're friends with her, you must be pretty cool. And I know you'll be great parents too, just like them."

Kyra leaned forward. "Is that why you're picking us, because we're Megan's friends?"

"No, I'm picking you because it's right. But knowing you're friends with Megan makes this easier. I respect her."

"Me too." Kyra swallowed hard and asked the question that burned. "Is the father around?"

Annabelle made a noise of disgust.

"Dane doesn't want anything to do with the baby. He told me it was my problem." Sienna wrapped her arms around her stomach. "But this baby isn't a problem. He's a blessing. Your blessing. It's not his fault Dane and I made a mistake."

"He is a blessing," Kyra said. David reached out, and Kyra took his hand in hers. "He absolutely is."

CHAPTER FORTY-FOUR
MEGAN

Another day of bed rest. Megan sighed, shifting uncomfortably on the couch. It was only ten o'clock, and already she was bored.

She had just decided on a new TV series to watch on Netflix when her cell phone rang. She picked it up, surprised. Christina? She never called during school hours. Megan paused Netflix and answered the phone. "Hey, what's up? Aren't you supposed to be in class right now?"

"I didn't go to work today." Christina's voice was thick and full of emotion, but dead somehow at the same time.

Megan pushed herself upright, gripping the phone. "What's wrong?"

Christina cleared her throat. "I went into labor yesterday and had the baby. A little girl."

Megan stood, already walking toward the door. "Christina, please tell me . . ."

"She's gone."

The hand holding her cell phone trembled. Megan slipped her feet into shoes and shrugged into her coat, closing the door behind her. "Oh, Christina."

"I wanted to tell you before you heard it from someone else."

"I'm coming over."

"No, really, it's fine."

"I'm already here."

The phone went silent, and Megan wondered if Christina had hung up. The front door slowly opened. Christina eyes were red-rimmed, her face devoid of makeup. Her red-orange curls splayed every which way, frizzy and uncharacteristically free. Megan disconnected the call and pushed her phone into her pocket.

"I'm so sorry," Megan whispered, holding out her arms.

Christina fell into them without a word, and for a moment they stood there, holding each other tightly. A baby kicked, and Megan closed her eyes tight. *Please keep them safe,* Megan prayed. *Oh, God, why?*

"What happened?" Megan asked.

Christina pulled back, wiping under one eye to clear away a tear. "Can you come in?"

"Of course." Megan stepped inside, and Christina closed the door behind her. Aside from the disheveled hair and makeup, she looked just as she had the last time Megan saw her, at church on Sunday. Christina's tall and slender frame hid her pregnancy well, and only a slight pooch at the middle gave any indication of her condition. That pooch was still there. How could the baby be gone?

"Where's Gary?" Megan asked.

"Upstairs sleeping. We didn't get home until four a.m. But I can't fall asleep."

Megan sank onto the couch next to Christina, her heart so full of sorrow and disbelief she thought it would explode. "What happened?"

Christina spoke quietly. Megan sat there for thirty minutes, asking questions as Christina explained.

"Her heartbeat was strong right until the moment I pushed," Christina said. Her hands were clutched in her lap, knuckles white. "But her lungs collapsed as soon as she was born. She was perfect, Megan. Beautiful." She picked up a photo from the end table and handed it to Megan.

Megan stared into the face of the tiniest baby she had ever seen. The skin was dark with what looked like bruising. The baby was clothed in a white dress that dwarfed her. As tiny as she was, Megan could tell she had Christina's cheekbones, Gary's oval-shaped face. A perfect blend of both their features.

"She's beautiful," Megan said, unable to keep the thickness from her voice. She handed the photo back. "I am so sorry, Christina. I don't even know what to say." How could something like this have happened?

Less than one percent, Christina had said. An incompetent cervix was present in less than one percent of pregnancies. Why did Christina's have to be one of them? They had worked so hard for this baby, gone through so much. Why them?

Please don't let it be me, Megan thought and instantly felt guilty. Here she was, with three babies growing healthy and strong inside of her. And Christina had lost the only one she'd ever had.

Christina played with the corner of the photograph. Her eyes were haunted, but Megan saw a strength in their depths. "I don't want you to feel awkward around me, Meg. Please don't shut me out."

"I won't."

"I need you to share your pregnancy with me. I want to feel like I get that much, at least."

The full magnitude of the situation hit Megan. They had gone through this together, every step of the way. They'd been each other's source of comfort and reassurance through the entire in vitro process and the early weeks of their pregnancies. But now their paths had diverged. Megan would continue on alone, leaving Christina to watch with anguish as Megan experienced everything they should have cherished together.

It wasn't fair.

Megan blinked, trying to force back tears. *Don't cry,* she commanded. She needed to be strong for Christina. A lone tear escaped and dripped down Megan's cheek. She brushed it away, hoping Christina wouldn't notice.

"Christina?" Gary's voice was frantic and worried.

"I'm in here," Christina said.

Gary appeared, shoulders sagging. "I woke up, and you weren't there. I got worried."

"I was telling Megan what happened."

"I am so sorry, Gary. If there is anything Trent or I can do for you . . ." The words felt empty, meaningless. How on earth could anyone heal this kind of hurt?

No one could except God, and that would take time.

"Thank you." Gary cleared his throat, and his eyes were suspiciously red. "It still doesn't seem real."

They talked for a few more minutes, and then Megan gave Christina a hug and left. Megan walked across the cold, frozen grass, letting the tears she'd been holding back finally fall. She went upstairs and collapsed on the bed, sobbing.

It was so unfair. Her heart broke for Christina. Megan held her stomach, cradling the lives within. *Be safe,* she prayed. *Stay healthy and keep growing.*

She heard the front door open and sat up, trying to dry her eyes. Trent must have decided to check on her during lunch. He'd been doing that a lot lately.

"Megan?"

"In the bedroom."

His footsteps creaked up the stairs. He paused in the doorway, then rushed to her. "What's wrong?"

Megan started to cry, then explained how Christina and Gary's hearts had broken.

CHAPTER FORTY-FIVE
CHRISTINA

Christina had been to her fair share of funerals—three grandparents, a few great-aunts, and even a co-worker to name a few. But she had never been to a funeral for a child. She had never imagined she would have to bury her baby.

The hospital had asked them, as delicately as possible, what they wanted done with Grace's body.

"We want to bury her," Christina had said immediately. She couldn't imagine doing anything less for her baby.

The grief counselor had nodded in approval. "Most couples find it helps the healing to have somewhere they can go to mourn."

They'd contacted the mortuary and made arrangements for a small graveside service, inviting only family and their close friends.

As they pulled up to the graveside, Christina looked at the small hole, covered by a green tent with a few folding chairs underneath. Gary parked and came around to help her out of the car. They slowly walked up the gentle incline to the grave. It had snowed the night before, and the ground was covered in three inches of white.

A tiny pink casket, no bigger than a doll bed, sat on the straps over the top of the grave. Christina placed her hand lightly on the casket and sighed. *I miss you, angel. I miss you so much.*

Christina would give anything to have Grace still inside of her, growing healthy and strong. If Christina had gone to the doctor earlier in the day, would Grace still be alive?

No, a voice whispered to Christina's heart. *It was her time.* Their pastor had prayed with them that morning, and she'd felt that very strongly. Grace's mission on earth was fulfilled.

But why couldn't she have stayed?

Family and friends arrived, one by one: Elauna and Alexander; a few random aunts and cousins from Gary's side of the family; Megan, Trent, Kyra, and David; Pastor Lynd and his wife. Gary and Christina greeted them with hugs and sad smiles. She barely held back the sobs when she watched a crying Elauna place a tiny stuffed pink bear next to the casket. Gary's parents had been an unexpected source of strength the last few days.

"I think that's everyone," Christina told Gary, looking around at the small crowd.

"Let's wait a minute longer," he said.

Normally Christina would have argued against starting late. But today was about them. If Gary needed a few extra minutes, he would get them.

A black SUV pulled to a stop behind their Lexus. Probably a mourner, come to place flowers on a nearby grave. Christina's mouth fell open when her mother stepped out of the vehicle, followed by her father. She started to tremble, then ran down the short embankment and threw her arms around her mom. Her mother's arms wrapped around Christina, and Christina leaned into her and sobbed.

"I didn't think you were coming," Christina said. She hadn't even considered asking them to make the trip from France.

"We couldn't stay away," her mother said. "We told Gary about our flight arrangements two days ago, but he wanted to surprise you." Tears trailed down her cheeks. "I'm so sorry, Christina."

Christina turned to her father next. Being encircled in her parents' arms helped soothe her aching heart in a way nothing else could.

Christina's mom held an arm tightly around her as the pastor started the services. He spoke a few words, and though Christina couldn't concentrate on what he said, a blanket of comfort surrounded her. Grace's death would never be something she got over or forgot. But she could move past the pain, with the Lord's help.

The pastor gave a moving sermon, and then Gary offered a prayer over the grave. He looked handsome in an expensive designer suit, but the hunched shoulders and haunted eyes made him seem broken. Christina turned her face into her mother's shoulder and sobbed. Gary folded his arms and began to pray. "Your mother and I love you, Grace, and look forward to the day we can be with you again." His voice choked on the words.

No man should have to pray over his child's grave, Christina thought as her shoulders shook. *Especially when he's not even thirty.*

It wasn't fair.

After the dedication, the pastor stepped forward. "Christina and Gary asked Megan Burke to play a piano rendition of 'All Through the Night.' She recorded it for us since we couldn't bring a piano here." He pushed a button on Christina's iPod.

The hauntingly beautiful strains of "All Through the Night" filled the air. Megan had played the song perfectly, even though Christina knew she'd only had a few days to learn it.

"All Through the Night." That was the song from Christina's statue of a mother rocking her baby. The one Gary had given her when she found out she was pregnant. It seemed fitting for the occasion.

Gary wrapped an arm around Christina, kissing her temple as the final measure of the song filled the air. After the final note, all was quiet. The pastor stepped forward and thanked everyone for coming.

People came forward with murmured condolences. Megan gave Christina a long hug, her stomach pressed against Christina's. Christina squeezed her eyes shut, wishing so badly they were still in this together. If only she could rewind time.

"Thank you for the song," Christina told Megan. "It was beautiful."

"Of course. If you need anything, call me."

Christina nodded, grateful for Megan's friendship. She would need her in the days to come.

And then it was just Christina and Gary and Grace. Gary wrapped his arm around Christina, and she leaned into him. The cold was biting, but she didn't care. She wanted to stay here with Grace forever.

"That was a beautiful prayer," Christina said.

"Thank you." He wiped at his eyes with the back of his hand. Christina squeezed her eyes shut at the sight of his pain. "It's going to be okay. I don't know how. I don't know when. But it will be."

"I know." Christina plucked a rose from an arrangement near the grave. She kissed it, and placed it gently on top of Grace's casket. "I love you, my little angel," she whispered.

One day, she would hold Grace again. She would raise her and do all the things she had dreamed about. But she had never imagined all those things would take place in the next life.

Christina gulped and let Gary lead her from the cemetery. It was time to leave.

CHAPTER FORTY-SIX
CHRISTINA

After a miserable Thanksgiving, Christina's parents flew home, and she returned to work.

Her hands gripped the steering wheel as she drove through the snow to school. How would she explain this to the students? How would she answer their questions without falling apart? They were six years old. They would have lots of questions, and most of them wouldn't be phrased in a sensitive and tactful way.

Christina's heels echoed in the quiet school hallways. Some of the tension of the last ten days drained away as she stood in the center of her classroom, breathing deeply. The familiarity of the twenty-eight little desks, the smell of dry erase and antiseptic, blended together in a comfortable harmony. Home.

It felt good to be back.

Stacey checked on Christina within minutes, followed by Principal Gardner and Linda. When the bell rang, Christina went to pick up her students. The kids followed her into the classroom, more somber than she'd ever seen them.

"Put away your things and meet me at the rug," Christina said. She needed to explain to them what had happened. Needed to help them understand. They'd been excited about the baby, too.

The students quietly did as instructed. Twenty-eight little faces stared up at Christina with concern and apprehension.

"I've missed all of you," she told them. "Do you know why I've been gone?"

A little voice spoke up hesitantly. "Mrs. Applegate said your baby died."

Christina blinked, trying to hold back the tears. She couldn't let her students see her cry. "That's right."

"Why?" someone asked.

"My body thought it was time for the baby to be born, even though it wasn't," Christina said. "The baby was too small to live outside my stomach yet."

"Mrs. Applegate said it was a girl."

"Yes. Her name is Grace."

For a half hour Christina answered their questions and reassured them everything in their lives would continue on as normal. A student brought her a giant envelope, filled to the brim with notes. Stacey had helped both her class and Christina's make while Christina was gone.

Christina felt happier than she had since losing Grace. She didn't have a baby to hold, but she did have her students. And even though it wasn't the same, she cared about them, and they cared about her. It felt good to talk about Grace with them. They didn't tiptoe around the situation. They weren't afraid to ask the hard questions. Their genuine love and concern helped heal Christina's broken heart.

After the discussion, the students resumed their typical noisiness, and the day went on as usual. Christina soaked the normalcy in like a balm. When the day ended, she reluctantly left for her empty home. She was surprised to find Gary waiting for her there.

"What are you doing home already?" she asked.

"I wanted to see how your day went." He took her hand gently in his. "How are you?"

"Surprisingly okay." Christina chewed on her lip, then admitted something she'd thought about all day. "I don't want to try again, Gary."

His eyes widened. "You don't want a baby?"

Christina cursed the tears that always seemed so close to the surface. "Of course I want a baby. But this . . ." She motioned vaguely to the room. "I can't bear the thought of going through this again anytime soon."

He shifted from foot to foot, seeming agitated. "The doctor said next time we'll do the surgery, and it won't happen. We'll—"

Christina put a hand to his lips, quieting him. "I can't. I'm not ready for any of it again, for in vitro, for worrying constantly about miscarriage, for the stress of the surgery. I want to wait, Gar. Please."

His eyes were pained. "I'm finally ready to be a dad. Grace helped me get there. I want a baby."

"I know. And you will be an amazing father. But I need time. I realized today that for now, my students are enough." Christina thought for a moment, not sure how to phrase what she needed to say next. "I want to make sure the next baby isn't just a way to replace the void Grace left. I feel like if we tried again now, we'd be trying to erase what happened. I don't want to forget."

"I never want to replace Grace. But your endometriosis gets worse every day. We might not be able to wait very long."

"I know." Christina put a hand on his chest. "I'm not talking about waiting forever. Maybe six months. We both need time to heal. Let's work on us for a while."

Gary leaned down and kissed her. "Six months, and then we'll re-evaluate. For Grace."

CHAPTER FORTY-SEVEN
KYRA

The next few weeks were stressful for Kyra, but blissful too. The only dark cloud was Grace's funeral. Kyra felt guilty preparing for the birth of her child while Christina suffered through the loss of hers. Kyra knew what it felt like to lose a baby, though not in the same way as Christina. It wasn't something she'd wish on her worst enemy, let alone a dear friend.

As Sienna's due date drew closer, she spent more and more time with Kyra. Sienna even surprised Kyra by requesting to help prepare the nursery.

They decided to see what could be reused from Sophie's baby stuff. Sophie had fallen in love with Sienna and sat by her side chatting as Kyra brought boxes up from the basement.

"Aunt Sienna, I can't wait until my baby brother is born," Sophie said as Kyra opened the first box. "Can I feel him kick again?"

"Sophie," Kyra said. She didn't want to make this any harder on Sienna than it had to be.

"It's okay," Sienna said. She took Sophie's hand and placed it on her belly. "Did you feel that?"

Sophie giggled. "He likes me."

"Yeah, I think he does."

They spent the next two hours going through boxes. Most of the clothing was too girly to reuse, but some of the receiving blankets and onesies would be okay.

"I think that's enough for today," Kyra said. "You look tired."

"I'm fine." Sienna struggled to stand. "Didn't you say you wanted to clear out Sophie's toy room today?"

"I want to get started at least." Kyra held out a hand. "Here, let me help you up."

"Thanks." Sienna stood, then gasped as her pants grew soaked. Sienna looked at Kyra in horror.

"Mommy, look." Sophie pointed to Sienna's wet pants.

"I swear I didn't pee my pants," Sienna said. "What happened?"

"I think your water broke," Kyra said. "Oh my gosh. Your water broke! We've got to go to the hospital."

"But I'm not due for another two weeks."

"I don't think the baby knows that."

Sienna motioned to Sophie. "What about her?"

"I'll drop her off at Cassandra's. Call your mom and tell her to meet us there. I think I have some sweat pants you can wear to the hospital."

Sienna changed, and Kyra rushed Sophie to Cassandra's while Sienna called her mom. Sienna was just hanging up when Kyra got into the car.

"Seat belt on," Kyra reminded Sienna as she started the car.

Sienna complied, tears streaking down her cheeks.

Kyra took Sienna's hand in hers. "Hey, it's going to be okay. I'll get you to the hospital as soon as possible. Are you having contractions?"

Sienna hiccupped. "I don't know. What does a contraction feel like?"

Kyra peeled out of the driveway and turned toward the hospital. "If you were having contractions, you'd know."

Sienna let out a gasp. "I think that was one. That hurt! Tell the doctor to make it stop, and we'll come back on my due date."

"It doesn't work that way." Kyra sped through a yellow light, then whipped into a parking spot near the front of the hospital. "Want me to get a wheelchair, or can you walk?"

"I can walk," Sienna said.

Kyra nodded, unbuckling her seat belt and reaching for the door handle.

"Wait." Sienna grabbed her arm. Mascara had smudged under her wide, fearful eyes. She looked so young. A child, really. And soon she would be a mother.

Soon Kyra would be a mother. Again.

"I'm scared." Sienna's hand cradled her belly. "He's not going to be mine anymore."

Kyra put her hand over the top of Sienna's. When she spoke, her voice was thick with emotion. "You will always be a part of his life. You're as much a part of our family now as he is, for as long as you want to be."

Sienna started crying. "You've been so nice to me. But I keep worrying once I give you what you want, you'll blow me off."

"We won't. I promise. Sienna, you're giving us the greatest gift we could ever ask for. And we'll never forget that."

Sienna leaned over and gasped, a contraction breaking their moment.

"I'll get a wheelchair," Kyra told her, opening her door.

"No, I can walk. I don't want to be alone."

Kyra helped Sienna across the parking lot, stopping once for a contraction. They took the elevator up to labor and delivery, and Sienna waddled to the admitting desk.

"I think my water broke," she told the nurse.

The nurse's mouth twitched, probably at Sienna's obvious youth. "Let me get some information, and we'll get you to a room as soon as possible. How far apart are your contractions?"

"I don't know. I just started having them."

The nurse looked to Kyra. "About ten minutes," Kyra told her. She'd been timing them, even if Sienna hadn't.

"Are you her sister?" the nurse asked, uncertainty in her tone.

"No." Kyra wondered how to answer.

"She's the baby's mom," Sienna said. "She's adopting him."

"Sienna!" Annabelle raced through the doors and hugged her daughter tightly. "Are you okay?"

Sienna nodded. "Kyra's been with me the whole time."

Annabelle turned to Kyra. "Thank you."

"Let's go," the nurse said. "We'll do a test to make sure your water really broke and admit you."

Kyra stood there, feeling lost. What was her role in all of this? She wanted to be there for every second of Sienna's labor and delivery. She wanted to be in the room when her son cried for the first time. But she also wanted to respect Sienna's privacy.

Sienna grabbed Kyra's hand, her fingernails biting into the flesh. "Come with me. I want you to be there when he's born."

Kyra blinked to hold back the tears and nodded. "Of course. Whatever you want. I'm here for you."

Sienna turned to the nurse. "I want her to have one of those wristband thingies or whatever so she can stay with the baby after he's born. My caseworker said to make sure you knew."

After Sienna was officially admitted, Kyra called David. Thirty minutes later he arrived at the hospital to pace in the waiting room. Kyra's heart went out to him, but they had agreed it would be uncomfortable to have him wait in Sienna's room.

Sienna's labor progressed quickly, and only five hours after arriving at the hospital the doctor told her, "It's time to push."

Sienna grabbed Kyra's hand. "Don't leave."

"I'm staying right here," Kyra said.

"On your next contraction, bear down," the doctor told Sienna.

"You can do it," Kyra said. She stood on one side of Sienna, and Annabelle stood on the other. Sienna gripped both of their hands. Kyra's fingers tingled from lack of blood circulation.

"Push now," the doctor commanded.

"It'll all be over soon, honey," Annabelle said. "Push!"

"I am pushing!" Sienna yelled.

For twenty minutes Sienna pushed. Tears pooled in Kyra's eyes as Sienna screamed and yelled and cried from pain and exhaustion. She wished she could switch places with Sienna and go through the agony for her. "You're doing so well," Kyra said over and over.

"His shoulders are almost out," the doctor said. "One more should do it."

Sienna let out a scream, bearing down. A moment later, a newborn cry pierced the air.

Tears fell down Kyra's cheeks. Her baby. Her son. He let out another cry, louder than before, and she wanted to rush over and soothe him. She felt exactly the same as she had with Sophie's first cry—completely and totally in love. It didn't matter that she hadn't given birth to him. He was hers.

Sienna collapsed against the bed, sobbing. "You did good," Annabelle said, rubbing Sienna's shoulders. Tears streamed down her cheeks.

"Seven pounds, two ounces," a nurse announced.

"You were amazing," Kyra said.

A nurse walked over, the baby in her arms. "Do you want to hold him?" she asked Sienna.

Sienna nodded. Kyra's heart wrenched as she watched Sienna take him. Would she change her mind? How on earth could she possibly give such a precious child away?

"Hi, little guy," Sienna cooed, putting her finger out for the baby to grasp. Kyra's arms ached to hold him, but he wasn't hers. Not legally. Not yet. Sienna needed this moment.

The baby's cries settled down as Sienna cuddled him close. The moment felt so private that Kyra wondered if she should leave.

"I have waited so long to see you," Sienna whispered. "There's someone I want to introduce you to." She reached out with her free hand, grasping Kyra's. Kyra stepped forward in surprise. "This is your mother," Sienna whispered in the baby's ears.

Kyra let out a sob. Annabelle buried her face in her hands.

Sienna transferred the baby into Kyra's arms. "He's your son now. Not mine."

Kyra stared in wonder at the baby. His eyes, gray and beautiful, were opened wide as he took in his surroundings. His face was red from the trauma of birth, his head slightly misshaped. Kyra had never seen a more beautiful baby boy in her life. "Hi, little guy," she whispered. "I'm your mommy. And I love you so much." Kyra turned to Sienna, unable to hold back the sobs. "I can never repay you for this. Thank you feels inadequate."

"We need to take him to the nursery," a nurse said. "Hospital procedure says he needs to be transported in the bassinet."

Kyra nodded, leaning down to kiss his head before placing him in the bassinet.

"Are you coming with us to the nursery, Mom?" the nurse asked.

Kyra glanced over at Sienna. Annabelle sat on the edge of Sienna's bed, her daughter's head buried against her chest as both their shoulders shook with sobs. Kyra turned away, her own shoulders shaking with emotion. "Yes." The baby was her priority now, and Sienna needed time with her mother.

The nurse wheeled the bassinet, and Kyra followed, her eyes glued to the baby inside. Her son.

"My husband's in the waiting room," Kyra told the nurse. "Can he come to the nursery too?"

"Sure. I'll send a nurse to find him."

"Thank you." Kyra wouldn't leave the baby's side, but she longed for David to meet their child.

Kyra watched as the nurse checked the baby's vitals and helped bathe him for the first time. He screamed and screamed. "He's got a healthy set of lungs on him," the nurse said with a laugh as she wrapped him in a blanket. "We're done for now. Would you like to hold him?"

Kyra nodded eagerly. The nurse transferred him to her arms. "Hey, little guy." Kyra bounced him gently. "It's okay. Mommy's here."

His cries stopped. He looked up at Kyra with beautiful dark gray eyes and let out a coo.

"He knows his mother's voice," the nurse said. She pointed outside the nursery window. David stood there, his expression one of awe. "Looks like the nurse found Daddy. Shall I let him in?"

Kyra nodded. The nurse opened the door, and David hurried inside. He peered over Kyra's shoulder and down into the baby's face. "He's absolutely beautiful."

"He is." Kyra gently placed the baby in David's arms.

David's face glowed as he stared at their son in awe. "Hey, buddy." He held the baby with the expertise of someone who'd already had a child. "He's beautiful, Kyr."

"He's our son."

He blinked. "I can't believe it. A month ago, we hadn't even been placed with Sienna. And now he's here."

"Congratulations, Daddy." Kyra kissed him softly on the lips. "We're officially a family of four."

CHAPTER FORTY-EIGHT
MEGAN

Megan anxiously stared at the ultrasound screen. "Well?" she asked. "Can you or can't you?" She was twenty-four weeks, and they still weren't certain what the genders of their children were. They were pretty sure there was a boy in the mix, but despite all their ultrasounds, they had yet to get a clear shot of each child. Apparently their kids were too darn modest.

"I definitely can tell," Dr. Johnson said.

"For absolute certain?"

"For absolute certain."

"What are they?" Megan demanded.

"It's three boys," Trent guessed.

Dr. Johnson shook his head. "One boy and two identical girls. Congratulations."

Trent and Megan stared at each other in amazement.

"I can't believe it." Megan laughed in pure joy. It was all becoming real.

Life had changed so much in the last month. Christina had lost a child, and Kyra had gained one. Megan had reached a big milestone in pregnancy—twenty-four weeks, the age of viability. She was on complete bed rest now due to pre-term labor, and knew there was a big chance she'd soon be hospitalized for the rest of her pregnancy. But they were hopeful she could go at least another eight weeks before the birth of their children.

At home a few hours later, Megan wandered into the guest bedroom and lay down. She looked around the room. The guest bed disappeared, replaced by three cribs. The reading alcove she'd so desperately wanted in Logan materialized in one corner of the room. Mobiles hung above each crib.

Megan closed her eyes, smiling with pure joy. She softly hummed a lullaby. Maybe she'd paint the walls a pale yellow or green, something gender neutral. A music theme would be perfect. She'd find canvases with music notes and hang them over the cribs.

Nine months ago, she'd stood in an empty room in Logan, her heart longing for what could've been. Now all she could see were the possibilities, and what the future held.

Trent sank onto the bed next to Megan, brushing back her hair. "What are you doing in here?"

"Trying to decide what to do for the nursery. Guess it's time to sell this bed." Megan patted the mattress. She lay in bed on her left side, just as Dr. Johnson recommended to alleviate possible contractions.

"We never have guests anyway." Trent kissed her neck. "I'd rather have three babies."

Megan laughed. "Me too."

Christina and Kyra came over that night so Megan could share the good news with them.

Kyra arrived first with baby Hunter, her face alight with the joy of new motherhood. "Did you find out for certain?" she asked, leaning down to hug Megan.

"Yes," Megan said with a grin. "But you have to wait until Christina gets here to find out." Megan motioned to the tiny infant, asleep in his car seat. "How's Hunter doing?"

Kyra set the carrier on the floor. "He's doing amazing. Sophie absolutely adores him."

"And how's Sienna?" Bed rest meant Megan regrettably had to let her piano students go—for now, at least. She missed the weekly contact with Sienna, but she'd be in Pennsylvania soon anyway. Megan had texted her a few times over the week since Hunter's birth, but mostly Megan had tried to give Sienna space.

"Struggling," Kyra admitted. "She had to relinquish her parental rights twenty-four hours after his birth, and that was really hard."

"Has she been over to see him?"

"Once. I think it hurts too much right now. She's really looking forward to leaving for Philadelphia in a few weeks."

"I can't even imagine. I'm happy for you, but my heart hurts for her."

"I know." Kyra sank into a chair by Megan's bed. "I've never felt such joy and pain simultaneously."

There was a knock at the door, and Christina walked in. "Hi."

Kyra rose, giving Christina a hug. Christina bent down to hug Megan. "Well?" she asked, sitting down.

"Well what?" Megan said.

Christina gave an exasperated sigh. "Did you find out or not?"

"Yes." Megan couldn't stop the silly grin from splitting her face. "I'm planning a gender reveal photo shoot for Friday."

"You can't make us wait," Christina said.

"I don't know . . ."

"Megan Burke!"

Megan grinned. "You have to act surprised at the party. But . . ." She pulled back the blanket on the bed, revealed three pairs of baby booties—two pink, and one blue. "We're having two girls and a boy."

"Ahh!" Kyra hugged Megan.

Christina hugged Megan too. "Congratulations." Her eyes couldn't quite hide the pain. "They would've all had so much fun together. Hunter and Grace and your triplets."

Megan frowned. "If this is too hard for you, Christina . . ."

Christina shook her head. "No. I want you to tell me everything. I'm so excited for you."

Megan reached for Christina's hand. "You and Gary will have another child one day. Our kids will play together then."

"We need time to heal," Christina said.

Kyra nodded. "Of course you do. No one expects you to jump back into it immediately."

Christina brushed back a tear. "We don't want to replace Grace. And that's what trying again right now feels like. We'll wait a few months, and then see how we feel about things."

"Of course," Megan said. "You should take all the time you need. When it's right, you'll know it."

"And you can come over and hold Hunter whenever you need to," Kyra said. "Or not come over. It's your choice."

"Same with these three," Megan said, pointing to her belly.

Christina laughed, reaching forward and taking Hunter from Kyra's arms. "Oh, I definitely need to hold the babies. All of them." She nuzzled Hunter's neck, breathing in deeply. "When the time is right, we'll try again. I have faith that God has something more in store for us than this pain."

"I know he does," Megan said.

Kyra linked her arm through Christina's. "And in the meantime, we'll all be living our someday."

DISCUSSION QUESTIONS

1. In Chasing Someday, each woman's perception of herself is closely tied to her inability to have children. Do you think motherhood is an appropriate indicator of self-worth?

2. All three women in the story take a different approach to infertility. Christina and Kyra are both very secretive, and Megan is very open. Which approach would you take, given their situations? Is one approach better than the other?

3. Infertility is often a taboo subject in our society. How do the characters in the story reinforce or fight that stigma? Should infertility continue to be a subject that is kept quiet?

4. At one point in the story, Megan says she doesn't just want to be a mom—she wants to have a baby. How are the two different?

5. Motherhood is a theme throughout Chasing Someday. How has the book influence and changed your ideas about motherhood and womanhood?

6. Throughout the story, Kyra is worried someone will find out she's struggling to have another baby. Why does she want to keep her infertility quiet?

7. After the move to Riverton, why is Megan resistant to beginning fertility treatments again?

8. At the beginning of the story, we find out Christina went off birth control without telling Gary. Do you feel she was justified to do this? Why or why not?

9. Which of the characters did you connect with the most? Why?

10. Which of the characters grew the most over the course of the story? How was this growth shown?

11. How does Megan's perception of unwed mothers change as she teaches Sienna?

12. After Grace's death, Christina and Gary decide to wait instead of trying immediately for another baby. Do you agree or disagree with their reasons for waiting? What would you do in their situation?

13. How has this book changed your perception of infertility?

14. None of the women get the ending they imagined at the beginning of the story. As a reader, do you feel the ending was emotionally satisfying? Why or why not?

Lindzee Armstrong is available for book club visits. Email her at lindzee@lindzeearmstrong.com for more information.

FREE DOWNLOAD

Nothing slows down love like the friend zone.

"This was the book I've been looking for!"
—Angela, reader

Get your free copy of *Meet Your Match* when you opt in to the author's VIP reader's club. **Get started here:**

http://lindzeearmstrong.com/claim-your-free-book

Enjoy Lindzee's #1 Best-Selling Series!

"This heartwarming, feel-good romance will leave you swooning and cheering for the characters as they fight for true love." -InD'Tale Magazine

Strike a Match: *Out of the ashes she might find true love.* When Kate's husband dies in a fire, she doesn't expect to fall for Taylor, the handsome firefighter who gives her the news. But past relationship fears and old habits threaten to tear them apart before they've even begun. Can the ashes of their pasts hold their happily ever after? *Melt into this sizzling romance today!*

Meet Your Match: *Nothing slows love down like the friend zone.* Brooke's convinced all boys are trouble. Luke's a player who loves the thrill of the chase. Can a set of crazy rules keep these two safely in the friend zone? *Enjoy this witty and fast-paced romance today!*

Miss Match: *Playing cupid may break her heart.* With the matchmaking company she works for in decline, Brooke is desperate to sign Luke, her billionaire best friend, as a client. But Luke is more interested in capturing Brooke's heart. *Escape into this lighthearted romantic comedy today!*

Not Your Match: *Sometimes it takes dating Mr. Wrong to find Mr. Right.* Dating the wrong people has convinced both Ben and Andi that what they really want is each other. All that's standing in their way is a fake boyfriend, a jealous ex-fiancée, and being afraid to risk their hearts. *Explore this emotionally-charged romance today!*

Mix 'N Match: *Fire and ice aren't meant to mix.* Zoey and Mitch couldn't be more opposite. One passionate kiss has convinced them they'd never work. But three weeks in Paris could change everything. *Take a trip to Paris in this fun-filled romantic comedy today!*

Mistletoe Match: *A kiss shouldn't be this complicated.* When animal rights activist Michelle kisses a mystery man underneath the mistletoe at a holiday party, she's horrified to realize he's the new marketing director of the pharmaceutical company she's trying to destroy due to their nasty habit of animal testing. Can one impulsive kiss be the foundation for a happily ever after? *Curl up with this delicious holiday romance today!*

OTHER BOOKS BY LINDZEE ARMSTRONG

Sunset Plains Romance Series

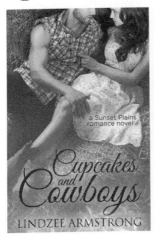 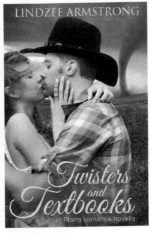

Other Works

Cupcakes and Cowboys (A Sunset Plains Romance): *He's everything that broke her heart.* Cassidy wants two things—to make her cupcake shop a success, and to forget that her fiancé traded her for the lights of Hollywood. When Jase—best friend of her ex and A-list actor—shows up at the ranch to research an upcoming role, forgetting is the last thing she can do. Can Jase convince her he's really a country boy at heart? *Devour this deliciously romantic story today!*

Twisters and Textbooks (A Sunset Plains Romance): *Some storms can't be outrun.* After the death of her parents, chasing tornadoes is the only thing that makes Lauren feel alive. Each storm gives her the adrenaline rush she craves, but it can't make her forget Tanner, the country boy she left behind in Oklahoma. When a tornado brings the couple back together, Lauren and Tanner are caught up in a cyclone of emotions neither is sure they want to escape. Can they weather the storm of their past, or will they let it consume them? *Get caught up in this wildly romantic story today!*

First Love, Second Choice: What happens when you impersonate your identical twin sister to score a date with your long-lost high school crush? *Enjoy this delightfully sweet case of mistaken identity today!*

ABOUT THE
AUTHOR

LINDZEE ARMSTRONG is the #1 best-selling author of the No Match for Love series and Sunset Plains Romance series. In case it wasn't obvious, she's always had a soft spot for love stories. In third grade, she started secretly reading romance novels, hiding the covers so no one would know (because hello, embarrassing!), and dreaming of her own Prince Charming.

Lindzee finally met her true love while at college, where she graduated with a bachelor's in history education. They are now happily married and raising twin boys in the Rocky Mountains.

Like any true romantic, Lindzee loves chick flicks, ice cream, and chocolate. She believes in sigh-worthy kisses and happily ever afters, and loves expressing that through her writing.

To find out about future releases, you can join Lindzee's VIP reader's club on her website, www.lindzeearmstrong.com.

If you enjoyed this book, please take a few minutes and leave a review. This is the best way you can say thank you to an author! It really helps other readers discover books they might enjoy. Thank you!

ACKNOWLEDGMENTS

There are so many people who have made this book possible. I happened upon the idea for CHASING SOMEDAY at the most inconvenient time possible. I was a new mother to twin boys, sleep-deprived and exhausted. But the idea wouldn't leave me alone, and I knew I had to write it down. The wounds of infertility were still fresh, barely healed from the birth of my sons. It was cathartic to write this book. I had battled infertility and survived. I wanted other women to feel the hope I felt.

So I wrote the book. And I edited the book. And I published the book in a small niche market. It had scarcely been out a year when I felt a nudge to pull it from publication, send it through another round of edits, and republish it on a wider scale. I fought that urge for more than six months before giving in. I didn't want to return to this book. It's such a big part of my heart, but so hard for me to work on. I have personal experience with almost everything that happens in CHASING SOMEDAY, and the memories are raw and painful. But I fought through the pain, because I believe there are woman who need to read this book as much as I needed to write it.

This book never would've happened without the support of my sweet husband, Neil. He cheers me on every step of the way and constantly reassures me that the time I spend writing is worth it.

To Liz, my accountability partner. If not for her, I would've given up on this book a long time ago.

To my critique group, The Authorities—Darren, LaChelle, David, and Jacob. The book would've been a complete disaster without them (and it was).

To all my beta readers. There were many of you! To my friends at iWrite who answered questions and provided encouragement. To Tristi Pinkton, one of my editors, who helped me in so many ways, but especially by convincing me to change the entire book from first person to third.

To my parents, especially my mother. They don't understand my burning desire to write, but they wholeheartedly support it anyway. They never doubted that one day I'd be published.

And to all my sisters in the Land of IF. I thought about you every time I wrote this book. I cried for you, ached for you, and rejoiced with you. So many of you shared your stories with me so that I could make this book better. Keep chasing your someday!